DURESS

A BIRCH FALLS NOVEL

POPPY FITZGERALD

To all the women who deserve better. It's not too late.

TRIGGER WARNINGS

Duress is a dark romantic suspense, with dark themes, including intimate partner violence, gaslighting, manipulation, sexual assault, and the death of a parent. I did my best to handle these topics with care and compassion for the victims, but please tread carefully if any of these subjects are upsetting for you.

Visit the National Sexual Violence Resource Center for more information or help if you have been a victim of sexual assault.

National Sexual Violence Resource Center
https://www.nsvrc.org

CONTENTS

CHAPTER 1
DANE

I stare at the message on my phone, brows knitted together in confusion, trying to make sense of the words on the screen.

I need you to come over tonight. Have an issue I need your help with.

Individually I understand the words. Combined as a text message from my mostly estranged half brother who barely tolerates me is the part I find bewildering.

We haven't spoken in months. We try not to unless our jobs force us to cross paths. The last time we were in a room together, it nearly resulted in us coming to blows.

Before I have the chance to type out a response, a cup of coffee appears on my desk, stealing my attention away from the demanding message. Glancing up, I see my new rookie partner, Serena Roberts, leaning her hip against my desk, dangling a to-go bag from Brewed Awakening in front of my face. The tantalizing scent of orange and cranberries wafts from the bag.

"Oh fuck. Is that one of Marge's cranberry-orange scones?" I toss my phone to the side, frustrating older brother immediately forgotten in favor of fresh baked pastries. I reach out to snag the bag from Serena, but she jerks it away at the last second.

"What the fuck, Serena?" I shoot her a petulant glare.

"What the fuck, indeed, D. You can have it, but only if you tell me why you took my sister-in-law on the most awkward date ever. She said you *shook her hand* when you dropped her off and said goodnight. Like you were closing a business deal. If you didn't want to go out with Naomi, you could've just said so." Serena's full lips press into a disapproving, thin line as she stares down her nose at me.

Closing my eyes, I slump into my seat and hide my face in embarrassment. Serena has been trying for weeks to set me up with her husband, Kai's sister, Naomi, and I finally relented, thinking maybe just getting back out into the dating pool would be good for me. Naomi is wicked smart and fine as fuck, with a smile that could light up the night sky. She also has an amazing sense of humor. There was absolutely no reason for me to say no, at least on paper, so I took her out on Saturday night. The date was one awkward disaster after another, and I'm the only one to blame. I knew when I drove away after the world's lamest handshake that there would be zero percent chance of Serena not giving me hell about it.

"Do you know how weird game nights are going to be now? What the hell, D? I thought you were interested in getting to know her?" She gives a sharp flick to my fore-head, shaking her head which causes her curly hair to dance around her face. She is younger than me by a couple of years, but being lectured by her feels a lot like letting my mom down.

My cheeks heat in shame at Serena's chiding. She and Kai host a weekly game night where Naomi and I both regularly attend. There has been some light flirtation between the two of us, and in my defense, I thought I was interested in getting to know her. But once we were on our date, my mind kept going back to a certain set of enigmatic hazel-green eyes that belong to the one woman I can't have. The one woman I've been longing after for almost a third of my life. The woman married to my shithead older brother.

"I thought so too, Serena. I swear. But…" I huff out a sigh as I shrug helplessly. Serena's eyes narrow, her arm still holding the bag full of pastry out of my reach.

"But what, D?"

"It's not Naomi; it's me. I'm just not ready to date right now. I thought I was, but I was wrong. I'll call her and apologize."

Serena holds my gaze for a long moment, the gold of her irises reminding me of a lioness, causing me to shift uncomfortably in my seat. She's a natural at this, and it's why she will make an excellent cop once she gets some experience behind her.

"Fine, but do it before game night. I don't want shit to be weird next time you're both in the same room." Serena plunks the bag down on my desk, stealing a scone from it before moving over to her desk across the aisle.

"Yes, Mom," I respond, around a mouthful of scone.

"Boy...do you want to die today?" She shoots me another glare from her desk as I almost choke on the scone, holding a laugh back.

Serena and I have an interesting history together. She's not just my partner; she's a friend and the ex-fiancée of my former partner Dominick Reeves. I had a bad feeling about Dominick pretty much as soon as I joined the Birch Falls PD, and spent the better part of a year trying to come up with evidence of his shadiness. Unfortunately, Serena fell into his clutches before I could come up with anything concrete to use against him, but his abuse of her and harassment of Kai, then her best friend, was the final piece of the puzzle needed to put him away.

Serena has made it her personal mission to make sure other victims have someone safe to turn to, while I've become disillusioned of the whole idea of upholding the law. Between cops like Dominick, and shady as fuck defense lawyers like my brother, some days it feels pointless to even try. Dominick is already working on an appeal of his sentence, and some days it feels like this nightmare will never be over. I'm sticking it out though, at least long enough to help Serena get her footing on the force. It's tough breaking in as a rookie. And as a female rookie? Forget about it. So here I am, going through the motions, hoping the spark that made me want to get into law enforcement will reignite, while Serena settles in and learns the ropes.

* * *

My phone buzzes against my desk again as I finish off the last of the coffee Serena left for me. Flipping it over, I roll my eyes when I see it's another text from my brother.

BRYCE

Leaving me on read? Very mature Dane.

BRYCE

Be at my house at 7.

My back teeth are on the verge of cracking from how hard I'm clenching my jaw. I want nothing more than to tell him to fuck off. This is how it's always been with us. Bryce says jump and expects me to ask how high. The only reason I go along with his demands is because he supports our mom with his big flashy lawyer salary. After my dad's death, Mom slipped into a pretty severe depression and became a recluse. She no longer works, and Bryce pays the rent for her small cottage. He loves to hold this over me, like he's some benevolent ruler caring for his people, instead of being a son doing the bare minimum to help his own mother out. He knows I can't foot the bill on my police officer's salary, but it doesn't stop him from threatening to cut off her funding if I don't play along.

It's been like this between us our entire lives. Bryce blames my dad for being the reason his dad left Mom. Never mind his dad was a cheating piece of shit and mom was better off without him. Bryce will never see it that way, and considering the apple hasn't fallen far from the tree, I've given up on trying to forge any kind of relationship with him. He's been resentful of me since day one.

You'd think maybe he'd have grown half a heart after my dad died in a tragic accident, leaving our mom an emotionless husk of the woman she used to be, but nope, his attitude has only gotten worse. The only silver lining to going to see Bryce is that Everly will be there.

Everly with the hazel-green eyes, hair the color of a starless sky, a constellation of freckles dusting her cheeks. Everly with the smile that pulled me out of my darkest depression when my dad passed. I was sixteen at the time of his accident. Sixteen, with a brother who tormented me, a dead dad, and a mom who refused to get out of bed. I don't know what possessed an angel like Everly to date my dickhead brother, let alone marry him. She's everything he isn't. Kind. Supportive. Empathetic. I've tried a few times over the years to see what she sees in him. Why she continues to stay married to him. I can see he doesn't love her. Not in the way she deserves. But any time I try to bring up the topic of my brother being an ass, she gets this look in her eyes. Like she thinks he's all she deserves, and she changes the topic or beats a hasty retreat.

There was one time, right after I graduated high school, where I thought maybe I might get an answer out of her. It was my graduation party, and we were both tipsy from overpowered canned cocktails snuck in by some of my friends. Bryce had disappeared, and we were sitting by the fire chatting. I asked her what she saw in my brother, when I could tell he didn't appreciate her the way she deserved. The way she looked at me then in the firelight, like she could see me, *seeing her*... It felt like watching a flower bloom in real time. Like she might actually spill her secrets to me. The way her eyes locked in on my lips, causing her tongue to dart out—moistening her own—made my dick hard. I was seconds away from leaning in and kissing her before we were interrupted by my buddy Scott drunkenly crashing into me, ruining the moment.

Shaking away the memory, I blow out a frustrated breath as I tap out a reply to my brother.

ME
See you at 7.

I see that my message is read immediately. I wait for the three bouncing dots to indicate an incoming response from Bryce, but none comes. Of course not. Heaven forbid if I leave the fuckwad on read, but he has no problem doing the same to me.

"Hey, you ready to go?" Serena's honeyed voice drags my attention from my phone. It's time for our patrol shift, so I gather up my badge, radio, and gun and follow her out of the station, ready to start my shift.

CHAPTER 2
DANE

"Bro... BRO! Two o'clock. Hottie in a red dress." My buddy Scott jabs his elbow into my ribs, causing beer to slosh out of the red solo cup I'm currently filling. I extend my arm just in time to avoid getting soaked in shitty light beer.

Glancing up, I turn my attention to the direction he indicated, but all I see is some of our teammates from football. I'm not sure what hottie would even be here. My mom agreed to let me host a party as long as I kept it under control, so I just invited some of my closest friends from football, their girlfriends, and a few other friends from Forensics Club. Most of the girls here are either in a relationship or are practically like a sister to me.

"No, your other two o'clock," Scott slurs, as he not at all discreetly gestures with the hand holding his own red solo cup full of beer. He had a flask under his gown during our graduation, so he has a head start on all of us. I predict he will be passing out by the firepit first.

"That's eight, dipshit. Not two. How in the hell did you manage to graduate without having to do summer school?"

"Fuck if I know." Scott shrugs, chugging his beer before swiping the keg tap out of my hand and going back for more.

The hottie in the red dress turns around, and I realize it's Everly, my sister-in-law. Well, that doesn't change anything. All of the girls here are spoken for or like a sister to me. Or *are* a sister.

"That's my sister-in-law, you jackass," I mutter under my breath.

Everly is married to my dickhead half brother for some unfathomable reason. She is sweetness and light, where he is cold and dickish. I don't get what she sees in him. Sure he's some up-and-coming hotshot lawyer and is decently good-looking. I guess. But he's also the biggest douche in existence. I gave up on us having a brotherly relationship years ago, when I finally was old enough to realize he wasn't just ignoring me because of our age gap, but because he actually seems to hate me. He puts on a good show for appearance's sake for Mom, but we both know the score.

If Everly is here, that means Bryce is too. I scan the crowd of people scattered throughout our backyard but there is no sign of him. I watch as Everly scans the party, a canned cocktail in hand. Her posture is stiff and uncomfortable, like she knows she doesn't belong here, at a party full of high schoolers. Her face lights up with relief when her hazel eyes land on me.

"I'm gonna go say hi to her. I'll be back." Scott shrugs and takes his beer across the yard where a game of Asshole is happening.

"CONGRATULATIONS!" As soon as I'm within reaching distance, Everly wraps me up in a hug. Her hair smells like the flowers from Mom's garden. She presses a brief kiss on my cheek before pulling away and beaming up at me with genuinely proud smile. "Graduating with Summa Cum Laude honors! We are so proud of you, Dane!" She says *we* but I know Bryce gives zero shits about what honors I graduated with. I'm surprised he's even here, based on how he couldn't leave the graduation ceremony fast enough.

"Thanks, Ever. I appreciate it." Glancing around, there is still no sign of Bryce. I don't wanna leave Everly alone feeling awkward at a party where she doesn't know anyone, so I keep the conversation going. "I didn't know you all were coming to the party. I figured Bryce had more important things to do than hang with a bunch of drunk eighteen-year-olds."

Everly flinches a little at the barb directed toward my brother. I think she knows we don't get along, but she tries so hard to fix the rift between us. There is some innate sense of goodness in her that insists on trying to fix broken things. Even if it isn't her fault it's broken. There is so much empathy in this woman; I don't know how she can carry feeling so much for everyone all the time. Or how in the hell she wound up marrying a cold-hearted dickhead like my brother.

"We are heading to dinner soon, but I wanted to come by and congratulate you in person. Bryce dragged us out of the football stadium as soon as the ceremony ended, and I didn't get to tell you there. You know how he is. Impatient and irritable in crowds." Everly gives me an apologetic shrug before sipping from her drink.

"Where is he now?" I grab one of the canned cocktails from the drink cooler, and we drift over to the fire, finding a pair of empty chairs next to it.

"Inside, talking to your mom. Said he had to talk to her about the house or something. So what are your plans for the summer? Caroline said you weren't fully committed to the college thing?" She turns toward me, our knees barely touching, her expression nonjudgmental and genuinely curious.

When Everly gives you her undivided attention, it's like the sun is shining only for you. She has the ability to give you her focus so completely it makes the rest of the world disappear until it's just the two of you. Her ability to make me feel seen and heard is probably the biggest reason why I agreed to go to therapy after my dad's death and stop my asshole spiral. God knows Bryce threatening to send me to some sort of military school after I was almost expelled for fighting didn't help. I get he was just trying to scare me straight, but I was grieving and angry, and my mom was lost to her own grief. I needed someone to care about how shitty my life was. Not tell me to suck it up and be strong.

"I'm gonna take the summer to work and save up. I

want to avoid student loans as much as possible. But I've got a lot of college credits already thanks to dual enrollment, so I think I'll just get an associates in Criminal Justice at BFCC before joining the police academy. By the time I finish the associates and graduate from the academy I'll be twenty-one, the minimum age to become a police officer."

Everly's eyes widen in surprise at my plan. I hadn't told anyone I was thinking of going into law enforcement. Especially not Bryce. I don't want to deal with his judgment of my career choice.

"I didn't know that was something you were into."

"My granddad, Mom's dad, was a cop. He retired with a good pension. The pay is decent, and it doesn't require a four year degree or a lot of student loan debt. I figure it's best to get a career going ASAP so there is less stress on Mom supporting me. She's not working, and Dad's life insurance policy won't last us forever."

Everly's eyes soften at the reminder of why I have to think so practically about my transition into adulthood. She is so pretty in the firelight right now. I lick my lips absently, wondering what it would be like to kiss her.

"Oh Dane, you know Bryce and I are always here. We are more than happy to help if you really want to go to college." Her hand rests lightly on my forearm, and it lights me up in a way it absolutely shouldn't. I know she only sees me like a brother and wants to take care of me because of that, but I can't help but wonder what it would feel like for her to touch me in a very *non-brotherly* fashion.

I let out a derisive snort at her earnestness that feels

mean. "As if Bryce gives two shits about me going to college. No, I won't rely on him for anything." Everly's gorgeous mouth pops open as she sucks in a surprised gasp at my retort. There is a flash of hurt that barely registers on her face before she pulls her hand back. I reach out and stop her, holding her hand in mine, not ready for her to break contact the between us. The high ABV of my drink, making me forget how to hold my tongue around her.

"You are so sweet, Everly. You are the kindest, most empathetic person I have ever met. How in the hell did you wind up marrying an asshole like Bryce? You're too good for him."

Everly bites her bottom lip, and her eyes shine brighter with tears. Shit, I made her cry. I open my mouth to apologize, but Scott, the drunk fuck, barrels into me from behind, wrapping his arms around me in a sloppy bro hug.

"Dude, come on. They're gonna start playing Truth or Dare. You don't want to miss this. I'm gonna dare Grayson to streak across the football field tonight."

I want to stay and apologize to Everly for being a dick, but she's already up and moving away from me.

"I should find Bryce. Go have fun with your friends, Dane. Congratulations again." And with that, she's gone, and I might have irreparably changed the dynamic between us.

CHAPTER 3
DANE

I pull into the circular drive of Bryce's ostentatious McMansion at 6:59 p.m. Being on time is the absolute maximum granule of respect I am willing to give him, considering how little he respects me. If it weren't for our mom, I wouldn't afford him even that, but I try to be the bigger man and keep the peace. The door opens as I approach; Bryce's wife, Everly, greets me with a warm smile and a hug.

"Dane! What a surprise. I didn't know you were coming over tonight." Everly's light jasmine-scented perfume clouds my senses as we embrace. It takes a moment longer than appropriate for me to come to my senses and pull away from her when I hear her clear her throat awkwardly.

"Er, sorry for dropping by on you unexpectedly. Bryce didn't mention I was coming?" I sheepishly grasp the back of my neck as I pull away, trying to find some place for my hands to be other than wrapped around Everly's soft curves. The faint scent of jasmine still lingers in the air around us.

"No, it must have slipped his mind. He ran out for some work emergency around five." Everly scrunches her nose up in the most adorable way, like she's trying to remember if she's the one who forgot I was coming over. For a woman approaching forty, you'd never know it. Between her big doe eyes the color of peridot, the freckles that dust her cheeks, and the penchant for wearing T-shirts featuring her favorite cartoons from the '90s, she could easily pass for someone closer to my age. It's not until you get her to smile that you notice the laugh lines in the corners of her eyes, or when the light catches her onyx hair just the right way, highlighting the few silver strands near her face that give away her true age.

Momentarily distracted by the beauty in front of me, it takes a second for her words to register. "He left for a work emergency? Bryce isn't here? You gotta be fucking kidding me. He's a fucking lawyer, what kind of 'work emergency' does he have on a Tuesday night?" Figures the shithead would demand my presence, then ghost me just to be a prick. Exasperated, I turn to leave, but Everly stops me with a gentle hand on my shoulder.

"Stay. I'm sure he'll be back soon, if he's expecting you. I was just getting ready to have some wine on the patio. Come sit with me and have a glass." Everly's hand slides from my shoulder, down my bicep, setting all my nerve endings on fire with her touch when her fingers meet the bare skin of my arm. I still have half a mind to leave as a *fuck you* to my older brother, but when her delicate hand folds around mine in a tentative grasp, I let her tug me along, powerless to say no.

Our footsteps echo on the marble tile. Their house is huge, mostly white, and devoid of almost any sign of life, much like my brother. There are small touches of Everly. Pops of color from the fresh flower arrangements from her greenhouse. Some of her smaller pieces of art that Bryce has deemed tasteful enough to display where anyone can see them. The occasional gaudy embroidered throw pillow with a silly phrase like, "If you don't have anything nice to say, come sit by me." or "I'm the problem."

I know my brother hates them. I've heard him, time and time again, berating Everly for her "silly hobbies". Why a woman as kind, creative, and as funny as Everly is, is married to my brother, I will never understand. No amount of money or good looks could possibly make up for his personality.

She makes a quick pit spot to the kitchen to grab another wine glass before we continue on through the French doors out onto their patio. The sun is just setting over the mountains, so the pool lights have kicked on, illuminating the outdoor space. The sound of running water from the rock waterfall and soft music playing causes a gentle ease to roll through me. I can feel my shoulders relax as I take in my surroundings. Everly has one of her smaller easels set up on the table with paints lined up next to it. It appears to be a half-finished outdoor scene of the very sunset in front of us. The canvas features a sky shifting from pink and orange to indigo to navy to midnight blue, almost exactly how the sky appears right now.

"Damn, Ever. Wow. That's good. Great. Fucking amazing. Really." I feel my cheeks heat at how I stammer over my words, making a fool of myself. I glance at her out of my periphery hoping that my compliment sounded as sincere as I meant it to be and see her biting her bottom lip, looking up at me from under her lashes, a bashful smile playing at the corner of her mouth. Immediately my mind imagines that might be very close to what she'd look like if she were on her knees, sucking my dick.

"You think so?" Her question sounds sincerely hesitant. Like she can't tell how good it is.

I turn to face her and look directly into her eyes when I say, "Yeah, Ever. I really fucking do." It feels like my heart forgets to beat during the time it takes for my words to sink in to her. "Why would you ever think that it's not?"

Her cheeks flush at my final question, and I swear I catch the telltale shimmer of tears before she turns away. Everly busies herself pouring the wine, and I decide to let it go. For now. I know why she thinks it isn't good. My douchenugget of a brother has always scoffed at her art. He met Everly when she was a junior and he was in law school at BFU. I think he saw this beautiful, creative, free spirit and thought he could mold her into his perfect wife. He's succeeded some. Outside of the house, Everly plays every bit the "respectable attorney's" wife. At home, in her studio or her greenhouse, she still shines as brightly as she ever did. I think Bryce entertains it only because her art does have some respect in the community. That and her dad is a judge, which I suspect is the real reason he started dating her in the first place.

"I've been sitting out here every night, watching the sunset. I am trying to capture a time lapse effect to show how it evolves as the days get shorter..." Everly trails off, taking a sip of her wine. I'm sure Bryce doesn't bother to listen to her when she's talking about her art, so I show her I'm paying attention.

I wait for her eyes to drift back to mine before I say, "The way you captured the shift of green to blue on the mountains is incredible."

I'm rarely alone with Everly. These days, I never have a reason to be around her without Bryce present. So being able to speak so openly to her about her art feels meaningful. Everly and I used to talk. When I was in the police academy, still living at home, she would come visit mine and Bryce's mom and do art therapy with her twice a week. I usually found a way to hang around in the kitchen with them while she was there, and make enough dinner for her to have some too. I learned a lot about Everly in those months. Her sessions with mom brought back the woman I remembered from my childhood, before my dad's death. Before the depression caused her to retreat into herself, becoming a ghost of the mother I used to have. I will always be grateful for Everly for that reason alone.

I reach over and place a hand on her shoulder, gently cupping her neck, to keep her attention on me as I try to convey how serious my next words are. "You are so insanely talented, Ever. Don't ever doubt that, okay?" Another fraught moment passes between us, where I swear it feels like the air is charged. It reminds me so much of that moment by the fire at my high school graduation. Her pulse flutters rapidly under my fingers, and I wonder if it's racing for the same reason as mine. I wonder if she feels this connection between us. The moment is shattered by her phone's ringtone going off. Ever gives me a small smile before turning away to answer the call. As she puts the phone to her ear I see my brother's picture on the screen. Great.

"Hey, when are you gonna be home? Your brother is here." I see her shoulders stiffen at whatever response my brother has. "He said you told him to be here at seven. Okay... How long?" I can feel my frustration rising when she shoots me an apologetic glance over her shoulder. I can't hear the words my brother is saying, but he's loud enough that I can pick up on his self-important tone. Everly winces at whatever his last words are before hanging up.

When Everly turns around, she's biting her bottom lip in worry. "So, Bryce is caught up at work, and he doesn't know when he will be able to leave."

Rolling my eyes, I turn toward the door, my anger threatening to get the better of me. My boiling frustration is immediately squashed when Everly says, "Will you still stay? I could use the company. Bryce has been working a lot of long hours lately." My heart softens when I see the pleading look in her eyes, and I know I can't say no to her.

"Sure, I'll stay."

"Wait, so you're telling me these frat bros actually thought Serena was a stripper they ordered?" Everly cheeks are flushed from a combination of wine and laughter as I recount the story of one of mine and Serena's recent noise disturbance calls. The bottle of wine sits on the table between us, mostly empty. The pool lights reflecting off of Everly's face give her an ethereal glow.

"Yeah, and she played right into it too, walking in and giving the boys that stern cop look and telling them they've been very bad. I was standing on the porch off to the side, so they didn't see me at first. I wanted to see how she'd handle it. But one of the drunk Chaddington McDouche-bros reached out to try to undo her top, so she put him in a standing arm lock. Then she told him he was under arrest for assaulting a police officer, and suddenly they didn't have any trouble turning down the music."

"I would have loved to be a fly on the wall in that room." There is a note of admiration in her voice. From what I've gathered during our conversations tonight, Bryce works a lot, and Everly doesn't have many close friends. Just a few other attorneys' wives she's forced to socialize with to keep up appearances for Bryce. There is an air of loneliness to her, and it breaks my goddamn heart.

"You'd love Serena. You should come over for game night sometime. She hosts one weekly. It can get a little rowdy, and more than a little cutthroat, but it's a good time."

Ever's smile falters at my invitation, like she'd love nothing more than to accept it, but can't. The idea of her sitting in this big house alone, or forcing smiles around people she doesn't like, kills me. I reach across the table and grab her hand, emphasizing how serious I am about my invitation. "The next game night is Thursday. I'll send you her address, and if you want to come, you can. There's always plenty of food, and someone is always bringing a new friend to join. It won't be weird." She gives me a small nod, and I squeeze her hand before letting go. Glancing at my watch, I realize it's nearly eleven and Bryce still isn't home.

"Shit, it's getting late. I need to go soon. Does Bryce normally work this late?" I can't stay forever, but I don't love the idea of leaving Everly alone either.

"Sometimes. I usually get bored waiting up for him and go to bed. I'm sure he'll be home soon. It's fine if you need to go." She gives me a helpless *what can you do?* shrug and another crack forms in my heart. My fucking spoiled asshole brother has no idea what an amazing woman he has waiting for him at home. My first instinct is to stay and keep her company until he gets home, then give him a piece of my mind, but her next words put a stop to that particular train of thought.

"You should probably go. I am tired, and Bryce might think it's weird if you're still here when he gets home. I'll just go to bed. Thanks for keeping me company tonight." Everly stands, collecting the wine glasses to take them back inside. I open the patio door for her and follow her inside the house as she deposits the glasses in the expensive looking stainless steel dishwasher. She walks me to the front door, and I lose the fight against the impulse to hug her. I pull her in for a quick hug and drop a chaste kiss to the top of her head.

"I'll text you the details about game night. I hope you come; I think you'd really like Serena. Lock the door when I leave." Bryce and Everly live in a gated community. I know she'll be fine, but the idea of her being here all alone still worries me.

"Yes, sir." She gives me a playful salute, but hearing those two words come out of her mouth shoots a jolt of arousal straight to my dick. Great, I know what I'll be thinking about when I rub one out tonight.

When the door closes behind me, I wait a beat to hear the lock engage before walking to my car. On the drive home, I realize I'm not even that mad about Bryce blowing me off. I'm just wondering how I can have more nights like this with Everly.

CHAPTER 4
EVERLY

"*You are so insanely talented, Ever. Don't ever doubt that, okay?*"

The memory of Dane's rough fingers resting gently on my pulse point as he stared into my soul and told me I am talented plays on a loop in my mind. The ease of our conversation. How free he was with his compliments. How sincere. His gentle touch. His smell. Sandalwood with a hint of something citrusy. The way he looked at me like he saw me. Truly saw me.

The shrill whistle of the tea kettle pulls me from my reverie, startling me back into reality. My cold, lonely, reality. Pulling the kettle from the heat, I pour it into my favorite mug, one of the first hand-thrown pieces I made. It's slightly lumpy, there's a weird dip in the lip, and it wobbles just slightly, but it fits into my hands perfectly and it is a reminder of how far I've come with my art. In my life. It's not perfect, but it's still useful. That's how I like to think of myself.

Bryce got home last night after midnight. I was lying in bed, pretending to be asleep, when he came into our bedroom. I didn't want to deal with his excuses, or his questions about Dane. I also didn't want to know if he smelled like *her*. The real reason I suspect he didn't come home until late last night. I don't have proof that he's having an affair. Only suspicion. But there have been signs. More late nights working. The strange perfume on his dress shirts. The mysterious calls he won't take in front of me that he claims are work related.

Honestly, I don't even care if he has an affair. I haven't felt love for my husband in a very long time, but leaving isn't an option. Not with our...*history*. I don't think he loves me either. To him, I'm a trophy. A pretty, shiny trophy he displays when convenient and neglects most of the time.

"Damn, Ever. Wow. That's good. Great. Fucking amazing. Really."

My cheeks heat again as Dane's forest green eyes flash in my mind. The way he honestly looked impressed by my painting made my heart skip a beat. Bryce hasn't spared my art more than a passing glance in years, unless he has to pretend to be impressed by it in front of clients.

Taking my tea, I venture into my studio to begin my day. I have a few pieces I need to finish glazing. I used to do art therapy when I was fresh out of college, but Bryce didn't like the idea of me working. He said, "No wife of mine will ever need to work." And so...I don't. I stay at home and work on my art. Sometimes I sell a piece. Or have something on display at the local gallery. But most of my work languishes in my studio.

I think he thought I would stay home and raise our children, but after ten years of marriage and trying, I've never gotten pregnant. The doctors haven't found an explanation for my infertility, and honestly, I consider it a blessing. The idea of bringing a child into our loveless marriage turns my stomach. I would never subject a child to the type of childhood I had growing up. I wouldn't want them to settle for the first pretty boy that shows them some kindness, tying them to a narcissist for the rest of their life.

My phone dings with an incoming text message just as I put my last piece into the kiln. Picking it up, I'm surprised to find a text notification from Dane staring me in the face. Why would he be texting me? I swipe my thumb across the lock screen, opening the message.

DANE

Game night tomorrow. 7 sharp. 615 Bloom St. Bring your A game. Hope you can make it. Serena is looking forward to meeting you.

I bite my lower lip, fighting the smile that is threatening to break free. Why is an innocent text message from my brother-in-law, inviting me to game night, causing me to feel like a giddy teenager? Maybe because his brother hasn't shown any interest in me beyond what I can do for his public reputation or the favors I can help him get from my dad.

My mind conjures up what a game night with Dane and his friends would look like. Would he be competitive? Carefree? Would those dimples of his make an appearance? Would his friends welcome me? Friends. God. What a novel concept. I had friends at one point, back in college. Back before I let Bryce consume my whole life. Now I have acquaintances. Fellow attorneys' wives that meet for boozy lunches. That talk about the tuition costs for their kids' private schools, or the trips they take with their husbands, and gossip about how one of their husband's got so-and-so off from serving time for silly charges like DUI or domestic violence.

ME

Thanks. I'll see what I can do.

Sighing, I tuck my phone away after sending my noncommittal response. It's not like I can go. Bryce would throw a fit if I wasn't home with dinner ready for him. But I can't quite bring myself to crush the fantasy I have building in my head of a normal night, with normal people, doing normal shit like playing board games and drinking cheap beer.

Instead, I pull out a canvas and throw myself into my art. A portrait slowly takes form in front of me as I work. A portrait of a masculine face featuring impossibly green eyes, sandy blond hair that's fallen out of place and dangles across one piercing orb, and full, pouty lips quirked up in just a hint of a secret smile.

HOURS LATER, I hear the front door open, and slam shut. The noise startles me out of the hyperfocus I fell into while painting. Jumping back with a gasp, my paintbrush makes an errant blue mark across the canvas. Shit. I'll have to fix that, but there's no time right now. I am shocked when I take in the portrait I was working on and realize it's nearly complete. Holy hell. It's been years since I've gotten in the zone like that and knocked out an almost completed piece in a day.

The clock on the wall reads 8:07 p.m. Oh fuck, I really did lose track of time. Bryce is going to be so pissed that dinner isn't ready. Thinking quickly, I rush out of the studio and head to our bedroom to change out of my paint spattered clothes and throw on a cute dress. Maybe if I convince him to go out for a date night, he won't be too grumpy about dinner not being ready.

I tug on a dark blue maxi dress that I know is one of his favorites. It shows off an ample amount of cleavage that I hope will be distracting enough for him to go along with my plan. After fixing my hair into something that resembles a romantic messy bun and swiping on some lipstick, I take in my appearance, hoping it doesn't look like I just spent the day painting. No errant paint colors are on my face—a minor miracle, normally I wind up covered in paint—and I look presentable. Satisfied with my reflection, I head out of the bedroom to find Bryce.

Bryce is sitting at his desk in his study, whiskey tumbler in hand and a pensive look on his face. My husband is a handsome man. I could never deny that, even if the passion and love between us has fizzled away. A five o'clock shadow perpetually dusts his strong jaw. His dark hair has just started to silver slightly at the temples, giving him a distinguished edge, while his tanned olive skin makes it look like he's always just got back from vacation. He takes so much after his father it's hard to believe he and Dane are related. The Mediterranean genes are strong on that side of his family. His once warm brown eyes now burn with a hard intensity that will make anyone squirm under their gaze. Useful in the courtroom, but I miss the sweetness I used to see in them when he would look at me.

Leaning against the door frame, I clear my throat before speaking, nervous to disrupt him. "Hey, you're home…"

When he turns his attention to me, I feel myself wilting like a flower. His gaze is cold. Hard. He's looking at me like someone he needs to cross examine in the witness chair, not his wife of twelve years.

"What's for dinner?"

No 'Hi honey, how are you? I missed you.' Just straight to the point. I do my best not to let my disappointment show on my face, desperate not to start an argument.

"I was thinking we could go out tonight. It's been so long since we've gone out on a date… I thought it might be good for us." I stammer through my words, hoping he will go along with my idea.

His stare rakes over me, examining me with his lawyer's eye for detail, seeing if I am selling him a line or if I'm telling the truth. His eyes linger on my chest, and I feel my skin heat under his scrutiny. Holding my breath, I wait for his answer. I don't want another tense night. I don't want to fight. I know our marriage doesn't have any love in it anymore, but that doesn't mean I don't want to keep the peace. If I'm stuck in this sham of a relationship, I want it to at least be somewhat amicable.

After a long, tense moment where my lungs begin to burn from the lack of oxygen, he finally nods. The breath I had been holding whooshes out as I heave a sigh of relief. He doesn't say anything as he swallows the last of his bourbon before standing and walking toward me. He stops when he reaches me, leaning over me, caging me in with his arms. The smokey, charred caramel scent of the alcohol he was drinking fills the space between us. He lowers one hand, and traces a finger along my cleavage, causing a hitch in my breath and my pulse to spike. The hunger in his eyes is unfamiliar. I haven't seen him look at me like this in so long. Like he wants me. Needs me.

"You look good, Everly. I can't wait to take this off of you later." My eyes flare at his compliment. It's been so long since I've been noticed by him, I can't help the tiny thrill of excitement it sends jolting through me. Maybe… maybe our marriage isn't dead after all. Smiling, pleased that my plan has worked, I cup his jaw in my hand and lean forward to dust a kiss on his lips.

"Thanks, I wore it just for you." He doesn't kiss me

back. Just takes the small peck I give him with no further show of emotion. Wordlessly he pulls away and heads toward the front of the house, and I bury my disappointment, trying not to let it show as I trail after him.

CHAPTER 5
EVERLY

We go to Bryce's favorite bar for dinner, The Blind Pig. It's one of those bars that fancies itself as higher class and charges minimum $20 a cocktail. The food is also nontraditional, deconstructed takes on typical bar fare. Pretentious and insufferable. A lot like my husband.

I am picking at the Bahn Mi sliders I ordered, wishing it was an actual Bahn Mi sandwich from my favorite Vietnamese restaurant. These are a sad imitation of the real thing. But that place is a tiny hole-in-the-wall, and Bryce wouldn't lower himself to going somewhere with only three tables and two employees for dinner. No one would see him there. Bryce likes to be seen and feel important. I feel like that's eighty percent of the reason he is still married to me. Being connected to me equals being connected to my dad, and he is gunning for his job eventually.

"Are you even listening to me, Everly?" Bryce's clipped

tone pulls me from my distracted thoughts of actual good food. When I look up at him, his face is an annoyed mask. Shit, I tuned him out. I've been doing that a lot when he talks about work. Mostly because it doesn't affect me, and he never asks me how my day was.

"Yeah, sorry. I zoned out for a second. What were you saying, darling?" The smile I give him doesn't quite reach my eyes. I put my slider down and give him my full attention.

"I said we need to go to the Harringtons for a dinner next Friday. Skip is fund raising for his campaign for re-election. We need to make an appearance and a donation. Also, Veronica wants you to join her for a luncheon on Sunday. You will need to go to that."

I fight the urge to roll my eyes at his demand. The Harringtons are some of the most shallow, superficial, pretentious busybodies I've ever had the misfortune of knowing, and for some unfortunate reason, Veronica has been trying to recruit me to be her best friend. My gentle brush-offs and reluctance to make plans never seems to phase her. She persists in inviting me to do things, and if I brush these plans off, Bryce will know and give me a lecture about not doing my part networking to support his career.

Forcing another smile, I respond, "I'll give her a call this weekend." I shove a large bite of slider into my mouth while returning my attention back to my plate, hoping that is the end of that conversation. Maybe I'll get lucky and come down with a gnarly case of food poisoning from this subpar pork slider and have an excuse to stay home.

Eventually, a couple of attorneys Bryce works with come in and spot us. Bryce proceeds to spend the next forty-five minutes ignoring me while glad-handing and chatting with them. I throw back two more overpriced cocktails and scroll on my phone, waiting for him to remember I am there. This is almost always how it is when we go out for dinner. He goes somewhere to be seen, is seen, then proceeds to ignore me in favor of whomever he can connect with for whatever case or pet project he is working on.

Once I finish my third cocktail, my bladder decides it's time for a trip to the ladies room. My seat is tucked against the wall, and I'm blocked in by Bryce's colleagues. Shane and Rob? Steve and Bob? Shit, I can't remember their names. There's no way I'll be able to sneak past them without disrupting their conversation. Bracing myself for the awkwardness, I clear my throat and stand.

"Sorry, gentlemen, I need to slip past to go to the ladies room." Steve—or is it Shane?—turns to look at me, and the look he gives me more closely resembles a leer. His eyes rake down my body, lingering far too long on my chest, and I suddenly feel self-conscious about the dress I chose to wear. It's one thing for my husband to ogle me. Another for his older, balder, also married colleague to do it. This man is in his late fifties and could easily be my dad.

"Sure, Everly. Squeeze on by." He gives me a smile that causes my stomach to turn and my dinner to threaten a reappearance. Taking one step back, he gives a minuscule amount of space for me and my ample ass to scoot between him and the table. Bryce's attention is fixed on Rob or Bob, or whoever he is. Blowing out an exasperated sigh, I move to slide past Shane/Steve. As I step in front of him, I feel his hand fall to my hip, grasping it tightly as he pushes his crotch into my ass. I freeze, shocked by his brazenness. He has his hands on me, right in front of my husband, and he doesn't even seem to give a fuck.

Low, so only I can hear, he whispers into my ear, "God, what I wouldn't give to take this for a ride. You should call me sometime when he's working late. I'll take care of you."

Bile rises in my throat, and I finally come to my senses enough to move out of his grasp and escape to the bathroom. I glance over my shoulder as I beat a hasty retreat, and see him checking out my ass shamelessly, like he isn't even trying to hide his interest from my husband. What the fuck? I spend the next ten minutes in the bathroom, hiding in a stall, trying to calm my racing heart, hoping Shane and Bob are gone when I come back. I can't bring myself to get within groping distance of that pervert again.

My phone buzzes in my hand. A text notification from Bryce pops up on my screen.

BRYCE

Where are you? I paid the check. Time to go.

I let out a relieved breath and step out of the stall. After washing my hands, I make my way back out into the dining room and find Bryce waiting by the door, tapping his foot with an impatient, irritated look on his face. Great. I made him wait to leave for five minutes after he ignored me for the last hour, and now I'm the bad guy.

Bryce's jaw is clenched; a slight tick is all the indication I get that he's irritated with me as we drive home. I debate if I should mention what Steve did. Would Bryce even believe me? I'm not entirely sure he would.

When we arrive home, I get out of the car without a word and head straight to our bedroom. All I want to do is hop in the shower and wash off the slimy feeling of Shane/Steve's touch. I don't trust myself not to start a fight. Not with this much alcohol coursing through me. As I get to our bedroom, Bryce catches up to me, grabbing me by the arm. He spins me, backing me into the wall so he can cage me in.

"Where do you think you're going?" His voice is cold, harsh, but there is a fire in his eyes. He's looking at me like he can't decide if he wants to fuck me or throttle me.

"I'm going to take a shower. Do you mind?"

"I do mind. I told you I was going to take this dress off of you." His grip on my arm tightens, causing me to wince. When I try to look away, his other hand comes up and grips my neck, directing my gaze back up to meet his.

Annoyance at being manhandled again surges through me. "Get your hands off me. Do you really think I want to fuck after you spent most of our date ignoring me? After your friend fucking groped my ass and said he wanted to take me for a ride? You're delusional." Oops, the alcohol has loosened my tongue. So much for not starting a fight.

"*Who* said they want to take you for a ride?' Bryce's grip tightens to the point of pain, and I let out a yelp.

"Steve! Shane! Whatever the fuck his name is!"

"Shane said he wants to take you for a ride?" Bryce's voice drops to a low, scary tone.

When I look him in the eyes there is a manic gleam to them. I can't tell if he's angry or excited or turned on.

"I'll have to keep that in mind. Too bad for him, I'm the only one who gets to fuck this pussy." The arm that was holding my throat drops, grabbing my dress and hiking it up on one swift move. Bryce grips my sex, slipping one finger past the edge of my thong into my wet pussy. I'm disgusted with myself for being turned on by his caveman behavior, but my wetness is all the permission he needs. A feral grin splits his face right before he yanks my dress off and tosses me to the bed.

I watch, chest heaving, as he stalks across the room, unbuttoning his pants, freeing his cock. It's been so long since Bryce has shown any interest in me that my mind can't decide if I should be excited by the inferno burning between us, or angry at how he's treating me. Bryce crawls onto the bed nude, his erection jutting out in front of him. He is still as gorgeous as he ever was. I lick my lips as he settles over me, the heat from his body scorching mine.

Hiking up one of my legs over his shoulder, Bryce notches the head of his cock at my entrance.

"This pussy is mine. I am the only one who gets to fuck it. No one touches it without my say-so." He punctuates his statement by thrusting, sheathing his full length inside me. My eyes fly open at the intrusion, and it takes a second for his words to register in my brain. No one touches me without his say-so.

The implication of those words sends dread coursing through me as he fucks me senseless.

CHAPTER 6
EVERLY

It's Thursday evening, a little past six. Dinner is rapidly cooling on the table. Bryce is nowhere to be seen. He left for work early this morning, without even saying goodbye. My texts to him have gone unanswered. I pick at the pasta on my plate, my appetite nonexistent. The comment he made last night about no one else fucking me unless he says they can keeps running through my mind. He seemed to get some sort of sick satisfaction out of knowing Shane wants to fuck his wife, and I'm not entirely sure he won't use that to his advantage at some point to make a deal with Shane. Surely he wouldn't...would he?

As time creeps by, food getting colder by the minute, I find myself staring at my phone, rereading Dane's invitation to game night, debating if I should go. Dinner is made, but it isn't my fault Bryce isn't here to eat it while it's warm. The frustration I feel at his lack of communication and his disrespect of my time courses through my veins. Why should I sit here, waiting for him to get home, like a doting housewife? I'm not a prisoner. What is he going to do? Yell? Be angry? Well, I'm already pissed, so that doesn't matter.

I take his plate, cover it with foil, and stick it in the fridge, leaving a note for him to look for it in there. I don't leave any details about where I'm going or what I'm doing. Let him worry for a change. I throw on my favorite denim jacket, grab my purse, steal an overpriced bottle of wine from the wine fridge so I don't show up empty handed, and head out the door, ready to live my life for me, if just for tonight.

PULLING up to 615 Bloom Street, I find a cute, craftsman-style house with a red front door and a porch lined with beautiful hydrangea bushes, still clinging to their color in the late summer season. It's been getting cooler the last few days, and soon the leaves will change and the flowers will die. I sit in my car, taking a moment to calm my nerves. It's been so long since I've gone out to meet new people with the intention of making friends. What if they don't like me? What if I'm too out of touch after spending so much time with Bryce and his social circle? Will I seem like a snob to them the same way Veronica seems like one to me? Fuck it—that's what the wine is for, right?

I march up to the front door and knock before I let my doubts get the better of me and convince me to turn around and go home. I hear boisterous laughter coming from inside the house. It's after seven, so the game night has probably already started. Biting my lower lip, I take a step back, reconsidering my decision. But before I can make my escape, the door opens, revealing a handsome young Black man with a dazzling smile. My mind temporarily glitches as I take in his appearance, from his neatly braided corn rows to the dimples in his cheeks and the gorgeous brown eyes that seem almost bottomless. His sepia brown skin still seems to glow from the joy radiating off him. I find myself immediately at ease with him.

"Hey, can I help you?" His tone is curious, but not unfriendly. His voice is rich like honey, and I wonder if he works in radio or perhaps sings.

"Um, yeah, is Dane here? He…he invited me to join him for a game night at this address? I'm Everly, his sister-in-law." I stick out my hand in offering, and my cheeks heat as the man in front of me holds back a chuckle.

Instead of shaking my hand, he grabs it and pulls me into the house, taking me by surprise.

"Hey, Dane, you can get that stick out of your ass. Your guest is here!" He turns, flashing me an amused grin, and waggles his eyebrows at me. "Hopefully he will stop being so damn pissy now that you're here. He's been in a mood since he got here. I'm Kai, by the way." Without any other choice, I follow him further into the house, getting closer to the sound of people laughing and chatting.

I follow Kai into a den, and find a group of people sitting around an oversized sectional couch. There is an easel set up on one wall, where a gorgeous woman with tawny brown skin, golden eyes, and a youthful face dusted with freckles stands with a marker in her hand, poised like she is ready to draw. She has a halo of curls that frames her face, and I immediately realize she must be Serena, Dane's partner.

Dane is sitting at one end of the couch, staring down at his phone, brows furrowed, scowling. Kai wasn't joking—he does look like he's in a bad mood. My feet freeze in place as doubt creeps in. Maybe I shouldn't have come. Kai stops short when he senses I'm not following him into the room.

Everyone but Dane turns toward us, and I suddenly have seven sets of eyes on me. I clear my throat nervously and throw my hand up in a wave. "Hi. Sorry to barge in but —" I start to introduce myself, but Dane's head jerks up when he hears my voice, and the scowl that had been etched on his face melts away as soon as our eyes meet.

"Everly, you came." He sounds surprised, but pleased to see me, and it sends a wave of relief coursing through me. Dane immediately jumps up from his seat on the couch and comes over to give me a hug. In a matter of seconds, I find myself wrapped in his arms, surrounded by his intoxicating scent, and I can't help but melt into him a little.

When Dane pulls away, I immediately find myself missing the warmth of his body. Has he always been such a hugger? I rack my brain trying to remember. "I wasn't sure if you were gonna come… Um, here, let me introduce you to everyone." Dane rests his hand on my lower back and guides me into the room. A slight thrill shoots through me at his touch, and I mentally chide myself for enjoying it too much. This was a bad idea. I'm going to spend the evening hanging out with my husband's brother, enjoying his company and torturing myself with something I can never have. Why did I do this to myself?

While my mind is doing mental gymnastics, I try to pay attention to the names of everyone he introduces me to.

"Seems like you met Kai already." Dane says, nodding to the man who has moved over to stand next to Serena. "That's his wife, Serena, cop-slash-undercover stripper extraordinaire."

"Boy, I swear to god, if you tell that story one more time." Serena's tone is threatening, but there is humor dancing in her eyes as she threatens Dane.

"You'll what?" Dane flashes his smirk before turning to the other people in the room.

"That's Gloria, AKA Mrs. G. Don't get her started on any stories about handcuffs or zucchinis unless you're really okay with TMI." The older woman with the over-sized glasses flips Dane the bird, and I immediately like her.

"Those two over there are Grace and Luther, Kai's parents. And next to them is Laura, Serena's mom." I stick my hand out to shake hands, but Grace leaps off the couch and pulls me into a hug.

"Honey, we hug in this house. We don't shake hands. Come, come, sit. We were just getting started!" Grace's hug feels like being wrapped up in my mother's arms. I give her a squeeze as I let the familiarity wash over me. She can't be much older than me, maybe ten or twelve years but her warmth reminds me so much of my mother, I can't help but feel a pang of longing. She passed from breast cancer shortly after Bryce and I married, and I still feel that loss on a near daily basis. When Grace lets go, I see Luther has scooted over to make room for me and Dane to sit on the couch.

When we sit, I find myself sandwiched between Laura and Dane, my body pressed firmly against his, the scent of his cedar wood cologne short-circuiting my brain.

"Hi, I'm Laura. Please don't get offended if I introduce myself to you more than once tonight. I had a brain injury, and my short-term memory is a little glitchy."

Despite not having the same skin color as Serena, it's clear as day that Laura is her mom. Her freckles mirror Serena's, and they share the same eyes and nose.

"Oh, that's okay. I'm awful with names, so there is a solid chance I'll forget someone's name tonight, and I don't even have the brain injury excuse." Shit. I cringe as soon as the words leave my mouth, and I hope they don't come across as glib and insensitive.

Laura just bursts out laughing. "Oh god, I can't tell you how handy that excuse is when someone comes up to talk to me and I don't recognize them. If I'm being honest, I've always been terrible with names too." Laura gives me a conspiratorial wink that puts me at ease.

Dane gives me a gentle nudge with his leg, pulling my attention back to him. "Is that just for you or for sharing?" He nods his head toward the wine I'm clutching to my chest like my own personal emotional support bottle.

"Oh, sorry! I brought this for sharing. I didn't want to show up empty handed." Sheepishly, I hold the wine out toward Kai, who takes it with an appraising look.

"Does this need to be chilled, or can we open it now?"

"It can be opened now if you want. I wasn't sure what you liked, but Riesling is usually a safe bet. It's on the sweeter side. If you don't like wine, that's fine. You don't have to open it." I'm rambling, and I can't seem to stop myself.

Kai throws me a bone with his response. "Awesome, Riesling is Serena's favorite. I'll go pour some. Dane, you wanna come give me a hand carrying back the drinks?" Kai shoots a look to Dane that says his request is more of a demand than a polite request for a favor. My heart clenches at the thought of being alone with a room full of strangers, but Dane gives my leg a reassuring squeeze before he stands.

"Don't worry. They won't bite." He shoots me an easy wink before following Kai to the kitchen.

"Speak for yourself, boy. Mr. G loved it when I would leave love bites on him!" Gloria calls after Dane, setting off a round of raucous laughter in the room.

CHAPTER 7
DANE

"Muscular hamburger man!" Serena yells, jumping up from her spot on the couch, animatedly waving her arms around.

As her nonsense answer, Kai looks at his wife like she sprouted a second head. "Woman, what part of this looks like a hamburger?"

"That part!" Serena waves her hand vaguely at the hamburger/humanoid's head.

"It's a stud muffin! His head is clearly a muffin, and he's a stud. I pointed to myself; you should've gotten that!" Kai throws up his hands in exasperation, and Everly doubles over in laughter, half collapsing on top of me. I'm not even a little mad about her proximity. She and Serena made quick work of the wine she brought over, then she switched to drinking ciders, and she has become progressively more comfortable touching me as the amount of alcohol coursing through her veins has increased. I should feel guilty for wanting to be this close to my brother's wife, but I have a hard time making myself care. I'm just enjoying being near her. I make a mental note that I'll need to drive her home when it's time to leave.

I wasn't sure if she would loosen up enough to enjoy game night with a bunch of strangers, but Everly immediately connected with Serena and Laura. When she mentioned she used to do art therapy when she was getting her B.A. in art, Laura told her they were looking for someone to start up a similar program at Whispering Grove, the assisted living facility where she lives. I could see the interest in Everly's eyes when Laura mentioned it, but then she brushed it off, claiming she was probably too busy to be the person to do it. In my heart I know it's because Bryce doesn't want her working. Doesn't want her having a life outside of him.

"Alright, kids, I think that's enough for us tonight. We are gonna give Laura and Gloria a ride home." Luther, Kai's dad, stands, lifting his fist to his mouth to cover an exaggerated yawn. His announcement causes Everly's giggle fit to calm down as she sits up, surprise written across her face. Her cheeks are flushed with alcohol, and tears from laughter shine in her eyes. I can't remember the last time I saw her looking so carefree and happy.

"What? How late is it?" She looks around on her seat, trying to locate her cell phone.

"It's ten-thirty. Luther is right—it's getting late. How about I give you a ride home?" I stand and offer her my hand. An expression crosses Everly's face that looks suspiciously like fear, before she schools it back into a facsimile of the carefree countenance she was wearing just a moment ago.

"Oh, you don't have to do that. I'm fine!" She jumps up from her seat and immediately sways on her feet. I wrap an arm around her waist, steadying her before she goes down. Kai and Serena follow their parents and Gloria to the front door while I stay behind to convince Everly to let me drive her home.

"I think it's a good idea if you let me drive you home. That wine hit you fast, giggle pants."

Everly rolls her eyes at my nickname for her. "I skipped dinner. Drinking on an empty stomach probably wasn't my smartest decision." She scrunches her face up in the most adorable fashion at her confession, and I can't resist the urge to give her a playful flick on the nose.

Her eyes fly open, and her mouth makes a surprised O. "You did *not* just flick me on the nose!" She smacks me in the chest, and I want nothing more than to grab her wrist, pull her into me, and trap her in my arms. Shit. I haven't even had anything to drink to justify thinking like that. I need to get her home before I make a mistake I can't take back. Shaking my head, I grab her by the hand and pull her toward the kitchen.

"Come on, Ever. Let's go. I think your purse and your phone are on the kitchen island. I'll drive you home in your car and Uber to my place." Everly follows without protest, the drunken haze that had momentarily lifted settling back over her.

After collecting her purse and shoes, we stop by the front door to say goodnight to Kai and Serena. Everly and

Serena hug like they're new best friends, and it warms my bitter, jaded heart. Serena has been through so much in her life, and Everly just seems so lonely now. I secretly hope they actually become friends, so I have more opportunities to see Everly.

"Thank you for letting me crash your game night. This was the most fun I've had in years."

I'm standing next to Kai, watching the girls say good-bye, and I swear it almost looks like Everly is holding back tears. When they let go, Everly turns to Kai and gives him a hug as well.

"For what it's worth, I knew it was a stud muffin." Kai barks out a surprised laugh before shooting Serena a glare.

"Next time you're on my team then. I can't with this one over here. We always lose when we are on a team!"

"Boy, you better watch your mouth. It's not my fault Archie has better drawing skills than you."

"ReRe, you leave my dog out of this!" Everly collapses into my side in a fresh wave of giggles at Kai and Serena's argument, and I take that as our cue to leave.

"Bye guys. See you tomorrow, Serena." They barely spare us a glance as their debate on Kai's artistry gets more heated.

I lead Everly out to her car, her clinging to my arm like my own personal koala. When we get to her sleek silver Mercedes, I lean her against the passenger door, keeping one arm around her waist to hold her steady.

"Where are your keys, Ever?"

"In my purse. It's push start. It should be unlocked now that I'm close." She pulls on the handle and the door pops open, causing her to stumble forward, her body pressing into mine. Instinctively my hands grab her upper arms to balance her, and the feeling of her soft breasts pressing into my chest momentarily short-circuits my brain. I don't immediately let go of her, instead taking a moment to get lost in the gold flecks of her hazel eyes. A small smile plays on her lips, causing her eyes to crinkle just a bit in the corners. I'm obsessed with those wrinkles. They are a testimony to all the reasons Everly has ever had to smile.

She lifts one hand and brushes a loose strand of hair away from my eyes. "I had fun tonight, Dane. The most fun I've had in a long, long time. Thank you for inviting me."

There is so much I want to say to that. *Why has it been so long since you had fun? Does Bryce never do anything fun with you? When was the last time you went out with friends? Do you have friends?* Instead, I just say, "Come on Ever, let's get you home."

CHAPTER 8
DANE

We drive to Everly's house, her drunkenly chattering the whole way. At first I was amused and happy to listen to her tipsy ramblings, but now she is talking about a date she and Bryce went on last night, and I can feel my jaw clenching harder and harder as I listen to her story of how he basically ignored her the whole night.

"So then after like forty minutes of watching him kiss ass, I finally decided to make my escape to the ladies room. The martinis were catching up to me… Anyway, as I tried to scoot past Shane, one of the guys talking to Bryce, he fucking grabs me! Puts his hands on my hip and rubs his nasty dick against my ass and told me he wanted to 'take me for a ride,' like that's supposed to be a turn on. Can you believe that guy?" Everly rolls her eyes, like she's recounting someone stealing her parking spot and not sexually harassing her.

We are just pulling into Everly's drive when she drops

that bomb, and I hit the brakes, stopping us suddenly in the middle of the driveway.

"Excuse me? He did what?" I throw her car into park so I can turn and face her fully, making sure I heard her clearly. "He put his hands on you? Jesus, Ever. Please tell me Bryce did something."

Everly lets out a derisive snort. "He was busy talking to Rob. Or Bob. Whatever his name is. He didn't see a damn thing, and when I told him about it later, it almost seemed to turn him on knowing some other guy wants to fuck me." Her cheeks turned pink at that admission, like she's the one that needs to be embarrassed in this situation and not my brother or his creeper friend. "He said, and I quote, 'This pussy is mine. I am the only one that gets to fuck it. No one touches it without my say-so.'" Her voice trails off on the last part as she turns her head to look out the window.

I feel my blood start to boil.

"Jesus Christ. I always thought Bryce was a shithead but this really takes the cake. Fuck, Ever. Why do you stay with him? Are you even happy? Do you love him?" Everly doesn't respond to my inquisition. Just keeps looking out the window. I watch her reflection in the glass as she lifts her hand to her face, wiping away a tear.

Realizing my anger might be scaring her, I take a deep breath and blow it out, trying to calm my temper.

"Shit, Ever, I'm sor—" She moves to open the door, not turning to look at me.

"It doesn't matter, Dane." Her words are resigned. Like she knows her fate, and she's made peace with it. "Thank you for inviting me tonight and driving me home. I'm gonna go now." Before I can protest, she's out of the car, shutting the door behind her. I sit, stunned for a second, before jumping into motion, chasing after her with an unshakable need to make sure she is okay.

"Ever, wait! Talk to me." She picks up her pace, digging through her purse, blindly looking for the house key.

"Dane, you should go. It's late." Her voice wobbles, like she's trying not to cry, and my heart cracks at the sound.

"Hey, hey, hey… Everly. Please." I catch up to her just as she reaches the front door. I grab her upper arm, turning her so she's facing me, her back to the door. Even in the dim outdoor lights illuminating their flowerbeds, I can see the way her eyes shimmer with unshed tears.

"Everly, I want to help you. If you are unhappy or in danger, please let me help you. You don't have to stay with the dickhead." Everly huffs out a bitter laugh as she tries to turn her gaze away from mine. I don't let her though. I gently use my free hand to cup her jaw, directing her eyes back to mine.

"He's my brother, but I know what a dick he is. I've never thought he deserved you. If you're afraid of leaving him, I'll help you. If you need me to kick his ass, I will. If you just need someone to talk to…talk to me. Please."

Everly's breath hitches at my words, her eyes going wide in shock. Of course, she knows he and I aren't close, but I don't think she ever realized the depth of animosity between us. I can tell by her eyes and the way they dance slightly that she is trying to convince herself of something. Of what though?

One heartbeat passes. Two. Then three. And then her lips are on mine. Her hands reach up, grasping my neck, pulling me down to her. Pulling me into her. My knees nearly buckle when I feel the sweet wetness of her tongue slide into my mouth. Without thought, I take one step forward, crushing her body to mine, pinning her against the door. Her body melts into mine, like we were designed to fit together. My hand glides around her jaw to the back of her neck, where I twine my fingers into her silky soft hair. She tastes like sweet apples, and I am immediately addicted. The hand that had been holding her by the arm slides down to her waist, cupping a soft palmful of her delicious curves.

My tongue licks into her mouth, and I want nothing more than to bury myself into her soul. I've been thinking about kissing this woman since I was eighteen, and it's... devastating. I'll never be able to go back from this. This is it. This is the moment where I throw it all away just to have this woman. I don't care if she's my brother's wife. He doesn't deserve her.

"Fuck... Ever..." My voice is barely above a husky whisper. I kiss along her jaw and down the column of her neck. Her fingers dig into my hair, tugging it just until it's painful, and my dick hardens. I can feel my length pressing into the thin fabric of her leggings. She lets out the sexiest whimper when I let my teeth graze along her pulse point. Just as I seal my lips to suck on her neck, the sound of a phone buzzing disrupts the quiet night air.

"Shit!" Everly jumps like she's been tased, her arms coming to my shoulders to push me away. Her face is a confused mask of surprise, terror, and shame. We stand, inches apart, panting, breathing the same air, trying to comprehend what just happened. The phone buzzes again, breaking the spell between us.

"Fuck, Ever—"

"I-I-I have to go. Please leave, Dane. You can't be here." She gives me another gentle shove, and I'm stunned enough that I stumble back a step, giving her room to turn around and open the door.

"Everly, wait, please!" I lunge forward to stop her from closing the door, but she slips inside and presses her body against it, preventing me from following her.

"No, Dane. Please. This can't happen. Just go."

Dumbfounded, I step back, letting her close the door in my face. I know she felt that charge between us. She was trying to climb into my skin just as much as I was into hers. She may think this can't happen, but after that kiss, there is no way in hell I am going to let my dickbag brother win without a fight.

CHAPTER 9
EVERLY

EVERLY - 21 YEARS OLD

"I *really* don't want to go to this party, Ana. Can't we just stay in?" I make prayer hands as I look up at my roommate, pleading to her from under my favorite blanket hoody. Already tucked into my favorite TV binging spot on the couch. My outgoing, extroverted, energizer bunny of a roommate flips her sleek black hair and puts her hands on her hips.

"*You* said, and I quote, 'I owe you one, Ana! I prooooomise I'll go to the next party. But I can't miss this premier of *Grey's Anatomy*! I have to know what happened to McDreamy!' Well bitch, it's time to pay up. I need a wing woman."

Ana narrows her blue eyes at me, and I know there will be no wiggling my way out of this excursion. Why did I have to wind up being best friends with an extrovert?

"If I remember correctly, you're the one who wound up

bawling your eyes out halfway through the episode." I quirk a brow at her, making a last-ditch effort to convince her to stay in.

"And *that* is why you owe me. I need to fuck these feelings out. Now come on; go put something slutty on, and let's go."

TWO HOURS later we are shoulder to shoulder in a frat house well beyond fire code capacity. We've been here for forty-five minutes, and I am regretting all of my life choices. It's so hot and crowded, I feel on the verge of hyperventilating. Ana forges ahead, dragging me by the hand through the crowd in search of...booze? Or dick? I have no idea. It's too loud to communicate in here. All I know is that I need to get some air. Suddenly I see a break in the crowd and an open doorway leading outside. I lurch toward it, letting go of Ana's hand in favor of fresh air. She looks back at me, eyes widened in surprise, as our connection breaks. We never separate at parties—buddy system in place until we find someone to leave with, that's always our M.O.

"I need air! Go get the drinks! I'll be out there!" I shout over the music, as I point to the inviting front porch. There is at least fifty percent fewer people out there, and I need space. Ana looks unsure, not willing to separate just yet, but I flash her a thumbs up, encouraging her to forge on. I really don't want my introverted ways to ruin tonight for her. She's been there for me so many times when dealing with my heartbreak after my high school sweetheart of four years, Cole, dumped me.

It happened at the beginning of our freshman year at BFU, before I had built a support system of new college friends. All I had was a roommate who loved the color pink and partying, but when she caught me sobbing under my comforter the night of the breakup, she offered up her stash of candy and put on *Legally Blonde*. We went from comically diametrically opposing roommates—nerdy, introverted artist versus extroverted, socialite business major—to best friends bonded over pints of Ben & Jerry's, shitty '90s rom-com movie nights, and a mutual dislike of our philosophy professor.

Ana returns my thumbs up and continues on her mission, and I make a break for the fresh air and open space calling to me through the doorway. Outside, I blow out a calming breath as I let the cool night air caress my skin. It's mid-October. The days are still warm enough not to require a jacket, but once the sun sets, the temperature drops to just this side of chilly. I'll wind up regretting my choice not to wear a jacket soon, but right now the fresh, crisp fall evening air feels like heaven.

There are drunk couples scattered around the porch, making out in the shadows, and a small gathering of people in the yard next to a fire pit. Not wanting to disrupt anyone's make out session, I move to head down to the fire, but a large male form appears in front of me, blocking my path.

"Where you going, gorgeous? You here by yourself?" Alarm bells immediately begin ringing in my mind as I take in his appearance. He's huge. Probably a linebacker for the BFU Wolverines. He towers over me by a good six inches, and his frame blocks out the light from the fire. His blond hair stands in sharp spikes, and his dull brown eyes have an unfocused look to them. I take a step back; he steps forward, forcing me to back up until I come to a stop against the wall, putting himself between me and my path to escape.

"You're pretty. Whatsh yer name?" He leans in, his large chest consuming my entire field of vision. He reeks of beer, way too much body spray, and a vague hint of stale sweat. Even in the dark, I can make out a large wet spot on his pink polo shirt. Great, he's fucking wasted.

"Please get out of my way," I say through gritted teeth, trying not to look as intimidated as I feel right now.

"Naw, you haven't told me your name yet. I wanna know yer name, pretty girl." He hiccups, letting a fresh wave of beer breath wash over me.

"Fuck. Off," I grit out, as I shove him hard in the shoulder. I manage to catch him by surprise and knock him off balance enough to slip by him. Almost. His large, meaty hand grabs me by the upper arm, dragging me back and slamming me hard against the wall. My head snaps back, hitting the brick, causing stars to burst into my vision.

"That wasn't nice, pretty girl. I was just trying to talk. No need to be a bitch." His grip tightens to the point of pain, causing me to let out a whimper. When my vision clears and he comes back into focus, his face his right in front of mine, a dangerous gleam to his eyes.

Shit. Fuck. Shit. Fuck. I need to get away from him.

"I said fuck off!" I yell this time, hoping there's someone not too busy trying to get laid to hear me.

He doesn't like that. A look crosses his face that tells me he's seconds away from really hurting me. Suddenly another hand is on his bicep, pushing him away from me.

"Hey, Brody, dude, back off. She's here with me. I'm gonna need you to step away from my date."

Brody, the gorilla sized douchebag in front of me, flares his nose as he directs his attention to my rescuer. His eyes track the newcomer slowly, his drunkenness becoming more apparent. The new guy moves so he is between me and Brody. His back is broad and muscular, well-defined under the tight black henley he is wearing, but not nearly as large as Brody. He has dark hair and smells expensive. That's all I can tell from this angle.

"Shezyours?"

"Yeah, man, she is. Now fuck off." My "date" keeps his hand on Brody's bicep and marches forward, backing Brody up enough that I can finally get away from the wall. I dash around him and head down the stairs toward the crowd by the fire, desperate to get back into the safety of light and fellow students. Plopping down on an upturned log, I bend over, tucking my head between my knees, trying to fight away the panic threatening to overwhelm my nervous system.

"Hey, hey, you're okay. He's gone." A warm hand rests on my shoulder as a soft, deep voice murmurs in my ear. I don't move right away, my mind still fixated on how close I just was to being assaulted. My muscles are locked tight in fear. The voice keeps repeating a soft, soothing mantra of

"You're okay," while his thumb makes gentle circles on my skin.

Gradually my breathing evens out, and I am able to sit upright and get a good look at my hero. He's hot. I don't know why that's the first thing my brain decides to notice. Maybe because it's still rebooting and not fully back online. His eyes are a warm brown, framed by thick, dark lashes, and sharp, well-groomed eyebrows. He looks like he might be a few years older than me. Grad student, maybe? His dark hair, olive tan skin, and gorgeous brown eyes remind me so much of Ardeth Bay from *the Mummy* that I temporarily forget why I'm upset.

"Hey, there she is. Welcome back." He flashes a smile, revealing unnaturally white teeth.

"Hi—hi. Thank you for that. He caught me by surprise." I don't know why I say that. Why am I making excuses for being manhandled by an ape?

"No thanks needed. Brody is notorious for not being able to keep his hands to himself. Not the first time I've had to keep him from doing something stupid while shit-faced." The guy shakes his head in disappointment. "Seriously though, are you okay? Do you want to leave? I can help you get home."

It's on the tip of my tongue to say yes. I really do want to go home, but I don't feel right abandoning Ana. Especially not if Brody is still at the party. "I can't; my friend is here. I don't want to leave her alone." My new friend takes in my words, his face taking on a calculating look.

"Okay, how about I go find her for you and bring her out here. Then you can go home together." I nod. I don't want to ruin Ana's night, but there is no way I can stay here any longer.

"Who're you here with?"

"Ana Price. Black hair, blue eyes, she's wearing a high-lighter pink halter top. Looks like Wednesday Adams if she were a Barbie." His eyes crinkle at the corners when he smiles at my description of my best friend.

"Yeah, I think I've seen her. Stay here…" He trails off, like he's waiting for me to fill in the blank. It takes a second for me to realize he wants to know my name.

"Everly. Everly Strauss."

His smile gets wider when he hears my name.

"Stay here, Everly Strauss." He stands up to leave, and I grab his hand, not quite ready to let him go.

"What's your name?"

"Bryce. Bryce Carmichael."

CHAPTER 10
EVERLY

I kissed Dane. *I* kissed Dane. I *kissed* my husband's brother. What the fuck was I thinking?

I stand, my back pressed against the door, chest heaving, heart trying to beat its way out of my chest, while my mind tries to reconcile what I've done. I kissed another man, right on my front porch. I kissed my *brother-in-law* on my front porch. Kissing Dane was a bad idea for many reasons, least of which is the fact that I'm married to his brother. God, if he knew what kind of person I really am, he wouldn't look at me with so much compassion. Or want. Or need. I can't remember the last time Bryce looked at me like that. Like he would do anything to make my world better. Like my happiness actually matters.

Something wet splashes against my collarbone and trails down the valley of my cleavage before disappearing. It's then I realize I'm crying. Full on, fat, unstoppable tears, snot running from my nose, ugly crying. Guilt churns in my stomach, and I force my limbs into motion, pushing away from the front door, trudging further into the still dark house. I become dimly aware that the house is still empty. Bryce *still* isn't home. He probably didn't even know I left. I wait for the anger to come, at realizing my husband would've just left me waiting all night without a check-in, but the guilt over kissing Dane is too strong. It is the overriding emotion right now. I can't even bring myself to feel relieved that Bryce isn't here. That he didn't catch us.

I don't bother with turning on the lights as I make my way through the house to our bedroom. I go through the motions of washing off my makeup, brushing my teeth, and changing into pajamas, my mind alternating between guilt over kissing the one man I have absolutely no right to be kissing and how good his lips felt pressed to mine. How his large, firm body felt pinning my body against the door. His taste as our tongues danced together.

Climbing into bed, I burrow under the covers, as if the weight of the fluffy comforter can smother the twin flames of shame and arousal burning through me right now. I lay there in the dark, watching the minutes tick by on the clock on the nightstand, the faint blue light from the display the only illumination in the room. It isn't until the clock reads 12:02 a.m. that I hear the sound of the front door opening, signaling Bryce's return home. I feel my heart rate spike at the sound of his movement through the house, terrified that somehow he will know what I did.

When he enters the bedroom, I close my eyes and will my breathing to slow down, trying to feign sleep. I don't want to face him. I don't trust myself not to give away what happened between me and Dane. I pray he will buy my ruse and try not to disturb me. Keeping my breathing steady and shallow, I listen to him move around the room, undressing. The *thunk* of his belt landing on the dresser, followed by his watch. My breath stills as I hear him go into the bathroom and the water turn on in the shower. Why is he showering at midnight? Is it so I won't know what he was up to? Or rather, who he was with? My mind whirls over those possibilities, and I focus on Bryce and his mysterious whereabouts instead of all of the reasons I should be feeling guilty over my kiss with Dane, or how amazing it felt to be kissed by someone who wants me. It's with the memory of Dane's lips skating down my neck with his body pinning me to the door replaying in my mind that sleep finally comes for me.

WHEN I WAKE the next morning, bleary-eyed and head pounding, Bryce has mercifully already left for work. Instead of being irritated that my husband is barely around, I find myself relieved. I'm spared from having to make small talk with him and make up a lie about what I did last night, from having to ask him where he was all night. I don't have to hope the guilt I'm feeling isn't written all over my face.

Turning on the kettle, I start rummaging through the fridge to find something for breakfast. The vague pounding in my head, I'm sure is related to last night. I'm just not sure if it's due to the alcohol or from the stress and anxiety I'm feeling over my actions. Nothing in the fridge is appealing, so I just grab a yogurt container and finish making my tea before heading out to the pool deck.

Our house is located in a gated neighborhood at the top of a hill. Our backyard has unobstructed views of the mountains that Birch Falls is nestled in. Normally this view brings me peace and clarity. When I'm having a block with my art or mulling over a problem, I come out here to drink tea and let my mind wander, letting it puzzle through the matter bothering me while I lose myself to the view.

Sipping my tea, I find myself thinking of the night that changed everything forever. I thought I was doing the right thing at the time, but now I'm not so sure. It was when Bryce and I were still newlyweds. Still so very much in love. At least I was. I would've done anything for him. With the way he treats me now, I find myself wondering if he ever did love me, or if I was just the most convenient stepping stone in the progression of his life plan.

I'M HUNCHED OVER, elbow deep in pottery clay, lost in the sensation of the slippery clap sliding through my fingers. My tongue pokes out between my lips as I concentrate on shaping the lip of the tall, thin vase I'm in the process of throwing. Pottery is my latest artistic endeavor, and I'm striving to master it so I can start using it as part of my art therapy program. Not everyone can paint or draw, and there is something soothing about the process of shaping and molding clay. I want to incorporate it for my clients who don't seem to do as well with the other art medi-

ums. I'm almost done with the lip of the vase when my phone rings, startling me. My hand jerks and dents the vase, causing the opening to collapse in on itself. "Fuck a duck." I turn off the wheel and let the clay collapse in a heap while I wipe off my hands.

Glancing at the screen, I see it's Bryce calling. He was supposed to be working late tonight. Something about having to go over a case with Richard, the senior partner at the firm.

"Hey babe, what's up?" I answer the phone on speaker so I can clean up my mess.

"I need you to come get me, Everly. Now." Bryce's voice comes through the speaker sounding...frantic. Like he's on the verge of a panic attack. So unlike the unflappable criminal defense attorney that rules in the courtroom. I've never heard him like this.

"What happened? Where are you?" I immediately abandon my task and pick up the phone so I can give Bryce my full attention.

"Come get me. I am on route 19, just past town limits. You know the turnoff that goes to the quarry?"

The quarry? Why the hell is he out that way?

"Yeah, I know it," I say, already in motion, gathering up my keys and slipping my shoes on.

"Hurry, Everly." His voice is strained, like he's fighting back tears.

"Are you hurt? Do you need to call for an ambulance?" My own heart rate spikes as worry floods my system. Was he in an accident? Why won't he say what's wrong?

"Just get here as quick as you can. Don't call anyone else." Without another word, Bryce hangs up, leaving me more questions than answers.

I break several traffic laws in my frantic need to see if Bryce is okay. My mind is reeling with scary possibilities. Did he get in an accident? Is someone hurt? Surely not, because why wouldn't he call 911 if that's the case? Maybe he went for a drive and hit a deer. Or someone's dog. I almost have myself convinced that I'm overreacting and he probably just has a flat tire by the time I get to the stretch of road that Bryce described. I slow down, looking for the turnoff to the quarry. I flick on the high beams, slowing the car to a crawl as I scour the road looking for my husband. Just past the unmarked turnoff for the quarry, I see Bryce stumble out from behind a tree looking disheveled, like he's been crawling on the ground. I hit the brakes, and the car throws me forward, even at my slow speed. Throwing the car into park, I am out in a second, without thought or care about leaving it in the road. Bryce looks hurt. He needs help.

"Bryce, baby, are you okay?" When I get to him, I see blood trickling down the side of his face from a gash in his forehead. His shirt is covered in dirt, and there is white powder dusted into his hair, probably from an airbag being deployed.

"We need to go. Now, Everly." He grabs my hand and stumbles past me, back toward my car.

"Wait. What's going on? What happened? Why are you out here?" I try to pull out of his grasp, not ready to leave without answers.

Bryce whirls on me and grabs me by the shoulders. The look in his eyes is one I have never seen before. Manic. Crazed. Desperate.

"Everly. We have to get out of here. Now. I'll explain when we get home, but please, baby, trust me."

I try to take a step back, unsure of who this man is in front of me, but Bryce tightens his grip.

"Please, baby. If you love me, take me home now. I promise I'll explain it all once we are home, but I can't be found here. We can't be found here." The desperation in his voice causes my resolve to crumble.

I jerk a nod and move forward, putting my arm around his waist, supporting him as we shuffle to the car.

"God, thank you, baby. I knew I could count on you." He looks up at me with so much love shining in his eyes as I deposit him into the passenger seat of our SUV. I give him a small, forced smile as I fight back the sick feeling that something very, very bad happened tonight.

THE BUZZ of my phone pulls me from the bleak memory, bringing my attention back to the present. My tea is half drunk and cold. The yogurt untouched. Glancing at the phone, I see a text from Dane that causes a pit of dread to open in my stomach.

DANE

Can we talk?

CHAPTER 11
DANE

It's Sunday morning, and it's been three days since Everly and I kissed. She hasn't responded to my texts, and Bryce hasn't stopped pestering me about needing to talk to me. I've been avoiding his demands for us to meet. After he blew me off, I was already done entertaining his ass, but now I don't want to see him until Everly and I talk. I don't blame her for needing time to process, but I need to know if she told him. Or how she feels about what happened. I just need to know that she's okay.

I'm walking around downtown on a gorgeous fall morning, trying to distract myself from the Everly situation. I spent my entire Saturday wallowing at home, hoping like hell she would call or text me. She never did, and I'm doing my best not to fall into a spiral wondering if Bryce knows what happened. Taking a break from my stroll in downtown Birch Falls, I pull out my phone and look at my text thread to Everly. Each message is read but ignored.

FRIDAY 9:07AM
DANE:

Can we talk?

SATURDAY 10:15AM

Ever, call me when you get a chance.

Please.

I did my best to keep my messages innocuous-sound-ing, in case Bryce looks at her phone, but now worry that maybe he saw them and suspects something happened creeps into the back of my mind. I decide to try one more time, with a message that might pique her interest.

DANE

Serena said she wants to talk to you about bringing your art therapy to Whispering Grove. She spoke to the director there, and they would love to have you there. They've been searching for someone to run a program like that. Can I give her your number?

There, a text that needs a response. And it gives me a cover story if Bryce has been looking at her phone and wondering why I have been texting her. Tucking my phone away, I resume my walk to Brewed Awakening, on the search for a decent cup of coffee and a slice of their cran-berry-orange loaf.

Just as I pass the outdoor dining area of Knead, a popular spot for brunch in Birch Falls, a familiar laugh catches my attention. There is Everly, sitting at a table with another woman. I stop in my tracks and take in the scene, making sure my eyes aren't playing tricks on me.

Yup, it's Everly alright. She's angled facing away from the sidewalk, but I can still see enough of her profile to know it's her. Her hair sits on her head in a sleek high ponytail. She's dressed up more than usual, wearing a navy-blue dress and heels. There is even a strand of pearls wrapped around her beautiful throat. She looks like she should be heading to some sort of office job, not out having brunch. Then I see her companion and realize she must be dressed up to match her. This must be one of the stuffy attorneys' wives she was complaining about being forced to hang out with. The other woman is wearing a fancy-looking shift dress and heels that look wildly impractical.

Stepping behind one of the trees that line the sidewalk, I take a moment to watch her. Seeing her face for the first time after our kiss is like seeing the sun come out after a week of rain and gloom. I didn't realize how deep my need to see her again was until just now. It takes all of my self-control not to walk into the restaurant and make her talk to me. I know that would not end well for her. Not with one of those gossipy housewives there to witness it. So I tuck my hands into my pockets, lean against the tree, and just watch.

There is a smile on Everly's face, and she's laughing, but she seems...off. Her laugh doesn't sound like it did on Thursday night, when she collapsed against me in a fit of laughter during Pictionary. It's a higher pitch and sounds forced. Her smile appears strained. The light in her eyes is dim. She's faking it. Putting on some sort of show for whomever it is she's with. The more I watch her, the more I notice. Her posture is stiff and uncomfortable. She's barely touched the food on her plate. The other woman says something I can't make out, and the smile slips off Everly's face briefly before coming back. It's clear she is not enjoying this meal or the company.

I decide to stick around until she is done hoping I can catch her as she leaves. I know it's a little creepy to lurk around waiting for her, but I need to talk to her. The need to check on her is steering this ship at the moment, and my rational brain can't seem to take back control.

Brewed Awakening is across the street from Knead, with a direct view of the patio where Everly sits. I continue with my mission for coffee and a slice of cranberry bread, but instead of taking it home, I sit at the counter that lines the window facing the street and wait for Everly.

After an excruciating hour of watching Everly fake her way through brunch with false smiles and barely disguised disinterest, the women stand from their table, having finally paid their check. I wait to watch them leave, to make sure they didn't arrive together. I won't approach Everly in front of her "friend" and risk it getting back to Bryce. The women share a brief hug once they exit the restaurant, then part ways, giving me my cue to follow Everly.

Even though my coffee is long gone, I keep the empty cup as a prop. An easy excuse to show it's just a coincidence that I'm running into Everly downtown. She doesn't need to know I've been a creepy stalker watching her for the last hour.

She walks toward the paid parking lot next to Brewed Awakening. Perfect. Timing my exit, I walk out just as she gets to my side of the street, forcing us to cross paths. She's distracted, looking at her phone, hopefully reading my text. I call out her name, garnering her attention. "Everly?"

She stumbles to a stop at the sound of my voice. When she looks up, her mouth drops open, and her eyes widen in surprise. Yup, she's definitely avoiding me.

"D-Dane. Hey…umm…" Not willing to let her off with an excuse to avoid talking, I take control of the conversation. I reach out and take her hand, pulling her off to the side out of the way of pedestrian traffic.

"Ever, can we talk?" I do my best to keep my voice calm. I don't want to give her any impression that I'm angry. I watch at she scans our surroundings, maybe looking for anyone who might see us. Blowing out a sigh, she nods, relenting to my request. I spy her car at the back of the lot, so I lead her toward it so we can have some privacy. Hopefully that will put her at ease.

Once we are in her car, I can see her visibly relax. She leans her head back against the head rest, closes her eyes and takes in a deep breath, holding it for a four count before slowly releasing it. I've seen her do this before. It's how she centers herself before starting an art therapy session. I think she called it box breathing. She used to do it with Mom before they began each session. I watch her do it two more times before she opens her eyes and directs all of her attention toward me.

"What do you want to talk about, Dane?"

"I just want to make sure you're okay. I know you feel like that kiss was a mistake, and I don't want you to feel like I'm going to pressure you into telling Bryce or doing it again. If you feel like you need to tell him though, then I'll deal with it. I want to know where your head is."

Apparently whatever Everly was expecting me to say, it wasn't that. Her eyes soften at my words, and a small smile plays at the corner of her mouth. I think she's so used to Bryce's demands and coldness that she didn't expect me to hit her with empathy and understanding.

"I haven't told Bryce. I don't plan to. I know your relationship with him is strained enough, and I don't want to make it worse. I was drunk and sad and…I made a mistake. I shouldn't have kissed you. I'm sorry, Dane."

"I'm not." I mean it too. I'm not sorry at all that she kissed me. I hope it's the catalyst she needs to realize she can do better than Bryce. That she doesn't have to settle for him. Even if she doesn't wind up with me, I can't stand the idea of a woman like Everly withering away under Bryce's shadow.

"I'm not sorry you kissed me. I think you are incredible, Ever. I've felt that way for a long time. Probably for way longer than I should have. You are so much better than my brother. You deserve someone who loves you for the light you shine into the world. Not someone who tries to make you dim it. I just want to be here for you. Help you find a way to shine."

Everly's eyes shimmer with tears. My words hit their intended target.

"Let me be there for you. Don't shut me out. Please." Everly closes her eyes, causes the tears to finally break free and trickle down her cheeks. Her mouth presses into a thin line, like she's fighting back a sob. After a long, tense moment, her head nods.

Not ready to push my luck, I decide to change topics. Pull us back from the same charged energy that was surrounding us Thursday night when we kissed.

"So can I give Serena your number?"

Everly huffs out a laugh as she wipes away her tears. "Yeah, sure. You can give my number to Serena."

CHAPTER 12
EVERLY

"I'm not sorry you kissed me. I think you are incredible, Ever. I've felt that way for a long time. Probably for way longer than I should have. You are so much better than my brother. You deserve someone who loves you for the light you shine into the world. Not someone who tries to make you dim it. I just want to be here for you. Help you find a way to shine."

Dane's words echo in my mind as I walk through the front door. After my brunch date with Veronica—that I went to at Bryce's insistence—running into him was the absolute last thing I expected. I had been ignoring his texts; the guilt from kissing him and then blowing him off had been eating me alive, but I knew continuing down that path was only going to lead to both of us getting hurt. I had hoped maybe he would take the hint and back off, letting my momentary lapse into insanity be forgotten. I had almost convinced myself I could pretend it had never happened. Apparently, I'm not that lucky.

Seeing him in person, being reminded of the way it

feels like he manages to stare straight into my soul, sent me right back to that desperate, lonely headspace I was in on Thursday night when I kissed him. His presence has a calming effect on me. He makes me feel…safe. Secure. Seen. My mind screamed at me to make an excuse to leave and not talk to him, but seeing the earnestness in his eyes, the worry. I couldn't bring myself to say no.

Then when Dane delivered his speech about how incredible he thought I was and how he wanted to be there for me, my stupid heart wanted nothing more than to leap across the center console and crush my mouth to his for a repeat of our last kiss. The kiss we shared on Thursday had been electric. Mind-blowing. Consuming. God, if Bryce hadn't called and interrupted it, I don't know where we would have stopped. My whole body lit up under Dane's touch. I felt like a live wire, sparking in a rainstorm.

Bryce used to kiss me like that. Years ago, when we were first married. I don't know when our kisses went from *that* to…whatever they are now. Mundane? Perfunctory? Obligatory? It's not the difference between new, exciting lust versus old love. I don't even know if love exists between Bryce and me any longer. We are tied together because of circumstance now. Our marriage is a ship that we will both go down with together, whether we like it or not.

"Everly, is that you?" Bryce's voice floats through the house, pulling me from my thoughts. Clearing my throat, I give my head a shake, treating it like an etch-a-sketch as I try to erase the memory of Dane's lips on mine, on the off chance Bryce has suddenly become a mind reader.

"Yeah, it's me." I kick off these godawful heels and toss them into the entryway closet before heading in his direction. He's probably going to grill me about my brunch with Veronica. Make sure I did my wifely duty and made a good impression on her, so she will give a positive report to her husband. Honestly, I would've rather been having my teeth extracted than share a meal with the likes of Veronica Harrington, but it's not like I get much say in the matter. I do what I must to make Bryce look good. That is my lot in life.

I find Bryce sitting in one of the leather wingback chairs in his study, whiskey tumbler in hand, staring out at the view of the mountains. I pause at the doorway to take in his appearance. He's still as handsome as ever, but he looks pensive and slightly disheveled. His hair is ruffled, like he's been running his hands through it, and his white button-down is undone halfway, with the sleeves rolled up. He told me he had an early morning meeting before I left for brunch but didn't mention who it was with. It doesn't seem like that meeting went very well.

"Hey, honey. How was your morning?" I lean down to plant a chaste kiss on his cheek in greeting. Instead of letting me move away, he wraps his arm around my waist and pulls me into his lap. I let out a startled *oof* when I land, feeling the hard rigidness of his length under my ass.

"To be honest, it wasn't great. I had a meeting with someone that didn't go the way I wanted, and my useless, lazy, piece of shit brother won't return my calls. I could use some cheering up."

My spine stiffens at the venom in his voice when he

mentions his brother. *He doesn't know. He can't know. He doesn't know.* I keep repeating the manta in my head as I contort my face into a concerned expression.

"I'm sorry, love. What happened?"

"Do you remember the case a few years back, a cop got busted for DV, stalking, kidnapping, inappropriate use of police resources?"

I wrack my brain trying to remember what he's referring to. "I'm not sure if I do. What about it?"

"Well, apparently the cop in question was Dominick Reeves, Skip Harrington's brother-in-law. Veronica is his older sister."

A light bulb goes off in my head as I remember Veronica mentioning how much she missed her baby brother during our brunch. She hadn't told me why he wasn't around, and I honestly didn't care enough to ask, but now I kind of wish I had. It seems like that knowledge would be pertinent to have right now.

"Okay..." I trail off, not sure where he's going with this story, but my spidey senses tell me I'm not going to like it. There is another reason why that name sounds familiar, but my brain can't place it.

"Skip wants me to head up Dominick's upcoming appeal. Dane was involved in his original conviction, but according to Dominick, there were some very sketchy legal circumstances involved in getting his partner to flip on him. He wants me to convince Dane to testify on his behalf at the hearing."

"Those sound like some pretty serious allegations. Do you think Dane would be willing to do that?" Nausea swirls in my gut at the thought of my husband working to get an awful man like Dominick out of prison just for politics.

"He may not be willing, but I'm going to find a way to get him to do it. If I get Dom off, Skip is going to endorse me when I run for judgeship. Between Skip being on the legislature and your dad's clout from his time on the bench, I'll be a shoe in. I just need to get Dane to meet with me. He's been avoiding me. Do you know why that would be?" I stiffen in Bryce's hold, and his grip around my waist tightens.

"W-why would I? I don't talk to your brother." I hope he can't tell how hard my heart is pounding, panic creeping in the back of my mind that somehow he does know about the kiss.

"He hung out here waiting for me the other night, didn't he? Did he say anything negative about me?"

It takes me several seconds to process his words and realize they aren't *I know you kissed him you lying whore.* I shake my head, trying to keep my expression as neutral as humanly possible.

"No. He didn't talk about you... Maybe he's mad because you stood him up?" I throw out the suggestion, hoping my voice sounds less guilty than I feel.

Bryce sets his rocks glass on the side table before sliding his fingers lift up the hem of my skirt. He leans forward, brushing his lips against my pulse point as his palm slowly glides up my thigh.

"Because...I know he wants you. He always has."

Sucking in a sharp gasp, my eyes slam shut, bracing for his next words.

"It wouldn't surprise me if he tried to make me look bad in front of you. He's always hated me. Hated that I have you and he doesn't."

My heart feels like it's going to explode from my chest. I keep waiting for the accusation. The venom. Instead, his lips trace along my jaw line before capturing mine in a rough, possessive kiss. My skin heats under his touch. He's not kissing me like he's angry. He's kissing me like he wants to devour me. I'm a confused mess of panic, guilt, and arousal. When his hand reaches my sex, he slips a finger past the elastic of my thong and runs it along my slit. The hand that was around my waist moves up to grip the back of my neck. Bryce jerks my head back, ending our kiss, staring me in the eye.

"You'd tell me if he tried to make me look bad. Wouldn't you?"

I nod, but Bryce tightens his hold on my neck, apparently not satisfied with my nonverbal response.

"Y-yes. I'd tell you."

His lips quirk up into grin that is devoid of all emotion. "That's my girl." In a motion too swift for my brain to recognize, he has me turned so I'm straddling his lap, and he's directing my hands to his erection with the hand that was playing with my pussy. His intentions are clear on what he wants me to do.

"Get my dick out and ride it, Everly."

My brain screams at me, trying to tell me something is wrong. After ignoring me sexually for so long, he's suddenly all over me. I want to ask him what's changed. I want stop this, but I'm afraid it will make him more suspicious of Dane.

The buzzing of a phone on the side table shatters the intensity of the moment. I pull away from him and glance at his phone. Dane's name flashes on the screen.

"Oh, uh, look there. You should get that." I scoot off Bryce's lap while he's distracted. Some subconscious part of my brain realizes how damn uncanny their sense of timing seems to be. Bryce looks at me like he's going to tell me to stay, but I back away, putting distance between us.

"I'm gonna go change; I want to get out of this dress. Come find me when you're done." I wink, hoping he buys my excuse so I can have some time to process what the hell is going on.

Running his hand through his hair, Bryce dismisses me with a nod before turning his attention back to his phone. Letting out a relieved sigh, I retreat to our bedroom to get this maelstrom of emotions under control.

CHAPTER 13
DANE

As I listen to the phone ring and ring, the only thought that runs through my mind is that I don't want to have this conversation. I don't want to talk to my brother at all. Somehow all of his pretentiousness manages to ooze through the phone, and he never fails to remind me how inferior to him I am. We've gone months without direct communication, which is what I thought was our preferred status quo. What the hell could be so important for him to be up my ass? The only reason I am relenting and calling him back is Everly. I know how Bryce is when he's in a shitty mood, and I don't want to be the reason he's in a shitty mood if he takes it out on Everly. If talking to him and being near him will allow me more time with Everly, then I'll grit my teeth and do it.

"Finally decide to be a mature adult and return my calls?" Bryce's smarmy greeting immediately sets me on edge. Would a *hey bro, long time no talk, thanks for returning my calls* kill him? I decide to be the mature one and ignore the jab.

"Nice to hear from you too, bro. Care to tell me why you've been hounding me like a debt collector?"

"I'm working a case that I need your cooperation with. My client seems to think there's been a miscarriage of justice and is seeking a new trial. Seeing as how you were involved in the original arrest, I thought maybe you'd be willing to review the case and see where any evidence might have been...fabricated. Set past mistakes right, to clear a good man's name."

I am unable to contain the incredulous snort that escapes when I hear his request. "Are you shitting me right now, Bryce? Is this one of your frat buddies who got busted with one too many DUIs and is now trying to escape the charges? Or one of your lawyer friends trying to get out of a sexual assault conviction? Get fucked. You know I won't do that."

Bryce seems unfazed by my outright refusal. "It's more complicated than that. Just come over for dinner, and I'll explain the situation. I'll have Everly whip something up for us, and we can figure out how to help each other."

"There's nothing I need your help with."

"Oh, I wouldn't say that, baby brother. Without my help paying Mom's rent, where would she wind up living? You can't afford for her to stay at Whispering Grove or pay rent on two places on your cop salary. I guess you could put her up in your bachelor pad and have her sleep on the couch..."

Fucking dickbag. Is he seriously using our mom against

me? Jesus, I knew he was willing to do anything to win a case, but this is a new fucking low.

"Are you seriously threatening to stop paying Mom's rent just to get me to talk to you?" I don't even bother trying to disguise the disgust in my tone.

"You're the one being stubborn and refusing to have a simple conversation. Look, I know you like to look at the world in black and white. Good and bad. It's that do-gooder in you. One day you'll learn the world exists in shades of gray, and the sooner you come off that high horse of yours, the sooner you'll realize how much more rewarding life can be. Be here at six. I'm sure Everly would love to see you."

My stomach drops at those words. Is he insinuating he knows what happened between me and Everly? Is that what this is about? Shit. I try to play it cool and not let him hear how his words affected me.

"I seriously doubt she cares, dude."

"Oh, I don't know about that. You two must've had a good time together last week when you came over. It was pretty late when you left..."

The taste of iron in my mouth lets me know I'm biting my lower lip way too hard in my effort to keep from going off on this asshole. I inhale deeply, trying to calm myself before I respond.

"I was waiting on you. You were the one who stood me up. When I realized you weren't going to show up at a reasonable hour, I left. It's not my fault you let your wife get lonely enough that she enjoys the company of a poor cop. Maybe you should spend more time at home and less time fellating whatever politician you think will advance your career."

So much for responding calmly.

"Everly understands I have to work to maintain our lifestyle. She knows I have goals, and she is happy to support them in whatever way I need. Be a good brother and put whatever petty grudge you have against me aside, and come over for dinner. Now if you don't mind, I've got a wife I need to attend to. As you so kindly reminded me. Your call interrupted me getting my dick wet in her tight little cunt. I'll see you at six."

The line goes dead before I can respond. That mother fucker.

As I PULL into Bryce and Everly's driveway, the mental image he left me with plays through my mind. I've spent the last few hours alternating between trying to scrub the visual of them fucking from my brain and worrying that this means he knows we kissed. He's rubbed his relation-ship with Everly in my face before. I think he's always known I have a thing for her, and I hope this is just him being a smug asshole trying to make me jealous of their relationship. He seems to take great joy in knowing I'm single and make way less money than him. I decide to be as aloof as possible around Everly tonight, so he doesn't sense that he actually hit a nerve.

This time when I knock, Bryce opens the door to greet me. For some unfathomable reason, he's still dressed in slacks and a button-down shirt on a Sunday evening. Though the shirt has a few buttons undone at the top and the sleeves are rolled up. I guess this is what passes for casual in Bryce's world. His hair is disheveled, like he's been running his hands through it...or Everly has. That thought turns my stomach. He's not wrong that I'm jealous of his relationship with Everly. His arrow definitely hit the mark there. Though my jealousy has more to do with how much of an undeserving dick he is to have a woman like Everly in his corner, than with her being with him. If he was good to her, I'd find a way to be happy for them.

Schooling my face to be as impassive as possible, I nod at Bryce in greeting. "Well, I'm here. What's so important?"

"Come to my study. We can talk while Everly makes dinner." As if summoned, Everly appears at the top of the stairs that lead to their master bedroom. She's wearing one of Bryce's button-down shirts and nothing else. Her hair is an unruly mess. Not the sleek high ponytail it was in earlier today. Aside from the fact that she's wearing Bryce's shirt, she looks sexy as fuck. Her legs are bare, all the way down to her toes. The shirt hits mid-thigh, just long enough to cover her, but not long enough to be decent for company. She lets out a startled gasp when she sees me standing in the foyer with Bryce.

"Oh! Um, Dane. Hi. I didn't know you were coming over." I see her take a hesitant step back, her cheeks flushing with embarrassment.

Bryce lets out one of his pretentious fake laughs. "Oh, haha, that's my bad. Sorry, babe, I forgot to mention I invited Dane over for dinner. Do you mind throwing some steaks on while we talk business?" I feel my teeth grind together as I fight to keep my annoyance with Bryce at bay. He absolutely fucked her and didn't warn her I was coming over so I would know what they had been up to. And now he's treating her like she's the help.

"Uh, yeah, let me just go get changed." Everly moves to go to their bedroom but Bryce waves her off, dismissing her sense of propriety like it's nonsense.

"Nah, don't worry about changing. I'm sure Dane has seen much more scandalous things on the job. Besides, we're all family here, right?" Bryce claps me on the shoulder a little too hard, and I have to fight like hell to keep my expression neutral.

Out of my periphery, I see Bryce studying me, like he's gauging my interest in his half-naked wife. With monumental effort, I tear my eyes away from the goddess on the stairs, feigning disinterest in her.

"Can we just get to the point of why you invited me over?" I shift my focus to Bryce and see amusement dancing in his eyes. Whatever kind of test this is, it seems like I'm failing it. Fuck, it's no wonder. He's excellent at reading people. It's why he's so good at his job. That, and he's not above blurring the lines of legality to get the result he wants for his clients.

I push past Bryce and head in the direction of his study, hoping to end this little display of him marking his territory. I won't lie, seeing Everly looking freshly fucked by him hurts. A lot. I know I don't have any fucking right to feel jealous or angry at her. She is married to him after all, but my Neanderthal brain doesn't understand that.

My base primal instinct screams at me to grab her and run.

Fortunately, Bryce follows me to the study with no further attempt to provoke me or belittle Everly.

"Alright, man. Why am I here?" I slump down in one of the leather chairs that face his obnoxiously large, bespoke solid oak desk. It looks like it belongs in the Oval Office, not some study in an overpriced McMansion. I'm sure he spent more than one of my paychecks on the gaudy piece of furniture. Whoever said money can't buy taste was right.

"Dominick Reeves." Bryce sits down in the chair behind the desk and steeples his hands under his chin. Could he look at more cartoonishly evil?

"What about him?" A sick sense of dread slithers through my gut at the mention of Dominick's name. He is Serena's ex-fiancé and an abusive piece of shit. Oh, and a dirty cop and a murderer. If Bryce thinks I'm going to help him get Dominick out of prison, he can get fucked.

"I heard a rumor that the confession by a one Brad Hopper was obtained under legally dubious circumstances. And without that confession, there's nothing linking Dominick to the murder of Todd Dennison. Without the murder conviction, Dominick could go free in as little as a year. I've been tasked to get Dominick a new trial that will overturn the murder conviction. This case could set me up for life. I need you to admit that you coerced the confession out of Brad so we can get a judge to sign off on a new trial."

I sit and wait for the punch line. A *gotcha* moment from Bryce. There's no fucking way he's serious about this.

"You're kidding, right? You want *me* to help you get Dominick Reeves out on a technicality? The main who beat my current partner and put a black eye on the Birch Falls PD? That Dominick Reeves? You've lost your fucking mind." I stand to leave, unwilling to hear any counter argument he has. I knew my brother defended scumbags, but this is beyond petty DUI busts or financial crimes. Dominick is dangerous. He is exactly where he deserves to be.

"Dane, sit the fuck down." Bryce stands, leaning on the desk, his hands pressed to the shiny, polished wood.

"You are going to help me with this case. If you don't, I'll stop paying the rent on Mom's house. I'll open my own investigation into how exactly it was that you obtained that confession. I'll look into your partner and her husband, Kai, and put together a story of how they conspired to put Dominick behind bars so they could be together. Do. Not. Test. Me."

I open my mouth to respond, but Everly appears in the doorway, her hair pulled up in a messy bun, still dressed in only Bryce's shirt. There is fear in her eyes as she takes in the scene before her. Bryce leaning aggressively over the desk; me with my arms crossed over my chest, jaw tight with anger.

"Dinner is ready, if you guys are hungry." Her eyes bounce between us, like we are two lions ready to fight over the same piece of meat. The anger radiating off Bryce melts away in an instant; his normal, polished, cool façade slips back into place.

"Thanks, babe." Flashing her his best *you can trust me*

smile, he saunters to Everly and backs her against the wall before crushing his mouth to hers in a possessive show of dominance. I try not to watch, but my eyes don't miss the way his hand slides up her thigh, lifting the shirt just enough to show some dark purple blotches. What. The. Fuck.

When Bryce breaks away from the kiss, her eyes are wild with…fear? His face splits into a feral grin as he shoots a wink my way. "Come on, little brother. Let's eat. You can think about my proposal." He walks out of the study, leaving me and Everly alone. Her chest heaving, lips red and puffy, and her eyes blinking rapidly like she's fighting back tears. I move to comfort her, but she shakes her head, halting me in my tracks.

"Ever—"

"Don't, Dane. Not here. Not right now." Her words are just loud enough for me to hear, but they freeze me in place all the same.

"But—" I begin to protest, but she looks up at me, a fierceness in her eyes I've never seen before.

"Not. Right. Now." She bites out each word then turns on her heel, following Bryce to the kitchen, leaving me feeling impotent and angry at this entire fucked up situation.

CHAPTER 14
EVERLY

EVERLY – 21 YEARS OLD

It's Thanksgiving, and the smell of roasting turkey wafts through the air. My mom and Aunt Clara are busy putting the finishing touches on the sides, while Dad and Uncle James are in the den watching football with my cousins A.J. and Nick. I'm busy pacing around the dining room, setting the table for eight. Bryce is coming to Thanksgiving dinner, and I keep having to wipe the nervous sweat from my palms between place settings. We've been dating for two months now, and this is the first time my parents will be meeting him.

I was surprised when he suggested we spend Thanksgiving together. I thought he would be going back home for Thanksgiving break, but he surprised me by saying he wouldn't be making the three hour drive to Birch Falls. He said he doesn't care for his stepdad and that holidays are weird for him, so he usually spends them with friends. He's mentioned in passing before about how his own dad left when he was twelve, when his mom gave birth to his brother, but it turned out the baby belonged to another man. His father was so blindsided by the revelation, he just...left. Thinking about the pain a young Bryce must've felt being abandoned by his father after his mother's affair, I don't blame him for skipping the holidays when he can.

The doorbell chimes as I finish setting the table. The clock shows 4:30 p.m. Bryce is right on time. Thank god. My dad, a federal district court judge, is a man big on punctuality. I've seen the lecture he's given lawyers, witnesses, and other court attendees when they disrupt court proceedings with tardiness. I did *not* want Bryce to be on the receiving end of Judge Strauss's *why are you disrespecting my time* stare. Not the first time they meet.

My dad has never approved of any of my former boyfriends, but I'm hoping the fact that Bryce is a law student will work in his favor. All the previous boys I've dated were like me. Creative. Musicians. Artists. Writers. All useless wastes of space in my father's eyes. As far as my father is concerned, I'm going to college for psychology. I haven't told him yet I'm planning to double major in psychology and fine arts so I can go into art therapy. I'm hoping the psychology half of the degree will make the art half more respectable in his eyes, but that's future Everly's problem.

When I open the door, Bryce is standing there with a bouquet of flowers and a bottle of wine. He's wearing a pale green button-down under a dark navy blazer, dark wash jeans, and Italian leather loafers. He looks every bit the up-and-coming hotshot lawyer he plans on being, and I know instantly Dad will approve of him. The nervous energy that has been jangling through me all day melts away, and I momentarily get lost in his warm brown eyes while we stand in the doorway. Bryce is so handsome, it's unreal. I still can't believe he noticed me—the shy, artistic introvert, of all people—at that party all those weeks ago.

"Everly, who's there?" My dad's booming baritone startles me from my stupor, reminding me I need to actually invite Bryce in. Stepping aside, I hold my breath as Bryce walks in, his face not betraying any worry about what verdict the Honorable Judge Strauss will bestow on him. Bryce deftly shifts the wine and flowers to one hand and offers the other to my father for a handshake.

"Judge Strauss, pleasure to meet you. Thank you for letting me join your family for Thanksgiving." My lungs begin to burn from lack of oxygen, but I don't move a muscle as I watch the two men in front of me. My dad grips Bryce's hand in both of his in a show of dominance, and I see the smallest twitch in the muscle of Bryce's cheek betraying how strong my dad's grip is.

"Bryce, nice to meet you. I've heard a lot about you from Everly. You're pre-law?" Dad smiles at Bryce, and just like that, I remember how to breathe. I let out a relieved exhale as Bryce glances at me out of the corner of his eye and gives me a reassuring wink.

"Yes, sir. I plan on focusing on criminal law. I'd like to work my way up to your position someday. Everly has told me a lot about you, and your career is one I aspire to have."

Oh, there we go. Bryce's humble southern charm melts away Dad's normally frosty demeanor.

"I like you already, Mr. Carmichael. Come join me in the den while the ladies finish getting dinner ready. Everly, will you go see how much longer it will be until we eat?" Dad takes the wine and flowers from Bryce, only to hand them to me. Bryce flashes me that megawatt smile that reassured me after Brody accosted me at that party, and I know now, like I knew then, that everything will be okay.

CHAPTER 15
EVERLY

I stare at the text Bryce sent me just after six, when I had already started cooking dinner. Of course he couldn't give me more of a heads up that he wouldn't be home. I don't even know why I bother trying to have it ready for him at a reasonable hour. The days of us having a nice meal together when he got home from work, then cuddling on the couch watching a movie are long gone.

Sometimes I find myself longing for the days when we still lived in a small two-bedroom apartment when he was just getting started with his law career.

My schedule was always more flexible, so I would finish up with my clients and get home early enough to make dinner. Bryce worked so hard, usually leaving the house by 7:00 a.m. and not getting home until seven at night. I'd have dinner ready for him, ask him how his day was, listen to him vent about his clients, and after we would just spend the evening unwinding together.

Things were simple then. We were enough for each other. Then he started making a name for himself, getting bigger and bigger clients to defend. Other lawyers, local politicians or their family members. This connected him with more influential people, and he started dabbling in politics. Now his entire purpose in life is to rise higher and higher on some imaginary ladder until... Who knows? I have no idea what his end game is. I feel like I barely know him anymore.

The smell of burning food brings my focus back to the pan in front of me and I realize I've cooked off almost all the sauce in my stir-fry. Disgusted by the charred mess in front of me and Bryce's complete lack of respect for my time, I pitch the food in the trash, vowing this is the last time I play the happy housewife making dinner for her husband like it's her entire purpose in life.

I'm getting ready to pour myself a glass of wine and settle in with my comfort show, *Schitt's Creek*, when my phone chimes with another incoming text. Glancing down, I see it's from Serena. Dane gave her my number, and we've been texting back and forth. She wants me to meet up with the program director at Whispering Pines, the assisted living/retirement village where her mom lives. She thinks my art therapy would be beneficial to many of the residents there. I've been putting off following up on it because Bryce doesn't like the idea of me working, but maybe it's time for me to start living for myself again.

SERENA

Game night! Will we be seeing you? Kai is making tacos!

I'M on the verge of responding that I won't be able to make it when I stop myself. Why shouldn't I go to game night? Bryce won't be home. I'll just be sitting here alone, bored and annoyed at my husband. Or I could hang out with some new friends...and Dane will probably be there. I haven't seen him since Bryce unexpectedly invited him over for dinner on Sunday after fucking me so roughly he left fingerprint bruises on my hips and thighs.

The look on Dane's face after watching Bryce kiss me flashes through my mind. It is a look I'll never forget. He was staring at his brother like he could set fire to him with the power of his mind. Then the way his eyes softened when he looked at me... It took all of my willpower not to let him make a scene in front of Bryce. All I wanted was to let him gather me in his arms and hold me. Let him give me the tenderness that Bryce seems incapable of now. Sure, Bryce's interest in me sexually has increased lately, but now it feels even more like I am just his possession. His plaything.

I miss feeling cherished.

EVERLY

I'll be there. See you soon.

"GIRAFFES DOING THE LIMBO!" I jump up and yell the answer as loud as I can, accidentally knocking Dane off the edge where he was sitting.

"Woah, Ever! This isn't full contact!" Dane exclaims incredulously from the floor.

Kai is at the drawing board armed only with a black Sharpie and his subpar drawing skills. He throws the marker behind him and runs over to pick me up. He spins us around in celebratory living room donuts.

"Now that's what I'm talking about. Everly, you're my new forever game night partner!" Kai crows victoriously.

Serena comes up behind her husband and smacks him in the head.

"Hey! It's not my fault Ever and I are connected on a level you and I aren't!"

Serena and I bust out laughing at the same time, both giddy from the margaritas Kai's parents brought over.

When I arrived two hours prior, I was equal parts pissed off and hurt by my husband's thoughtlessness. I wasn't sure if I would be able to have fun with my new friends. As it turns out, margaritas, tacos, and a weird, fucked up version of *Pictionary* is the perfect remedy. The Reynolds welcomed me into their home with a plate of tacos and a margarita, and my mood immediately lifted. It was the first time in...too long that someone seemed genuinely excited to see me. It felt *real*. Serena somehow managed to sense my foul mood before it completely slipped away, and she met me margarita for margarita as I tried to drown my acrimonious mood.

"Alright, pretty ladies. Time to hydrate." Dane swoops in between me and Serena, double fisting two glasses of ice water. He deftly wraps one arm around my shoulders and presents one of the water glasses to me, while handing Serena the other. He gazes down at me, his eyes dancing with mirth and a half grin tilting up his lips. Serena and I must be out of pocket if he's decided to start playing water daddy— *Daddy?* I nearly choke on the sip of water in my mouth when that thought hits me.

"Woah there, tiger. Don't choke on me." Dane turns his body toward mine, pulling me into a hug. He rubs my back as I try not to die after nearly inhaling the liquid. His innocent double entendre does nothing to help me control my hysterical wheezing. Oh my god, how much tequila was in those margaritas?

When I finally have control over my faculties again, my face is red and my cheeks wet with tears from laughter. I know I must look like a hot mess, but I am having so much fun I don't even care. It's been so long since I've laughed like this. All the people Bryce surrounds us with are stuffy, pretentious, opportunistic leeches. I haven't had a carefree night like this since college.

"Alright, you two are on water for the rest of the night. You'll thank me tomorrow." Dane steers me over to the couch to sit down. I plop down next to Laura, Serena's mom.

She grasps my hand excitedly when she asks, "Oh, Everly! Did you get a chance to talk to Serena about coming by to talk to Bethany about the art therapy program?"

"Yes! I'm going to call her tomorrow to set up an interview." I answer without even thinking. I hadn't actually made that decision before this moment, but it feels right when I say it out loud. I do want to start living for myself. I do want to make my own friends. Have my own purpose. I may be stuck in a miserable marriage, but that doesn't mean I have to make my whole life miserable.

AN HOUR LATER, we say goodbye to the Reynolds clan. Dane insists on driving me home in my car again. I've only been drinking water for the last hour, so I've begun to sober up but not nearly enough to drive. I also don't want to stop spending time with him. Seeing Dane in his element with his people has shown me an entirely new side of him. He's no longer the surly young man who lost his dad entirely too soon and had a brother who resented him his entire life. His sharp edges melt away, and his smiles come so easily.

I rarely, if ever, saw happy, carefree Dane during my early relationship with his brother. The only times I saw the softer, less bitter side of him was when I had my weekly therapy appointment with his mom. He still lived at home with her while he was in the academy. Bryce was never there for those because he was busy working. So it was just me, Dane, and Caroline. He was usually making dinner and would always offer me some. I took him up on his offer a few times and learned he was a surprisingly decent chef.

"You know what I miss?" We're in the car, only minutes away from my house. I turn my head to the side to take in his handsome profile as it comes in and out of view under the streetlights.

"What do you miss, Ever?" Dane cuts me a quick sideways glance, flashing me a smile.

"I miss brinner. Remember when you would make pancakes and eggs and bacon for dinner for you and your mom?"

"Yeah? I still do that. You don't eat brinner?" Dane laughs like I'm being silly but stops when he sees me shake my head.

"No. Bryce doesn't like it. He thinks it's not a good enough meal for dinner. Sometimes a girl just wants to eat some chocolate chip pancakes." Why am I getting up in my feelings right now about breakfast for dinner? The hurt and anger from earlier in the evening comes rushing back as we pull into my driveway. Bryce's car isn't here. Glancing at the clock on the dash, I see that it reads 10:42. My teeth clench, causing my jaw to tense. Dane must notice my shift in mood.

"He's not home, is he." It's not a question. Just a declaration of fact.

"No. Doesn't look like he is." I press my lips into a thin line, my mind at war over which emotion should be steering the ship right now. Anger? Hurt? Resentment? Or relief? Relief that I finally decided to stop waiting and that I made the right choice.

Dane gently cups my chin and directs my attention to him. "Talk to me, Ever. Tell me where your mind is right now." His eyes stare into me with such a solemn openness. Like he wants me to pour whatever is bothering me into him, so he can carry it for me. Has Bryce ever looked at me like that?

"I'm thinking I'm glad I came out tonight." Before he says anything, I hit the release button on my seatbelt and lunge toward him, capturing his lips with my own. He tastes vaguely minty, like maybe he freshened up recently. His lips immediately part, his tongue darting out, licking my own, seeking entry. I open for him, letting our tongues dance together as I slowly make my way over the center console and onto his lap. His hands hover over my body momentarily, like he's unsure of what to do, but when I grind my center down on him, he gets the idea, wrapping one hand around my waist and fisting my hair with the other.

His kiss is all-consuming. He doesn't kiss me like he's possessive or like he owns me. He kisses me like I am his very essence of being. He kisses me like he's a man dying of thirst, and I am the water essential to his survival. It feels amazing.

I am on the verge of losing myself completely to his intoxicating kisses when the flash of headlights illuminates the interior of the car. I pull away, and almost hit my head on the roof.

"Woah, Ever. Careful." Dane reaches up to put his hand between my head and the ceiling. The headlights are gone. It was just a car driving past. I collapse into Dane, suddenly overwhelmed with the reality of what I was doing. Am doing. And with whom. Fuck, I can't do this.

"Oh god, I can't do this. I can't do this to you." I shift to move off his lap, but his hands clamp me in place.

"Ever. Please. Don't run again."

"Dane, you don't understand. I can't do this with you." Again, I move to climb off; Dane tightens his hold more.

"Explain it to me then." He looks at me with so much earnestness that I almost cave and try to bury myself in him. He wants to know what's wrong. "Explain to me why you're so loyal to an asshole who doesn't even appreciate how amazing his wife is. You deserve so much more than what he gives you."

"Bryce takes care of—"

"More than what he gives you emotionally, Ev. More than scraps of his attention. More than countless late nights alone. More than using you for your appearance because you make him look good. You deserve someone who cares."

Dane's words hit me like a knife to the heart. He's not wrong. I do deserve more than what I get from Bryce. But Dane can't be the one who gives it to me.

CHAPTER 16
DANE

"You want the usual?" Serena asks, as she parks the squad car in front of Brewed Awakening. We are on the morning shift today and will likely spend our day giving out speeding tickets and consoling some old lady who will inevitably call in some college kid for being "suspicious" for studying outside. I just grunt in response as I continue to scroll rental listings on my phone. Day shift is dull as shit, but it'll give me time to research new living options for mom.

"God, you are extra grumpy today. You need to lose that attitude before you lose your partner." Serena rolls her eyes as she climbs out of the car to get our coffees.

"Sorry—"

She slams her door a little too aggressively, cutting off my apology, signaling she is absolutely done with my attitude. I wince as the car rocks in her departure and make a mental note to buy her lunch today to make up for putting up with my grumpy ass.

My mood has been sour since Bryce's ultimatum. I've been trying to come up with a way to tell Bryce to go fuck himself over the Dom situation, while figuring out how to support Mom on my meager salary. There's no way I'm going to help him and fuck Serena and Kai over like that, but he's been hounding me nonstop, putting me in a shittier and shittier mood.

It lifted briefly when Everly turned up at game night last night. Being around her is like having the sun shine directly down on you. And that kiss... Fuck... I was seconds away from pulling my dick out and letting her ride me and take everything she needed. There was no denying the desperate need for connection between us. If she hadn't gotten spooked by the car driving by, there is no doubt we would have fucked in my brother's driveway. Instead, she ran away—again—and I went home and beat off in my shower—again.

Everly is a good woman. She's not a cheater. She has a conscience. She won't be the one who takes it that far, no matter how much my brother sucks as a husband.

I, however, have no problem giving my brother the ultimate *fuck you* by stealing his wife. She deserves better than being his trophy, and I'm going to prove to her that I'm better.

AFTER AN UNEVENTFUL SHIFT, I head over to see Mom. I texted her that I would be coming by. I want to get a sense of how she might feel about moving...and maybe living with her son. She fell into a deep depression after Dad died, and became reclusive to the point that I was basically raising myself and taking care of her. It's one more reason why Serena and I have bonded beyond just being partners at work.

We both were dealt shitty cards growing up. Losing our dads at a young age and being forced to become caretakers for our remaining parent. Bryce should've been the one to step in and take care of Mom, seeing as how he was an actual adult at the time. But he did fuck all aside from helping with Dad's estate, stopping by on the holidays, and selling the house once I graduated from the academy. He claimed it was to use the proceeds to pay for a smaller place for Mom to live since she was no longer working. I think it was his way of kicking me out. He couldn't cut me off fast enough.

I haven't missed out on the irony of him needing *my* help with a case that will advance his career significantly. Once I figure out a viable solution to Mom's living situation, I'll talk to Serena about the evidence we had documenting Dominick's abuse. Make sure her and Kai's alibis are airtight, then tell Bryce to get fucked. I'm done with him thinking he can dictate my life.

I knock once on the front door before letting myself in. Mom is usually in the back yard tending to her garden when I come by. She'll probably be tending to the last of her blooms before fall fully sets in and makes the temperatures drop. She threw herself into gardening when she moved into this place and it's the main reason why I am loathe to make her move. It's the one thing that's brought her joy since Dad died. If I have to find a place for us both to live on my salary, it'll likely be a cramped, two-bedroom apartment with no yard.

When I step out on her small back deck, I find her watering her mums. There's a pitcher of lemonade accompanied by two glasses and a plate of cookies sitting on the wrought iron table.

A wave of nostalgia hits me seeing the set up in front of me. Lemonade and cookies used to be our routine when I would get home from school when I was young. She always had them waiting, and she would sit with me and help me with homework or ask me how my day was. That lasted until I was in high school and busy with sports and friends and chasing after girls. Then she would only bring out the cookies and lemonade when she needed to have a serious talk with me about grades or something. Then Dad died, and she stopped baking cookies. She stopped getting out of bed. She stopped living. I don't remember the last time we sat and had lemonade and cookies.

"Hey, Ma. The mums are looking good." I lean on the porch rail to get a better look at the purple, burgundy, and orange blooms that line the flower beds that surround the small porch.

Mom's green eyes, the very same ones I inherited from her, light up when she sees me. Her once charcoal dark hair is salt and pepper now, but her face still looks like the woman who raised me. Just with a few more lines in the corners of her eyes and mouth. Her mental health has improved a lot the past few years. Not so much that she's been able to bring herself to go back to work or really be around people, but she's gotten to a good place of pursuing some hobbies and interests at home to occupy her time. After setting aside the watering can and her garden gloves, she climbs the stairs and wraps me in a tight hug. She smells like dirt and flowers and home. I squeeze her tight, trying to hold on to this feeling of serenity before I shatter it with the news that she might have to move.

"What's with the cookies, Ma? You haven't baked in years." I snag a cookie as she pours the lemonade. Oatmeal chocolate chip. My favorite.

"The urge just hit me when you sent that text earlier. It sounded like you needed to talk. Everything okay, sweetie?" I fight the urge to cringe at the endearment. Around the age of twelve I decided I was too cool for my mom to call me sweetie, so I asked her to stop. Hearing it now just reminds me of how much I took for granted before our lives were completely upended. Suddenly I'm the same young boy who just wants his mom to tell him what to do.

This is the mother who used to listen to me when I complained about bullies in school. The woman who patiently helped me with algebra when I struggled thanks to my dyscalculia. This is the woman who tried so damn hard to keep the peace between me and my brother, even though the friction between us ran so much deeper than typical sibling rivalry. Now I get to tell her how no matter how much she tried to help us bond, it would never be enough.

I open my mouth to mention the move but surprise myself when a question comes out instead. "Why does Bryce hate me so much?"

Mom doesn't answer right away. Instead, she looks off to the trees that line the back of the property. Her eyes get that faraway look I became all too familiar with when she was so lost after losing her husband.

"I know he blamed Dad for Brian leaving, but why take it out on me?"

She lets out a deep sigh before turning her attention back to me, her eyes shining with unshed tears. "My relationship with Brian wasn't great. It started out okay. We were college sweethearts. He proposed as soon as we graduated. I thought we had it all figured out. We graduated, got married, bought a house, and got pregnant with Bryce all in the same year. Things were great. Then Brian got a good job in finance, and he had all these big aspirations to become some hot shot CEO. The more money he made, the more time he spent at work. It got to the point where he was traveling so much for business deals that we barely ever saw him. It was just me and Bryce for so long. He was such a momma's boy, but every time Brian came home from work, Bryce would look at him like he hung the moon.

Then one night, when he was home, I woke up, and he wasn't in bed. I got up to look for him and heard him talking in his office. He was talking to another woman. I won't go into detail, but needless to say, it wasn't just a business conversation." Mom pauses, taking a sip of her lemonade. She makes a face and stands up. "Hang on, this conversation calls for something stronger."

I wait as she disappears into the house. When she returns, she is carrying a small bottle of vodka. She pours a healthy measure into both of our lemonades before resuming her story.

"I was so hurt and so angry. I thought he worked so hard to provide for us, but it turned out he took all those business trips because he had a mistress in another city. Multiple in fact. I learned that after I did some investigating."

"Why didn't you just divorce him, Ma?" It hurts to see Mom relive some of her most painful memories, but I want to know the truth. I want to know why my brother hates me so much.

"Oh, I wanted to. I confronted him about it when I eventually worked up the courage. But Brian told me they meant nothing, and it was just a way to kill the time while he was on the road. He said all the right things, did all the remorseful husband duties. I didn't want to destroy the life we'd built together so I told him I'd give him another chance. Because I worked part time, only while Bryce was in school, I didn't make a lot of money and relied on Brian to provide for us. I was scared to get divorced. I wasn't sure how I would support the two of us on my salary. Bryce was still young enough that I would have to pay for before school and after school care if I got a full time job... It was complicated." Mom takes a long drink of her spiked lemonade before continuing.

"Eventually I discovered another affair. That time I did leave. I packed Bryce up, and we left while Brian was on a work trip. I left a note telling him I wanted a divorce. When he got back from the trip, he called the police and told him I had kidnapped Bryce. I was picked up at the grocery store when I was buying food and snacks to take back to the motel room where we were staying. Bryce was eight at the time. He got to watch his mother be arrested and put in the back of a police cruiser while his daddy came and rescued him."

My gut clenches at Mom's story as I realize the apple didn't fall too far from that particular tree. Bryce definitely inherited his dad's manipulative, narcissistic personality.

"After spending a night in holding, Brian dropped the charges and took me home. He told me if I ever tried to leave him again, he would sue me for full custody of Bryce and never let me see him. He had the money to hire the best divorce attorneys that I would never be able to afford to fight. So...I stayed." I watch as she wipes away the silent tears.

"Why wouldn't he want a divorce if he was busy dipping his stick in women all over the country?" Rage toward Brian builds inside me. My hand clenches into a fist as I imagine tracking him down and kicking his ass for treating my mother the way he did.

"Appearances. It's all about appearances. It was a lonely few years until I met Jake." A wistful smile appears on her face at the mention of her deceased husband. "We met when I hired him to do some repairs on the house. It was like a cheesy romance novel. He was working on renovating the bathroom and came to ask me a question. He caught me in the kitchen, crying because I was a depressed, miserable mess then. He was so concerned. He sat me down at the table, got me a glass of water, and sat with me. It had been so long since someone showed me that kind of empathy that I just opened up and let it all pour out.

We talked every day for hours while he was there working. I would find new repairs for him to do or change my mind on things he had already renovated. Anything to draw out our time together. I would make him lunch while he worked, and help at times too. I did whatever I could to come up with an excuse to be near him. He made me laugh… Oh, how he made me laugh. He listened to me. He made me feel seen. Eventually I realized I had developed feelings for him. I didn't act on them at first but…" Mom shrugs her shoulders sheepishly.

"What's good for the goose is good for the gander," I finished for her, not terribly interested in the more in-depth details of my parents' sex lives.

"Right. Well. I became pregnant with you. I honestly wasn't sure who the father was. Brian was still forcing intimacy between us when he was home. Jake begged me to leave Brian and let him raise you and Bryce, but I couldn't until I knew who the father was. It wasn't obvious until you were born and they typed your blood. I'm B+ and Brian was AB+. You are O+. I guess that was the final straw for Brian. He left. Just…disappeared one day. Left the divorce papers on the kitchen table. Jake stepped up in a huge way, but Bryce never got over being abandoned by his father like that. I think… I think the fact that it happened when you were born tied the two things together in Bryce's mind, and he blamed you instead of putting the blame where it really belonged. On me and your dad. We were the grown-ups in the situation."

Mom looks crest fallen. I don't want her to feel guilty for trying to find happiness in such a shitty situation. I reach across the table and take her hand. When she looks at me, she gives me a sad smile. "I'm so sorry, sweetie. I tried so hard to make it right, for Bryce. No matter how much I wanted to blame his father and tell him that Brian had abandoned us, I couldn't do it. I couldn't take that from Bryce. Jake did everything he could to try to make Bryce feel like he loved you both as his own, but Bryce never would give him a real chance. I knew you boys didn't have the best relationship but hate you? You really think he hates you? What happened between you?"

After having that particularly depressing truth bomb dropped on me, I'm not sure if I'm ready to bring up the fact that her son, who was irrevocably damaged by the failure of her first marriage, is using her as leverage to get me to help him. I don't think now is the time to tell her he is threatening to make her homeless if I don't do what he asks. Also, the irony that my situation with Everly is eerily similar to how my parents got together is not lost on me.

"Nothing in particular. It's just something that's been on my mind. Just wondering if there is any way I can fix it." I shrug, trying to play off the question while my mind whirls with all the new insight I have on my spiteful half brother, and how I can use it against him.

CHAPTER 17
EVERLY

"Do you think tonight is the night? Is Bryce finally going to shit or get off the pot?" I snort out an incredibly unladylike laugh at Ana's vulgar idiom. She's standing behind me, putting the finishing touches on my hair. We are supposed to be meeting with Bryce's mom, stepdad, and brother and my parents for dinner tonight in celebration of him passing the bar.

Bryce and I have been together for three years now, and Ana isn't the only one who has been wondering when he is going to propose. My parents have been dropping not so subtle hints about how much they would love for Bryce to become more than just a college boyfriend. My dad helped Bryce land his first job at one of his college buddies' firms.

They even let him come along on our annual family summer cruise for the past two years. They would love nothing more than for him to wife me up and put a bun in my oven. I can practically see the baby booties knitting themselves in my mom's eyes. Never mind I'm not even twenty-five and have barely gotten started with my own career.

But it seems to be some foregone conclusion from everyone in our lives that he's been waiting to propose until after passing the bar exam. I'm even starting to buy into the excitement, despite my best effort to make this celebration about Bryce's accomplishment.

"I'm trying not to think about it. I just want to celebrate him. If I spend the whole night wondering, it'll make the vibes weird." The butterflies in my stomach flit around, and I try to tamp down the excitement. I meant what I said. I want to celebrate Bryce. My eyes meet Ana's in the mirror, and she pops her shoulder in a half shrug with a bounce of her head.

"That's a good point. Plus you two do have that trip to Paris coming up! I bet he'll do it there!" Ana's blue eyes light up in excitement, and it's so contagious I get caught up in the feverish daydream she conjures up of Bryce proposing to me in front of the Eiffel Tower. We saved up all year to take this trip as a celebration for him finishing law school. What better time to take the next step of our relationship? By the time Bryce comes to pick me up, I'm convinced Paris is where I will become an engaged woman.

DINNER with our combined families is only mildly awkward. This is the first time our parents have met, and Bryce seems to have tucked away his usual simmering animosity toward his stepfather away for the sake of peace. I've tried over the last two years to bridge the gap between them, after noticing the toll it has been taking on his mother, Caroline. While she is clearly proud of Bryce, every time he ignores a conversational olive branch from Jake, her smile falters. Jake, to his credit, doesn't let Bryce's coldness get to him.

When Bryce and I first started dating, he made it seem like he had a hard home life with a stepdad who made his life hell. The truth seems to be less nefarious than that, and I think Bryce's main problem with Jake is that Jake isn't *his* dad. But every time I've tried to bring it up, he's shut me down with no discussion. The little boy who had his world upended when he was twelve is still inside there, and I don't know if I will ever find a way to soothe his pain enough to repair the rift in his family.

Fortunately, he has no hard feelings toward *my* dad. Ever since that first Thanksgiving when I introduced him to my family, Bryce and my dad have been thick as thieves. It's no secret that my dad hoped I would find someone like him—*respectable, career driven,* someone who could *provide* for me in relationship. Never mind that I don't plan on needing to be provided for. My dad is old-fashioned and it's just an area we will never see eye to eye. So it felt like I won the lottery when I saw how welcoming he was toward Bryce. It was a far cry from the stern father figure who did his best to scare away all the high school boyfriends he never approved of.

Just before the dessert course is set to arrive, Bryce stands, tapping on his wine glass, drawing the attention of not only our table, but most of the tables nearby as well.

"Family, and soon-to-be-family, I just wanted to take a quick moment to say thank you to everyone here tonight, helping me celebrate this milestone in my life. It's been a rough few years finishing out law school, but I wouldn't trade it for anything. Not the late nights studying or the hours spent writing case arguments or the asshole professors. Not when it led me to this moment, on this night, with the most perfect woman by my side." Bryce turns his handsome face toward me, and I find myself enraptured by his gorgeous smile. I'm so starstruck, it takes a moment for his words to process in my brain.

Soon-to-be-family...

"Everly, I knew the first night I met you that you would be my endgame. Who knew my buddy Brody being a drunk idiot would land me my dream girl?" Bryce lets out a *can you believe it?* snort laugh while I squirm, thinking of the night we met and how scared I had been of Brody. Sure, it led to me and Bryce meeting, and I'm not mad about *that*. But it still bothers me how Bryce never stopped hanging out with Brody. Bryce continues his speech, drawing my attention back to the present.

"...Everly has been my rock. My port in the storm. She has given me a sense of belonging and being loved that I haven't felt in a very long time…" My stomach flips at Bryce's touching words, but I can't help but sneak a glance across the table where his mom sits. There is a wobbly smile on her face, but tears in her eyes. Did she feel the sting from his words? Jake has one arm slung across her shoulders, idly rubbing reassuring circles on her upper arm, a bland, passive mask on his face, hiding any reaction from Bryce's speech. Dane, his younger half brother, sits slouched in his chair, eyes cast down, like he'd rather be anywhere but this dinner celebrating Bryce. Then again he's thirteen, so that could just be his default setting.

"Martin, Jennifer, you welcomed me into your home with open arms and made me feel like part of the family. Your support has been instrumental with helping me get my career off the ground, and I will always be grateful for that and the incredible daughter you raised."

My mom blushes at the compliment, and my dad beams with pride.

"I think it's time to stop feeling like part of the family and make it official." Bryce gives my dad a knowing wink before turning back to me, going down on one knee. I can't stop the surprised gasp that escapes when I see the shining diamond ring in Bryce's hand. It's a gorgeous, albeit flashy, oval cut center stone, surrounded by tiny stones in a halo around it, set in white gold. It catches the light from the chandelier above our table, flashing brilliantly.

"Everly Elizabeth Strauss, you have been amazing these last two years, putting up with my crazy schedule and grueling hours of studying. You have helped keep me focused on the prize, and now it's time to collect. It's time to put you first and take the next step of our relationship. Will you do me the honor of becoming my wife?"

My mom squeals in excitement at Bryce's proposal. My vision is blurry from the tears threatening to fall. I'm so stunned, it takes a few long seconds before I remember I'm supposed to give him an answer.

"Yes! I will marry you!" The tears obscuring my vision finally fall, revealing Bryce's face lit up like a Christmas tree. He slips the ring on my finger before capturing my mouth in a kiss that I definitely don't want my parents watching. When we pull apart, I see my dad beaming at us with a sense of fatherly pride that is wholly unfamiliar to me.

Well, at least I finally did something to make him proud.

CHAPTER 18
EVERLY

"I don't know what has you in such a shit mood, Everly, but I need you to adjust it right now."

Closing my eyes, I inhale deeply, letting Bryce's admonishment wash over me. I let the sound of the rain pounding on the car soothe me. I imagine it washing away all the hurt and anger I am holding inside. It doesn't work.

I am running on fumes after spending the previous night anxiety-spiraling over kissing Dane again. Every time I tried to close my eyes, all I could see was the way Dane looked at me. Like I was the only thing that mattered in his world. Right before I lost my mind and climbed into his lap as I shoved my tongue into his mouth. I could still feel the ghost of his touch. The way he gripped my hips. How his fingers twisted in my hair. How rigid and thick his cock felt under his jeans. Then the lights from a passing car lit up the interior of my Mercedes, breaking the spell between us, bringing me back to my senses.

When Bryce finally made it home, well past midnight, I

was lying in bed, staring up at the ceiling, my mind a swirling mess of guilt and arousal. I pretended to be asleep when he crawled into bed, so I wouldn't have to face him. It was starting to feel like I was living in my own personal Groundhog Day hell. Avoiding my inattentive husband after making out with his brother for a second time. How in the hell did I get into this mess again? This can't keep happening. Dane doesn't deserve to be hurt by my emotional recklessness.

Clearly, I haven't done a good job of hiding my emotional turmoil from my husband. "Sorry, I guess I didn't sleep well. You know how crabby I am when I'm tired."

Bryce pulls into the valet lane of The Magnolia Hotel, the nicest hotel in Birch Falls. Opened in 1909, built by the same railroad baron that built Whispering Grove, it is a majestic staple of downtown Birch Falls. It also is the site for all important social events hosted by the political elite of Birch Falls.

I move to open my door to escape the oppressiveness of being stuck in a car with my spiraling thoughts and my husband, but Bryce grips my arm, halting my escape.

"I need you on your A game tonight Everly. I want you to smile and be charming. Do *not* embarrass me. I have a lot riding on getting Skip Harrington on my side." His fingers bite into my flesh in a painful squeeze, quelling the urge to roll my eyes at him. "Do you understand?"

"I understand."

"Good." Before I have a chance to react, Bryce tugs me toward him and crashes his mouth against mine. I let out a shocked gasp that he swallows as his tongue sweeps into my mouth, overwhelming my senses with his dominance. My body wants to stiffen and pull away, but I force my muscle to relax and become pliant under his touch. Fighting with him now is not going to make this evening any more tolerable. When he breaks the kiss and leans back in his seat, there is malevolent hunger in his eyes that sends a chill down my spine.

"EVERLYYYYYY, YOU MADE IT!" Veronica greets me with an air kiss, nearly choking me with the cloud of perfume that surrounds her. Forcing my face into a smile, I return the gesture.

"Veronica, how lovely to see you again. Thank you for inviting us." I imbue as much false excitement in my voice as humanly possible. I can feel Bryce staring at me as I greet the hostess, the intensity of his gaze causing my skin to flush. After the dangerous look Bryce gave me in the car, I'm not looking to do anything that will cause him to be angry with me.

"Come, let me introduce you to one of my dear friends. She's one of my sorority sisters from college." Veronica loops her arm through mine and guides me away from tempest camouflaged as my husband. As we pass a server holding a tray of champagne flutes, I steal one, desperate for some sort of liquid oblivion that will help me get through the night. I risk a glance behind me and see Bryce watching me, his expression an unreadable mask. Then

Skip and Shane approach him, causing his icy exterior to melt away, leaving only the charming lawyer behind. It's frightening how his demeanor can change in the span of a heartbeat.

I let Veronica lead me around the extravagant ballroom, making introductions. I smile, laugh, and make the appropriate interested noises to every new face, but I wouldn't be able to tell you a single name, even if you held a gun to my head. My mind is too distracted, the swirling eddies of my conflicting emotions making it impossible to focus on the new faces in front of me.

After what seems like an eternity of making the rounds, Veronica gets caught up in reminiscing with one of her sorority sisters, so I make my escape to the open bar in the back corner of the ballroom. The two glasses of champagne I stole as we made our way around the room have done nothing to calm my nerves or make the people gathered here seem remotely interesting.

Just as I reach the bartender, I feel a large presence come up behind me, way too close for comfort. I turn to say something, but my mouth shuts when I see it's Shane, with a maniacal look in his eye. "There you are, Everly. Veronica swept you away before I got a chance to say hello." He wraps one large arm around my shoulders and pulls me into a hug, pressing my body so tightly into his, I can feel half-hard dick pushing into my hip. He holds me for longer than is appropriate for a friendly greeting, and I find myself looking over his shoulder, hoping to find Bryce coming to my rescue. As much as I don't want to be around Bryce, I want even less to be anywhere near this pervert.

Shane's nose grazes the shell of my ear as he inhales deeply. "God, you smell intoxicating. Your husband is a very lucky man."

Just then I see Bryce appear in the crowd, walking in our direction with a thunderous look on his face. I push away from Shane, with a fake smile plastered on my face. "Speaking of lucky husbands, there he is! Bryce, honey, you found me!" Shane steps back, but not far enough away for my comfort. Bryce slips in the space between us, capturing my lips with his, his hands sliding around my waist, claiming me in a possessive show of ownership.

"There's my gorgeous wife. I was wondering where you disappeared to. Thanks for finding her for me, man." He nods toward Shane, and Shane leers at me, not even acknowledging the fact that my husband is now here. What the fuck is wrong with him? I burrow further into Bryce's side, keeping him between me and Shane as we turn our attention back to the bartender, patiently waiting for our drink orders.

"I'll have an Old Fashioned, and a pineapple martini for the lady." The bartender nods and turns to make our drinks.

"I'll have an Old Fashioned as well!" Shane steps up on my other side, leaning so close his body presses into mine from behind. His breath tickles my neck, sending a shudder of revulsion down my spine. I am already as close as I can get to Bryce and suddenly feel claustrophobic being trapped between the two men and the chest high bar. Shane begins chatting with Bryce about some case they are on opposing sides of. He doesn't step away, just leans his body into mine discreetly while I mentally calculate how pissed Bryce will be if I make a scene right now.

"You know I've got your guy dead to rights. He's not getting off with anything less than twenty years if this goes to trial. There is DNA evidence and cell phone records putting him at the scene. Just take the deal and save us both some time." Shane's hand brushes against my thigh, where the hem of my skirt ends. I jerk at the touch, and Bryce shoots me an annoyed look before steering us away from the bar, drinks in hand. I let out a sigh of relief as we move away from Sleezy Shane.

He leads us over to a table off to the side, away from the crowd. My respite from Shane is short-lived when I realize he is following us. The table only has two chairs, so when Bryce takes a seat, he pulls me down on his lap, leaving the other chair directly across from me available for Shane. The skirt of my dress slides up my thigh, and Shane's eyes track the movement. Shifting uncomfortably, I try to tug the fabric back down but Bryce's hand rests on my thigh, blocking the way.

"Come on, Shane. You gotta do better than twenty years with the possibility of parole. I want manslaughter, five years, with time served. It was an accident. A stupid mistake by a young kid. He's got his whole life ahead of him. There's no reason to ruin a bright future."

Suddenly Shane's skeezy looks aren't the thing causing my stomach to turn. Bryce's casual defense of a man responsible for someone's death sends a chill down my spine. I take a long swallow of my martini, trying to quell the shudder my body wants to release.

"Got that girl wasted beyond reason, convinced her to have sex in a pool, and drowned her because he was too fucked up to realize he was holding her head underwater. I am sure I can get the jury to convict him." Shane leans back, resting his hands on his bulging stomach, a smug sneer on his face, like a cat who just got the canary.

"It was consensual sex; they were both fucked up. He said she told him she was into breath play and had read some kinky scene in a book that made her hot. It's not his fault she couldn't hold her breath. It's not worth ruining his life over. You know I can just bring up her dating history and past drug abuse and have him get a not guilty verdict." Bryce's hand trails up my thigh, tugging the dress up with it. I slap my hand on his, stopping his progress.

"Bryce, stop!" I hiss. I'm so distracted by his hand, I don't entirely process what he said.

"If you're so sure about that, why are you trying to make a deal with me?" Shane doesn't take his eyes off me as he speaks to my husband. Disgust roils in my stomach.

"I'm not opposed to the kid learning a lesson. Learning how to be careful and discreet is an important skill to have. He won't forget this lesson if he has a stint behind bars, but we need to be able to brush it off as a youthful indiscretion. This is the Governor's son, and having him owe me a favor would be quite a feather in my cap. I'll be happy to let him know how amenable you were to making sure his son got off with a warning. Surely we can come to some sort of agreement?" Bryce's fingers curl up more, dragging my skirt up another two inches. My muscles freeze, and I forget how to breathe as my brain processes Bryce's words and actions.

I'm sure we can come to some sort of agreement. His words ring through my skull like a klaxon. *Danger!* my mind screams, but I am paralyzed by horror as their implication sinks in.

I dig my nails into the back of his hand, praying this conversation isn't going where I think it is. Bryce in turn squeezes my thigh so hard I let out a whimper.

"F-fuck, Bryce…"

Shane leans forward, leering at me, a hungry look in his drab brown eyes. "What did you have in mind?"

That's it. I can't take this disgusting conversation any longer. I shove Bryce's hand away from my thigh and stand up from his lap, backing away, unable to keep the disdain off my face.

"Oh, my god. I can't believe you would sit here and so casually discuss the death of a young woman like that. You sound like you're making a fantasy football trade. Who even are you, Bryce?" I fling my arms out to the side, my voice rising to just this side of shrill. Bryce's expression is furious, but I don't give a fuck. I can't sit and listen to him barter over getting a rapist off with a smack on the wrist.

"Everly, sit the fuck down. You're making a scene." He stands, looming over me in an instant. He reaches for my arm, but I back away, out of his reach.

"Keep your hands off me, or I'll really cause a scene."

He reaches for me again, "Ever—".

"*No!* Do not fucking *Everly* me. I am leaving. Do not follow me. I don't want to look at you." I imbue as much venom into my voice as I can before turning and storming away from my husband. Tears threaten to fall as the realization that I am married to a monster I don't even know hits me.

I ignore the curious looks from the partygoers close enough to hear our argument and the chuckle Shane lets out at Bryce's expense. Suddenly the air in his ballroom is beyond stifling, and my only thought is *I need to get away.*

Storming down the plush carpeted hallway, vision blurry with tears of frustration and disgust, I pull my phone from my clutch and call the only person I can think of who won't tell me I'm overreacting and being silly. Ducking into the ladies' room to hide from Bryce, I wait—heart pounding from adrenaline—for my call to be answered. Relief rushes through me when I hear a confused but concerned voice on the other end of the line.

"Everly? Is that you? What's going on?"

"Dane—" My voice hitches as a sob escapes. "Can— Can you come get me?"

CHAPTER 19
DANE

When I pull my car into the circular driveway of The Magnolia, my muscles are tense from holding myself back, when all I want is to march into that ballroom and punch my asshole brother in the face. Everly sounded so distraught when I answered her call, my protective instincts for her took over, and I didn't think twice about coming to pick her up. I don't know what he's done to upset her to the point where she feels the need to run from him, but once I find out, I will make sure he suffers the consequences.

I pull out my phone and text Everly to let her know I'm here. She asked me to not come inside. She doesn't want anyone to see me and tell Bryce who she's with. It's taking all of my self-restraint to abide by her request, but I do it because I don't want to make this worse for her, and I don't want to be like my brother and ignore her boundaries.

A minute later, I see her rushing out the lobby doors toward my car. My breath catches when I see her. She's wearing a short black cocktail dress with a gauzy skirt that floats and shifts as her hips move, revealing tantalizing glimpses of her thighs. The top half is strapless, the sweetheart neckline accentuating her feminine curves, leaving her shoulders and neck on display. It's sexy but classy. It isn't until my gaze reaches her face that I see the tell-tale red blotches on her cheeks that reveal she's been crying, and my heart clenches at the sight. Shit, what happened to her?

Everly slides into the passenger seat of my car and doesn't look at me as she buckles her seatbelt. She just faces forward, a grim look of resignation on her face as she says, "Just go. I don't care where." Her voice is soft, buried under the weight of defeat, but lined with the sharp edge of bitterness.

Shifting the car into drive, I take her to the one place I'm sure Bryce won't look for her. My apartment. As far as I know, he has no reason to suspect she would call me for help, and she should be able to hide out at my place while she gets her bearings.

We ride in silence as I navigate the dark streets. The rhythmic swiping of the windshield wipers and her quiet sniffles are the only sounds to be heard. I resign myself to wait and let her decide when she's ready to talk.

I LEAD her into my modest apartment, and mentally cringe at how it probably meets the textbook definition of bachelor pad. It's a small studio with a bedroom loft that fits my needs but probably feels like a shoebox compared to the house she shares with my brother. The walls are white and bare on one side and exposed brick on the other. The furniture basic and utilitarian. One brown leather couch that has seen better days, a small dinette set with a table and two chairs, an oversized TV complete with gaming system, and a small galley kitchen stocked mostly with convenience foods. At least my mattress is on an actual bedframe and not on the floor.

Everly stops and takes a look around, still looking a little dazed. I watch as her eyes sweep across the space, like she's figuring out where she is and how she got here.

"Can I get you something to drink? Water? Coffee?"

"Got anything stronger?" Her voice is raspy and sexy from disuse. It goes straight to my cock, and I send a mental note to my dick reminding it now is not the time to get hard.

"Yeah, I got something stronger. Make yourself comfortable." I wave a hand to the leather couch with cracks in it as I head to the fridge to pull out two bottles of double IPA. It's not liquor, but it's strong enough to take the edge off, and I don't want to get her drunk. I make quick work of removing the caps before handing her a bottle and sitting next to her on the couch. She's curled up, legs tucked under, skirt riding up, once again putting her tantalizing, creamy thighs on display. God, my brother is a fucking idiot. He has no idea what he has.

Everly accepts the bottle with a grateful smile and takes a long swallow of the beer. I focus on my own, trying not to let my eyes lock in on the mesmerizing way her neck moves as she swallows, wishing it was my dick between her lips instead.

"So do you want to talk about it?" I shift my position so I'm facing Everly. She's looking down, picking at the label on the bottle. It's a long moment before she responds.

"I'm just coming to terms with the fact that I'm married to a soulless monster. I don't even know who Bryce is now...other than someone who's more concerned with using people to get ahead in his own life than doing the right thing. He wasn't always like this...was he?"

When she looks up and our eyes meet, there is so much agony in hers, like she needs to know she wasn't blind to his failings the entirety of their relationship. As much as I'd like to throw my dickhead of a brother under the bus, I can't. I don't want to hurt her more.

"No, I don't think he was. At least not when it came to you." It's not a lie. Bryce was good to Everly, even if he was a dick to me. "He's a man with goals and the determination to meet them, and he won't let anything get in his way. It's what makes him so good at his job. It's also what makes him a selfish asshole."

Everly nods and takes another sip of her beer. "Yeah, I'm beginning to see that now. I...I just don't know if I can sit by and be with someone like him. You didn't hear the disgusting things he was saying. How...dehumanizing he was toward the victim of his client. And the way he let Shane just leer at me like he was dangling a piece of meat in front of a starving animal." She closes her eyes, face scrunching like she's fighting the impulse to cry again.

"Hey, Ever, it's okay. You're safe here now. I've got you."

I reach out and cup her cheek, swiping a silent tear away with the pad of my thumb. I feel her body relax into my touch and take that as an invitation to scoot closer. I wrap an arm around her shoulders, pulling her into my side, and she rests her head on my chest.

"I'm just so disgusted by the man he is now. I can't believe I didn't see it sooner."

"Love makes us blind to a lot of things."

She looks up at me, her expression a confused mess of emotion, like she isn't sure how she's supposed to feel. "Thank you for coming for me, Dane. You…you make me feel safe." The corner of her mouth turns up in a small, sad smile, and I simultaneously want to punch my brother for making her feel unsafe and crush my mouth against her and make her forget all about him. I settle for placing a gentle, chaste kiss on the corner of her mouth.

"You are safe with me, Ever. Always."

When I pull away, she's looking at me like she's seeing *me* for the first time. There is a look of awe and disbelief on her face, like the concept of safety is new to her. My words hang between us like a promise. I want to kiss her. Make her forget the hurt she's feeling. But I wait for a sign. A signal that she wants this too. I don't want to push her if she's feeling vulnerable. Her small pink tongue darts out, moistening her bottom lip, and my eyes track the move- ment. Her breathing comes in short pants, and I know she feels this electric connection between us. She's been fighting it for weeks, and now that she knows what a terrible person my brother is, there should be nothing keeping her tethered to him.

She leans closer, bringing her lips close enough to mine that we are sharing the same air. She brings her free hand up to my jaw, and I shudder under her touch.

"Make me feel safe, Dane. Please." Her words are barely a whisper, but it's all I need. The tether on my self-control snaps. I take the beer bottles and set them on the coffee table as I lean into her, capturing her lips with mine. She lets me take control and leans back on the cushions, allowing me to cover her body with my own. I settle between her legs, one hand cupping her ass while the other tangles in her hair as our tongues dance.

I lose myself in the taste of her. In the breathy moans that escape from her mouth. The way her soft curves feel under my touch. The warm, wet heat from her center I can feel dampening my grey sweats. She is my rapture, and this time nothing is going to interrupt us.

Trailing my lips down her jaw, I nip and kiss her neck and along her collarbone as I move down her body. Her back arches, pushing her breasts into the path of my kisses. I pull down the top of her dress, releasing her breasts from the stretchy black fabric. She isn't wearing a bra, and I am momentarily stunned by the sight of her perfect, teardrop-shaped tits. They're just big enough to be a handful, and her dusky pink nipples are hard, begging to be sucked on. I capture one in my mouth while rolling the other between my fingers. The soft whimper of pleasure she lets out is music to my ears.

I take my time, lavishing each soft mound with attention, alternating sucking and pinching her nipples until she is a writhing, panting mess under me. She bucks her hips into mine, seeking friction. The needy responsive-ness of her body to my touch makes my dick so hard it hurts.

"Dane…god…more…it feels so good." Hearing her say my name while begging for more has got to be the sexiest goddamn thing I've ever heard in my life.

"Patience, sweetheart. I've been waiting a long time for this, and I am going to enjoy worshipping every inch of your gorgeous body." I shift lower, settling my face between her thighs. One of her legs rests on my shoulder, the other falls away, opening her sex to me. It's barely covered by a pair of black lacy underwear, and I can make out a damp spot in the center. I lean in and run my tongue up the wet fabric, savoring the taste of her. Fuck me. I'm done. This is it. If I die now, I'll die happy.

"Dane," she pleads, her hips bucking as she fondles her tits. She is as lost to this mindless need as I am. Her body seeking mine like two magnets drawn together.

Slipping a finger between her underwear and wet heat, I lightly tease her sensitive flesh, drawing out the ecstasy and agony of unfulfilled desire.

"Can I make you feel good, Everly? Do you want me to fuck you with my tongue until you forget why you're with the wrong brother?" I draw a gentle circle around her clit through her underwear with my tongue. She whimpers in response and grinds herself against my face.

"Words, Ever. Give me your words." I pull back, staring at her flushed and dazed expression. She looks at me, her eyes clouded with lust. This should be all I need, but I want verbal confirmation before we do something that cannot be undone. Once we take this exit, there is no going back. This is the point of no return.

"Please, Dane. Fuck me. Make me forget."

Fuck yeah. I know the grin that spreads across my face is nothing short of feral. With one swift tug, I rip the lacy undergarment from her body, then plunge my tongue into the most sinfully delicious pussy I've ever tasted.

With every swipe of my tongue through the slick, wet heat of Everly's pussy, her thighs clench tighter and tighter around my ears. She has one hand fisted into my hair, pulling my hair so hard it's *just* this side of painful, and it's making me rock hard. Her other hand is cupping one breast, squeezing and pinching her nipple. The way she rides my face—thrusting her hips up while dragging me closer with a fistful of my hair, her soft panting moans getting louder and louder—exceeds every fantasy of her I've ever had. By far. My imagination could never have expected how spectacular it would feel to make Everly shatter with my tongue.

"D-D-Dane...   Ohgodohgodohgod...   Don'tstopdontstopdontstop..." I keep my tempo as I slip two fingers in her pussy, curling them up and rubbing her G-spot, the sound of her pleas the singularly most erotic thing I've ever heard in my life. That does it. Her hips buck, and she cries out. Liquid gushes, coating my tongue and chin. I don't stop lapping up her release until her fist releases my hair, her hand falling limply to the floor.

Raising my head, I press a gentle kiss to her inner thigh. When I look at her face, she's watching me with hooded eyes, her cheeks flushed pink. God, she is beautiful.

I crawl slowly up her body, letting her watch me lick my lips, savoring the flavor of her. "You are magnificent." Her eyes widen in surprise as my compliment lands. Clearly, she hasn't been reminded recently how amazing she is. My fucking fuck of a brother doesn't deserve her. Before she can respond, I capture her lips with a filthy kiss, swallowing her protest. She wraps her arms around my neck, pulling me closer, deepening our kiss. She clings to me like she's afraid if she lets go, I'll disappear. Her leg shifts, and with an impressive show of flexibility, she slips her foot into the waistband of my sweats, pulling them down, freeing my cock. When it bobs forward it rests against her wet pussy, sending a shudder of desire through me. She's so slick and ready for me.

I rock my hips, rubbing the length of my dick against her sensitive clit. It causes another cascade of pleasure to ripple through her. I pause mid thrust when the head of my dick notches at her entrance, ready to push in and claim her fully. I break our kiss so I can look her in the eye when I say, "Tell me, Ever. Tell me you want this."

"I want you." Her words are quiet, but there is so much need and want in her eyes as she stares into my soul, I know in that moment I will give this woman anything she asks for. I watch her face as I push in, taking in how her expression goes from need to surprise to undeniable plea-sure as I fill her with my cock. God, she feels amazing. This isn't going to last long, and I want to make sure she comes one more time.

Hooking one arm under her knee, I lift her leg, bending her nearly in half, giving myself a better angle to fuck into her and hit her G-spot. I know I hit it when her fingernails bite into my back, and she cries out in surprise. Her hands find my face, pulling my mouth to hers, fusing them together.

Our kiss is desperate, like we are trying to blend our entire existence together. My hips piston in a relentless tempo, driving us both closer to the edge. Sweat coats our bodies as our frenzy comes to a head. She clenches around me, gasping into my mouth as her orgasm crashes into her. Her pussy tightens around my cock, pulling my climax out of me, and my body goes rigid as my dick pulses inside of her. Our chests are pressed together, hearts pounding, breath heaving as I revel in the perfection of this moment.

Everly Carmichael is now mine.

CHAPTER 20
EVERLY

The smell of frying bacon wakes me up from the deepest sleep I have had in weeks. I sit up, momentarily disoriented by my unfamiliar surroundings. After Dane and I…made love? Had sex? Fucked up everything in the most dramatic and irrevocable way? He carried me upstairs to his bed, tucked us both in, and held me while I fell apart. He thought I was crying over the death of my marriage. I was really crying over how I am the worst fucking person in the world for giving in to my selfish wants, and how much he will hate me if he ever finds out the truth I've been keeping from him.

THE SHRILL WHISTLE of the tea kettle shatters the tense silence of the dimly lit kitchen. I've been standing at the counter, head down, trying to calm my racing thoughts while Bryce showers. He didn't say a word the whole way home. Just stared pensively

out the window, one leg bouncing violently, while he clutched one of my hands in his. He said he would explain when we got home, but instead, he said he needed to shower and walked off to our bedroom. As I take the kettle off the burner to pour some sleepy time tea, my gut churns with a nervous feeling, while my mind tries to process what could have happened that lead to him being on the side of the road in the dark.

He was working late at the office. His office is in downtown. So how did Bryce wind up on the side of route 19 outside of town? Reeking of whiskey. There was no good scenario I could come up with that would lead to that situation. Did Bryce get drunk at work and get into an accident on the drive home? But where I picked him up is nowhere near our home or his office. Was someone else with him? Chill bumps explode over my skin as that thought floats into my mind. Oh god, did we leave someone behind? Are they hurt?

Warm arms wrap around me from behind startling me, causing my hands to release the mug of tea I had just poured. Nearly boiling water splashes onto my hands when it lands in a thud on the counter. "Fuck!" I scream, shaking my hand in pain.

"Shit, baby! I'm sorry!" Bryce jumps into action, turning the faucet on cold, pulling my hand under the frigid stream of water, soothing the burn. When he looks at me, there are tears in his eyes, mirroring my own. "I'm so sorry baby. I thought you heard me." His face is unusually pale, the angry red gash on his forehead peeks out from behind the wet clump of hair that fell over his brow. Bryce is shirtless, a diagonal belt shaped bruise in vibrant shades of purple, red and black, crosses left to right, shoulder to hip. Oh god, he was in an accident.

"*Bryce, are you okay? What happened?*" I cup his face, the pain from the burn forgotten.

Bryce returns the gesture, cupping my face gently as he leans in, pressing his forehead to mine. "*I fucked up, baby. I fucked up bad.*" Wetness drips down my cheek, and I realize it's not my tears but his.

"*Tell me what happened, Bryce. You're scaring me.*" My husband is always so calm and collected. I've never seen him rattled. He will face the toughest judge without flinching and defend even the hardest clients.

"*There...there was an accident. Jake's dead.*"

"Good morning gorgeous." Dane climbs up the stairs, interrupting my guilt spiral down memory lane, carrying a tray loaded with two plates full of scrambled eggs and bacon and two glasses of juice. My heart seizes when I take in his rumpled, sexy appearance. He's shirtless, just wearing the same gray joggers from last night. His hair is mussed, sticking up in every direction, and his usual two-day stubble has started more closely resembling a beard. But it's the smile he's sporting that causes my heart to stop beating. It's so open and relaxed and...happy. Like I gave him the best gift in the world last night. A sick feeling rolls through my stomach.

"You made breakfast?" I sit, stunned as he places the tray next to me on the bed. Dane plants a kiss on my forehead before taking one of the plates for himself. I can't remember the last Bryce did something as mundane as bring me breakfast in bed.

"I don't know about you, but I worked up a hell of an appetite last night." His green eyes sparkle as he winks at me. Memories from the previous night flash through my mind. Dane eating me out on the couch until I squirted on his face, then fucking me so well I forgot my name. Him carrying me into his bathroom where he did it all again, that time fucking me against the shower tiles until I was hoarse from screaming his name. I'm pretty sure there was one more lazy round of sexy spooning in the middle of the night when I wasn't fully awake, but I'm not entirely sure if that one was real or a dream. I am gloriously sore in all the best ways.

Tears spring to my eyes as I take in the spread for me. Eggs, bacon, and toast. So simple. But it represents something I haven't had in a very long time. Someone that wants to take care of me.

"Hey, hey, I know it's not much. I know I'm a terrible cook, but—"

I cut him off with a kiss. I cradle his face in my hands and kiss him with every fiber of my being, trying to convey how much this simple gesture means to me. I make a promise to him with this kiss. A promise only I know I'm making, but I will do whatever I must to keep it. I promise to right the mistake I made all those years ago, when I didn't turn Bryce in when he confessed to killing Jake.

CHAPTER 21
DANE

Breakfast is cold by the time we get around to eating it. Apparently, the way to Everly's heart is through her stomach. It also might be through her clitoris. It's hard to say what she appreciates more, the food or the orgasms.

She's in the shower right now. She insisted on showering alone this time, much to my dismay, but I take the time to check in with my conscience to see if I feel any guilt for sleeping with my brother's wife… Nope. Not even a little bit. Not after his attempt to blackmail me into helping him get Dom out of prison. Which is still a problem I need to deal with. I have zero intention of helping him, but I need to come up with a plan for covering Mom's living expenses if he does stop paying her rent. I'll continue to let him think I'm going to help him for now.

The only guilt I have is putting Everly in such a precarious position. I know Bryce. He doesn't like to lose. In the courtroom or outside of it. He hates losing to me even more. He's held a grudge against me my whole life, blaming me for his own shitty father's behavior, and he will not take letting Everly go lying down. He has the money and the connections to make things *extremely* difficult for Everly if she tries to leave. *When* she tries to leave. I will not sit back and continue to watch her languish away under his shadow.

The sound of the shower cuts off, pulling me from my thoughts. A few minutes later, Everly emerges from the bathroom dressed only in one of my T-shirts, her hair wrapped up in a towel, and smelling like my body wash. My dick stiffens in my sweats as I take in the mouthwatering sight in front of me. Everly in my clothes, smelling like me, is every fantasy I have ever had about her come to life. She gives me a wary smile when her eyes land on me.

"I hope you don't mind; I borrowed a shirt. I didn't want to put my dress back on yet." Everly approaches me slowly, nibbling on her lower lip in the sweetest, sexiest show of uncertainty.

Reaching up, I grab her hand and pull her onto my lap to cradle her against my chest. "Baby, you can borrow all of my shirts. I've never seen a more beautiful sight." Everly's nervous lip biting blossoms into a sweet, blushing smile, causing her eyes to crinkle in the most adorable way. I brush my thumb against the laugh lines, memorizing the feeling of happiness on her face. Happiness that I put there. How my jackass of a brother doesn't appreciate what he has with her just makes me hate him more.

I must caress Everly's face for an awkwardly long time, because she clears her throat, and I realize I've been staring at her, lost in thought. Thoughts about how I'll do whatever it takes to keep putting that smile on her face.

"So…what are you going to do now?" I ask, pulling my hand away and grabbing the back of my neck, trying not to look like a lovesick idiot.

The smile I was admiring falls away, and worry creeps back in Everly's eyes. "I…I don't know. I'll have to go home at some point, but I can't be around him anymore. He's… he's not the man I married anymore. I don't want to stay with him, but I don't know how to leave. He's not going to make this easy, Dane. Bryce doesn't like to lose."

"Tell me about it. He's been on my ass for weeks now to help him with a case that he has no business reopening, and I know he won't quit until he gets what he wants." I huff as I lean back into the overstuffed couch cushions. "I'll help you in every way I can, Ever. You don't have to do this alone."

Everly doesn't respond for a long moment. Instead she stares off, lost in thought. I don't tell her Bryce has texted me multiple times asking me to use my resources to find her. I've ignored his texts so far. I want to come up with a game plan before responding. I want to know where Everly's head is at. If she asks to move in here just so she doesn't have to go home, I'll let her. It's on the tip of my tongue to offer her that option when she finally speaks again.

"The Dominick Reeve's case?" she asks, surprising me.

"How do you know about that?" I didn't realize Bryce talked to Everly about his cases.

"He mentioned it to me, said he was trying to get you to help him with something, but you were avoiding him. Asked me if I knew why you weren't returning his calls..." She pauses, getting lost in thought again. "You don't want to help him because Dominick is guilty, right?"

I nod, my jaw clenched tight. "Dominick beat Serena. I will never do anything that would help him. Getting him locked up is the proudest moment of my career."

Everly nods, and I can see the wheels turning in her mind.

"That conversation he and Shane were having... Trying to cut a deal outside of the courtroom... That's not legal right? Especially how he was..." She trails off, her face scrunching up in disgust. "Flaunting me in front of Shane. Like he could use me as a bargaining chip to get the deal he wants for his client?"

"Not even a little bit. He also asked me to give false testimony on Dominick's behalf. He could lose his license and potentially be tried for conspiracy to commit perjury or witness tampering. The tricky part is proving it. Men like Bryce are good at covering their tracks and getting what they want."

"What if we could prove it?" Everly turns and looks at me with an inscrutable expression. I don't know if I like where this conversation is going.

"What do you mean? Prove what?"

"What if there is evidence for Bryce's backroom deals? What if I record him or something? Find something in his office? Proof of his evidence or witness tampering? We could put a stop to him, and if he's behind bars, it'll be a lot harder for him to fight the divorce."

My first instinct is to say *fuck no* to her suggestion. I absolutely do not want her back in that house with Bryce, and I don't trust his temper if he does catch her snooping around. I have no doubt he would make her life hell if he thought for half a second she was working against him.

I open my mouth to protest, but she shushes me with a finger to the lips. "I want a divorce. Bryce won't grant me one. I know he won't. We have too much history. But maybe if I can help you prove he's dirty and get him disbarred and maybe even locked away, he won't be able to hold me hostage in this sham of a marriage. I'm so tired, Dane. So tired of pretending to be happy with whoever this power-hungry asshole is. I haven't been happy in a long time, and I don't want to be the woman who stands behind a monster while he hurts people to get what he wants. I can't do it. Not anymore. I want to do the right thing. I need to do this." Everly stands and walks toward the staircase that leads to my bedroom loft.

"Where are you going?" I stand to follow her.

"I'm getting my clothes, then calling an Uber. I'm going to do this. It'll be easier if you help me, but I'm going to do it regardless. I have to do this, Dane." She's frantic now. Like this is the most important thing in the world. I don't know what's come over her. I catch up to her and grab her by the shoulders, stopping her.

"Hey. Ever. Stop. Think this through."

She shakes out of my grip, fury transforming her face into a determined mask. "I have thought about it. I'm tired of not doing the right thing. Are you going to help me do this or not?"

The fire in her eyes as she speaks about taking down my brother is officially the second hottest thing I've ever seen, and I know there is no way I can ever deny this woman anything.

"Alright, Ever. Let's do the right thing."

CHAPTER 22
EVERLY

When Dane finally relented to letting me go back home, an idea he was reluctant to go along with, I had him drop me off at Brewed Awakening before I ordered an Uber to go home. I had turned my phone off when I left the party and didn't want Bryce to connect my whereabouts to Dane. While waiting for my Uber and drinking the coffee I ordered, I scroll through the messages Bryce left overnight.

A queasy feeling rolls through my stomach at his last message. It's a threat. Not even a thinly veiled one at that. There are also at least a dozen missed calls and voicemails from Bryce. There is even a message from Ana, my friend and roommate from college. She doesn't live in Birch Falls, but she's only an hour away. Bryce must have assumed I called her for a place to stay or someone to talk to when I stormed off. I ignore the messages left by my husband but listen to Ana's.

"Hey, is everything okay? Bryce just called me at damn near midnight asking if you were here. He sounded frantic. Did you guys have a fight? Do you need me to come pick you up? I told him I hadn't heard from you, and I won't say a word if he calls me back. Just let me know you're okay. Love you."

A feeling of relief settles over me as I listen to her message. Ana has been my closest friend since our freshman year of college, and she knows I've been unhappy lately with Bryce. We don't get to see each other much with her job keeping her busy with travel, but we keep up with sporadic texts and phone conversations. Every time we talk, it's like no time has passed, and I know if I needed her she would drop everything to help.

My ride is almost here, so I shoot her a quick text to let her know I'm okay.

ME

> Hey, can't talk right now, but I'm fine. It's a long story. I'll call you when I can. XO

WALKING into the house feels like walking into a tomb. It's deathly silent. I know Bryce is here. His car is out front. I considered my options on how to play this on the ride over. Do I come in meek and apologetic and ask for his forgiveness? Or do I come in, head held high, completely unbothered with zero fucks to give? I know which option I *want* to choose, but for my plan to work, Bryce can't suspect that I'm thinking of leaving him or planning on betraying him. I need him to still feel like we are on the same team. That I'm still letting our dark secret shackle me to him. I need him to trust me, or at least be willing to be careless around me. I don't know what kind of evidence of wrongdoing I will find or how long it will take me to find it. I could be playing a long game here.

Slipping off my heels, I take quiet, measured steps through the house. I keep my head down and my steps quiet, like I'm a teenager again, sneaking in from a party. Only this time it's not my dad I'm worried about catching me. It's my husband.

Bryce isn't in the living room or the kitchen. I don't find him in his office either. Maybe he really isn't here. Maybe he's with someone and that's why his car is here. Some of the tension in my shoulders eases at the idea of getting a small reprieve from seeing him. Having more time to formulate a game plan would be amazing. I also want to shower again to make sure I don't smell like Dane.

When I enter the bedroom, I begin to unzip my dress. I'm tired of wearing the uncomfortable cocktail number and am dying to slip into some leggings and a T-shirt. My mind is already planning the conversation I'm going to have with Bryce when he gets home. Just as my dress hits the floor, a large hand wraps around my neck and squeezes, cutting off my oxygen. With a firm tug, I am yanked backward into a rigid, muscular chest. Bryce's signature cedar, tobacco, and leather cologne infiltrates my senses. Fuck, I must've been so lost in thought that I didn't hear him.

My heart rate skyrockets, and I don't even have to pretend to be afraid or remorseful. He's never grabbed me like this before. I can feel the anger radiating from him, and it is terrifying. My hands reach up on reflex, trying to loosen his grip. I can feel my face turning red as my lungs scream for air.

"Where. The. Fuck. Have. You. Been?" Bryce punctuates each word by squeezing harder and harder. My vision gets hazy as I dig my nails into the back of his hand.

"Everly, I swear to fucking god, you are going to regret pulling that little stunt." My eyes burn, and my cheeks feel damp. I realize I'm crying. I don't know if it's from the lack of oxygen or the terror from his anger. I've never seen him like this. I don't know who this man is. Just as my vision begins to go completely black, Bryce releases his hold. I stumble forward, landing on all fours on the bed, gasping for air. My whole body trembles in shock.

"I'm sorry. I'm sorry! I just needed space." I gasp out my apology between sobs as snot and tears run down my face, dampening the duvet.

"Space from your husband?" Bryce's voice is low and menacing.

I shake my head, clenching my eyes shut, trying to calm the terror cascading through my limbic system. I need to make him believe me. I need him to forgive me.

"Yes!" I turn around, and scoot backward on the bed, putting space between us. He's looming over me, dark circles under his eyes, his pupils the color of pitch. His jaw clenched; his face a mask of cold fury.

"I needed space from you. The way you spoke about that girl...the victim, it made me think of the night we met. When Brody wouldn't leave me alone and I thought he would do to me what happened to that poor girl. You *saved* me from that. How can you be so cruel and heartless about it now? It hurt hearing my husband be so dismissive. That's why I needed space." The tears don't stop streaming down my face. I bite my lower lip to keep it from trembling, waiting to see if there is a shadow of the man I married still lurking in the monster in front of me. I watch as Bryce's face softens a minuscule amount. He tilts his head to the side, as if he's considering my words.

"Bryce, I love you. But that man last night? The one showing me off like I'm a piece of meat? The one willing to let a woman suffer while her rapist goes free because of who he's related to? I don't know that man. I got overwhelmed and needed time to think." Even though the idea thoroughly repulses me, I crawl toward him and place a tentative hand on his chest, trying to calm the raging beast.

"I'm sorry."

"Where did you go?" His voice is cold and laced with suspicion, but he doesn't move to touch me again. I consider my options. He can check our credit card statements, so he will know I didn't get a hotel room. Telling him I was with Dane, having my guts rearranged, is most definitely not an option.

"I stayed with a friend."

"What friend? I called Ana. She said she hadn't seen you." It's depressing to realize that Ana is likely the only friend I have that I could turn to in a situation like this. How did my life become so isolated? I consider using Serena as an alibi, but then I remember how he's trying to get Dane to help get her ex-fiancé out of jail. That won't help rebuild my trust with Bryce.

"It was Ana. I told her not to tell you I was with her. She happened to be in town visiting her mom, so she picked me up and took me to her place for the night." I hold my breath, hoping he buys the lie. I'm not used to lying to my husband. I've never had to before. Will he see through me the same way he sees through a witness on the stand? Or will all the lying I've done *for* him work in my favor?

I decide to push my luck. "She talked me into coming home. She said whatever you were doing was probably just posturing to get Shane to make a deal and that I needed to remember who the man is that I married. She reminded me that everything you do is for our benefit. To make our life better. I'm sorry I overreacted."

Ana has always had more in common with Bryce than I have when it comes to ambition. He's always liked that about her, and it's probably the reason why he didn't mind our friendship. He probably hoped her cutthroat business sense would rub off on me, helping me understand why he works the way he does.

"Forgive me?" Leaning forward, I brush my lips against his in a tentative ghost of a kiss. I watch as the stony expression on his face melts away. My body feels like it's ready to collapse as the adrenaline that has been racing through me fades away, relief replacing it.

"You scared me, Everly. I can't lose you. We share too much now. It's you for me, always. Don't ever do that to me again. Understand?"

I nod and bury my face into his chest as he wraps his arms around me. My throat hurts, my head is throbbing, and I feel like I could throw up from guilt. Still, I can't help but feel like I just scored a victory in the war to absolve my soul for the lies I've been carrying for so long.

Just when I feel like I have bought myself a reprieve from Bryce, I feel his lips graze my neck as his hand slips down my back until he's cupping my ass. The feeling of his fingers trailing down my bare skin reminds me that I'm only wearing my bra and panties. I had been so caught up in diffusing the situation, I forgot I was nearly naked. Bryce snakes his hand under the lace of my panties and grips my ass, pulling me firmly against his body. I let out a gasp as the rigid length of his erection presses into my stomach.

Shit, shit, shit... My mind begins to panic for a new reason as Bryce trails hot kisses along my neck, down my shoulder, and to my breast.

"Bryce... Wait... I was going to shower." I push against his chest, but he ignores my protests and captures my wrists in one of his large hands, then holds them down behind my back as he continues to kiss across my sternum to my other breast.

"Shh, baby. Let's just forget about this fight and start over. Let me remind you why you never have to doubt me. Let me in. Fuck, I need to be in you."

"Bryce, n—" He silences my protest with his tongue, capturing my mouth with his. He shifts the hand cupping my ass to my pussy, letting his fingers tease at my entrance and apply pressure to my clit. My body responds to his touch even as my mind recoils in horror. Bryce has always known how to touch me. To make my body thrum with pleasure. I try to pull back again.

"Plea—" I gasp, trying to slow things down, but Bryce just continues his assault on my senses, his tongue sweeping in, stealing my words as his fingers deftly slip between my folds, pushing into me until he's pressing against my G-spot. My thighs clench involuntarily as he begins to stroke my G-spot mercilessly.

"Come for me, Everly. Come on my hand baby. I want you soaked before I fuck you." Bryce growls in my ear as his thumb circles my clit. I can feel the pleasure building in my core and fresh tears make my eyes burn. I can't get out of this. Not without triggering his anger again. He adds a third finger and lifts, pressing firmly into my G-spot, triggering my orgasm.

"Fuck! Oh god…Bryce!" I collapse against his chest, panting. My body trembles from the aftershock of the orgasm but also from the realization that I'm going to have to give up a bigger part of my soul than I expected if I want this plan to work. I may have to go all the way to hell to absolve my soul for the sins of my husband.

CHAPTER 23
DANE

DANE – 16 YEARS OLD

"Hey, Dad, can I stay at Jason's house tonight? We're gonna go to the game." I wait as my dad stares at his computer, completely zoned out.

"Hello? Earth to Dad?" I lean over and wave my hand in front of his face.

Jerking in surprise, Dad leans back and slams the laptop shut before I can see what he's looking at. "Where'd you come from?"

Smirking, I take a seat across from him at the table. "Mom's vagina. I thought you knew that? Or do we need to have a talk about the birds and the bees?"

Mom comes up behind me and smacks the back of my head. "Technically you were an escape hatch baby. Your big head wouldn't fit through my vagina even after two hours of pushing. You're lucky you don't have a cone head after being stuck in my birth canal for so long."

"Ew, Mom! Don't say that!" I cover my ears with my hands and begin singing off-key.

"Technically you're the one who brought up my vagina. Don't start something you can't finish."

"That's not gonna be the last time a woman says that to you, son."

"Dad!"

Sure, now he's paying attention. Mom leans down and kisses Dad, and I make an exaggerated gagging sound at their gross PDA.

"What's wrong, son? I thought you knew all about the birds and the bees?" Dad taunts.

"I don't need to see my parents' birds or bees co-mingling. Gross."

Dad just smirks as he gropes Mom's ass, and I bury my face in my hands.

"Ugh, just kill me now…"

"Oh, don't be so dramatic." Mom rolls her eyes in my direction.

Truth is, I'm only mildly grossed out by my parents. Mom was in an unhappy marriage when she met my dad, and my douchebag older brother's dad treated her like crap. She doesn't talk about it, but I found her blog one time and read it. She doesn't know I read it. It hasn't been updated in years. I think it was a therapy thing or some-thing; she stopped posting to it when I was in kindergarten.

I found it because I was bored one day and googled my mom's name. It was mostly poetry. Sometimes short stories or diary-like posts, but it was all sad. She was unhappy when she was with Brian. But then she stopped posting for a while before she started writing happier posts and stories. The dates line up to when I was born and she and Dad got together. So if Dad makes her happy, then I'll deal with some gross parental PDA.

"Anyway, can I? Go to the game and stay at Jason's?"

"Yeah, sure. I'll drop you off. I need to go see your brother anyway."

"Will you be back for dinner, honey?" Mom is making that face at dad. The one that means they're five seconds away from making out, so I jump up from my seat to leave the room.

"Should be. I'll let you know if I'll be late." Kissing sounds follow me out of the room, and I roll my eyes. They're worse than Jason and his girlfriend.

"Come on, Dad! The game starts soon! I don't wanna miss kickoff!"

THE NEXT MORNING, a gentle hand shaking my shoulder pulls me from sleep. My head is pounding from lack of sleep. Jase and I stayed up until four in the morning playing Call of Duty. I don't know what time it is, but it's way too freaking early to be up.

"Huh… Whaaa?"

"Dane, sweetie. Wake up. Your mom just called. You need to get up." Jason's mom's face comes into focus. The room is dark, and only a dim light is seeping from behind the curtains. It's definitely still early.

"What's going on?" I croak out, voice hoarse from too much hollering and shit-talking last night.

"I'm not sure, sweetie. Your mom just said something's happened and you need to come home."

I can tell from Mrs. Graham's tone whatever happened is serious. I kick off the blanket and sit up, fully awake now. The Graham family has been my second family my entire life, and I know Mrs. Graham's mannerisms and tone as much as my own mother's. The look on her face tells me everything I need to know.

When we pull up in front of my house, there is a police cruiser parked in the driveway where Dad's truck should be. The sun has barely risen, and Dad doesn't go to work on the weekends. Where is his truck? A sick feeling settles in my stomach. I must sit there, not moving, for a while.

"Hey, Dane. Do you need me to walk you in?" I look over at Mrs. Graham, and her eyes are full of concern. I shake my head, not wanting any witnesses to whatever bad news I'm walking into.

"No, no. I'll be okay. Oh, look, see, Bryce is here." I point to my brother's car that is pulling into the driveway. No one outside of my family knows how much of a dick my older half brother Bryce is to me, so I use his appearance as an excuse to send Mrs. Graham on her way. Fuck, if he's here it must be really bad. I hop out of the car as Bryce and his wife, Everly, get out of theirs. Everly's eyes are red and puffy; it looks like she's been crying. Bryce has dark circles under his bloodshot eyes, and he looks pale, like he's sick.

"What's going on?" I run up to Bryce and grab him by the arm. He flinches and pulls his arm out of my grip.

"You should go inside. Go find Mom." His tone is flat and dismissive.

Everly throws him a side eye and comes up to put her arm around my shoulder. Her floral perfume wafts around me, momentarily distracting me. How my dickhead of a brother landed an angel like Everly, I'll never know.

"Come on, Dane. You should hear this from your mom." I let her guide me through the front door. We find Mom sitting in the living room, two uniformed cops standing over her hunched form. Her shoulders are shaking, and she is making the most inhuman, broken sound.

It's the sound of someone's heart shattering.

"Mom? Mom? What's going on?" I collapse on my knees in front of her, gently pulling her hands away from her face. The look of heartbreak she gives me, is like a knife to the gut.

"Oh, baby. There was an accident. You-your father..." She chokes on a sob and can't finish. She just pulls me into her arms, cradling my head against her chest as she holds me the way she used to when I was small.

She doesn't have to say the rest. I know what happened. My dad is dead.

It feels like time stops. My body forgets how to function. My lungs forget how to breathe. Mom speaks, but I can't hear the words she's saying. There's a ringing in my ears drowning her out. I can only feel the vibrations of her words and sobs as my cheek rests against her sternum, and the soft stroke of her fingers through my hair. She used to play with my hair when reading me bedtime stories, and I feel like that little boy again as I cry into my mom's soft flannel robe, that smells like her favorite gardenia lotion.

Slowly the ringing in my ears dissipates, and I hear a soft sob behind me. Glancing over my shoulder, I see Everly, tears streaming down her face. Her hand covers her mouth, stifiling her sobs. Momentarily, I'm confused by how broken she looks over my dad's death. She didn't know him well. Bryce has always kept his distance from us after leaving for college.

Everly turns her head toward Bryce, a pleading look in her eyes. Like she's telepathically begging him to do something that would somehow make this nightmare not real. Bryce stands next to her, one arm wrapped around her shoulders, his face a blank mask. He stares at our mother with cold indifference. I never thought it was possible for me to dislike my brother more than I already do, but seeing the lack of emotion from him while our mother breaks in my arms turns dislike into hatred.

CHAPTER 24
EVERLY

EVERLY - AGE 26

My legs threaten to give out as my brain processes Bryce's words. "What do you mean Jake's dead? What accident? I thought you were at work? Why were you out on route 19?" The questions come out of my mouth in a torrent. None of this makes sense. Bryce was at work. He never mentioned seeing Jake. He avoids seeing his stepfather as much as humanly possible. I can barely get him to agree to visit his family at the holidays.

"Bryce, please. Talk to me." Cupping his face in my hands, I force him to look at me. I stare at my husband's face, studying his expression for clues to this bizarre riddle. His eyes are bloodshot, his nose red, cheeks wet with tears. I've never seen him cry before. Ever. He said once he stopped crying after his dad left and he realized he wasn't coming back. He said he'd never let himself get so attached to someone ever again, because he never wanted to feel that kind of pain when they left.

That was, until he met me. He even included a line in his vows to me that being with me was worth the risk of feeling that kind of pain, because he couldn't imagine a life without my love. It was so romantic. It was the moment I lost my battle to keep the tears at bay until after the ceremony, and my mascara was a mess as we walked back down the aisle, arm in arm.

Bryce closes his eyes and lets out a heavy sigh. "Jake came by the office. Said he needed to talk to me, man to man. Said it was important. He asked me to go on a drive with him so we could talk. Richard and I had just been sharing some fancy new bourbon he picked up while in Kentucky, so I guess I was tipsy enough to agree to go with Jake."

Richard is one of the partners at Bryce's law firm. Bryce has been working his ass off day and night to get on Richard's radar so he will be recommended for higher profile cases. That explains why Bryce didn't come home right after work.

"Where did you go?" I ask, gently prodding Bryce to continue with his story.

"Went to the quarry. It's where Jake used to take Dane and me when we were kids, to go fishing. When he tried to make me like him by doing normal dad stuff, in an attempt to make me forget he was the reason my dad left." Bryce lets out a derisive snort at the memory. "Guess he thought maybe being there would make it easy to break the news to me." His voice takes on a bitter, acerbic edge.

"What news?"

"That my dad is dead." Bryce looks away from me as he spits out the words, laced with the kind of anger one has when they know they've lost their chance at something for good.

"Oh god, baby. I'm so sorry." Fresh tears spring to my eyes. I wrap my arms around Bryce and pull him into a hug. I squeeze him, trying to give him some sort of comfort. I know he had hoped one day his dad would reach out and reconnect with him. He never gave up on that dream. Now it would never happen.

"He showed me the obituary. Dad died from a sudden heart attack. He was fifty-two. Left behind a wife and three kids, all younger than Dane. No mention of his first son…" Bryce's voice cracks as he chokes back a sob. I finally understand why he's crying and so broken. It's because *his* dad is dead. He's dead and had a whole new family. He had never planned on reaching out to his first son. Bryce buries his face in my hair, and I feel his tears on my scalp. I just hold him, stroking his back, trying to comfort him while he falls apart in my arms.

It's an eternity before Bryce speaks again. His voice cold and detached. He doesn't lift his head up or move away. He just mumbles his confession into my hair. "Jake drove us to the quarry and we sat and talked. He spun some bullshit about how he always wanted to do right by me and my mom and he never wanted to replace my dad. He said he always thought of me as a son, even when I was angry with him. Then he pulled out the sheet of paper with the obituary. I read it and…I don't know. Saw red. I got so angry. I'd lost my chance to reconnect with my dad forever. If it wasn't for Jake, I would still have a dad. I hit him. I just fucking lost it. Jake tried to wrestle me to the ground, but I overpowered him. When we went down his head hit a rock. I didn't notice at first. I was so lost to my anger. Then I saw the blood…"

Bryce pulls away from me. My arms fall limply by my sides, letting him go. I'm too shocked by his confession to move. He turns, leaning against the kitchen island, giving me his back. Like he's too ashamed to face me.

"He was just lying there. His eyes open. Staring at me. But there was nothing there. I fucked up, Everly. I didn't mean to kill him. I was just so angry. So hurt. I didn't mean to do it."

I watch his shoulders shake, as sobs wrack through his body. Nausea roils in my stomach, the reality of how dire this situation is settling over me. Then I realize I picked Bryce up by the road. There was no sign of Jake's car. Bryce looked like he had been in an accident. This isn't adding up. I have to know the truth. "Bryce… Where's Jake?"

"I put him in his car and drove it down an embankment just off the road. Put him in the driver's seat. Made it look like a car accident."

My world turns sideways. Then I'm sitting on the floor, my back to the cabinets. My head between my knees as I breathe in through my nose and out through my mouth, fighting the urge to vomit or pass out.

"Everly. Hey. Look at me. Look at me, baby. You can't tell anyone." Bryce is kneeling in front of me. This time he is cupping my face, forcing my eyes to meet his.

"You killed him!"

"It was an accident. God, baby, you know me. I'm not a murderer. I just lost my temper, and it was a tragic accident. If you go to the police, they'll arrest me. They'll charge me with murder. Then my mom will lose her first husband, second husband, and son in the same day. She will lose everything. You can't say anything. Promise me. Promise me you won't say anything, baby. Please."

I see the fear in Bryce's eyes as he pleads for my understanding. My compassion. My silence. My heart and my mind are at war. I don't know what the right thing to do is. The only thing I know is I don't want to cause any more pain, so I nod. Bryce lets out a relieved sigh and scoops me into his arms. We sit on the floor in silence, both lost to our own thoughts. Reconciling ourselves to the fact that our lives are now forever changed.

CHAPTER 25
EVERLY

Gray clouds hang heavy in the sky, threatening to open and unleash a torrential downpour. The funeral home planned ahead and set up two pop-up canopies on either side of the grave, to cover those in attendance. I'm sitting in the front row, next to Bryce, who is sitting next to his mother, one arm wrapped her shoulders as her body shakes with silent sobs. Dane is on the other side of Caroline, staring at the casket hovering over the open pit in the ground, waiting to be lowered into its final resting place. His face is an emotionless mask. Only the silent tears dampening his cheeks give away his anguish.

Since Jake's death a week ago, I've barely stopped crying myself, torn apart from the inside with grief and guilt. Watching Caroline, a once vibrant and engaging woman with a smile for everyone, fade into a mere ghost of herself has been heartbreaking. I've come over every day after work to deliver meals for her and Dane, clean her house to keep it presentable for the random well-wishers and mourners who keep stopping by, and just to be there if she needs to talk. During these visits I've managed to keep my composure, careful to be a safe space for Caroline to dump her grief into, rather than burdening her with my own.

Bryce has even been coming by every day to check on his mother and brother in an unusual show of compassion. We've spent more time with Caroline and Dane this past week than the previous five years of our relationship combined. Bryce has sat patiently with his mother while holding her hand and letting her sob into his Oxford button-downs, letting her pour her heartbreak into him. He's even offered a few words of comfort to Dane, but his brother, in true teenage boy fashion, has retreated into himself. He only appears from his room to eat and take out the trash, only offering head nods and grunts in greeting, refusing to actually talk to anyone.

My relationship with Bryce has been tense since his confession of what really happened the night Jake died. The first few days I begged him to find a way to come clean, the burden of carrying such a huge secret crushing me under its weight. Even though it was an accident, Bryce assured me in the eyes of the law it would not be seen that way. Not after he covered it up. There would be no way for him to confess and not have it look like it was premeditated. Bryce would at the very least be charged with manslaughter—at worst, first degree murder. That would result in a catastrophic domino effect that would ripple through both our families, taking away one of Caroline's last remaining pillars of support, and causing an uncomfortable backlash against my dad, who has been very involved in Bryce's career so far. Holding this secret in feels like a cancer eating me from the inside, but Bryce is right. Telling the truth will only cause more hurt for everyone involved.

The crowd in attendance is small. Caroline only wanted immediate family for the graveside service. It's us; Jake's parents; his siblings, Michael and Sara; and their families. Bryce talked so little of Jake that I didn't even know he had siblings until he died. They don't live close by, but judging by the devastation on their faces, they clearly adored their brother and had a close relationship with him.

The priest recites the closing scripture, Psalm 23, before asking if anyone would like to say any final words before Jake Wilcox is laid to rest. Caroline lets out a devastated wail, like she's somehow been holding in the worst of her pain this entire time and the announcement that it is time to put Jake into the ground is the final crack in the dam holding back the full force of her grief. The priest flicks a concerned look her way, waiting to see if she will speak, but Bryce just nods for him to continue on, while holding his mother tightly to him. I notice Dane snake one of his hands over to her lap so he can hold her hand too, but he doesn't move to say anything. Just as the coffin begins its slow descent into its final resting place, the sky opens up, fat raindrops pelting the canopy above us in a deafening barrage. Under the cover of the downpour, I finally let my own sob burst free, unable to hold back my own tortured grief any longer.

CHAPTER 26
DANE

It's been seven days since I last saw Everly. One agonizing week since the best night of my life. 168 hours since I felt her lips on mine. I've texted her a few times since she left my apartment, but her responses have been short and casual. She told me she was going to play it safe around Bryce until she was sure he didn't suspect it was me who had picked her up from the fundraising gala. I know she has a plan and having Bryce trust her implicitly is vital to it working, but it doesn't change the fact that she's the only thing my mind has been willing to focus on all week. The way her face looks when she comes. The way her eyes shone with surprise and happiness when I fed her breakfast in bed. The way her body fit so perfectly against mine when we slept. I can't stop thinking about her, and if I don't see her soon, I might lose my fucking mind.

"Earth to Dane. Are we gonna respond to that call or what?" Serena's voice breaks through the Everly fog clouding my thoughts, bringing me back to the here and now. To the crackle of the radio alerting us to a 10-16, domestic disturbance, in progress.

"Shit, yeah, sorry. I was just…"

"In your head. Yeah, I know. You've been there all week." Serena rolls her eyes at me as I shift the cruiser into gear and head to the address on the computer.

My stomach dips when I realize it's an address in Everly's gated community. I stare at it for a long moment, trying to remember her exact address, trying to assess how close this disturbance is to her.

"Watch the road, not the computer." Serena snaps out a command just as the passenger wheel touches the edge of the road, causing the cruiser to bump onto the shoulder. I correct my course slowly, careful not to jerk the wheel and send us into oncoming traffic.

"Seriously, what's with you? If you're gonna be so distracted you can't drive, then I'm taking the wheel. Kai will be pissed as hell if you get us in an accident, and I won't stop him from kicking your ass." I can feel Serena's irritation radiating from her. It's almost palpable how annoyed she is with me. I've been keeping her at arm's length since sleeping with Everly. Between that and Bryce trying to get me to help him with Dom's case, which I still haven't mentioned to Serena, the secrets are taking their toll on our partnership. In our line of work, if you can't trust your partner, you're going to wind up hurt. Or worse.

I decide to give her a partial truth. I don't want to worry her about Dominick just yet. I remember the toll his trial took on her, and I do not want to bring that stress on her unless it's necessary. And if I have any say in it,

Dominick will never walk out of prison as a free man. I tell her about Everly instead. I know she won't tell anyone about us, and I need someone to talk to. As a woman who's been in a similar situation, Serena might have some useful insight.

"I slept with Everly." In my periphery, I see Serena whip her head around, eyes wide in surprise.

"I'm sorry, you *what?*"

"Everly and I slept together. Spent the night in the same bed. Had sex."

"Everly your sister-in-law, Everly? Everly the woman married to your brother, Everly?"

My jaw clenches at the judgement in her tone. "You got a problem with it? Because I could use your advice." I turn to look at Serena, giving her a pleading look.

She narrows her eyes at me, studying my face, searching for sincerity. She must find it because she shakes her head. "I don't guess so. I know you. I know you wouldn't fuck a married woman for kicks, so what happened?"

Before I can get into the full story, the house we are heading to comes into view. I recognize it as the Harrington's house. Great. Another knot in the tangled web that is my life now.

I park the cruiser in the driveway and radio in that we are on the premises and will check in if we need backup. From the outside, everything looks normal, but I've been on too many calls where respectable family homes held dark secrets to trust outside appearances.

As we approach the front door, it swings open, Skip

Harrington standing there looking every bit the slimy, glad-handing politician he is. He's got the small town *awe, shucks, I come from humble roots* act down cold. It's how he keeps getting elected. Qualifications or policy don't actually matter if people can see themselves having a beer with you.

"Officers. How can I help you?"

"There's been a disturbance reported at this residence. Do you mind if we come in and check things out?" Normally I'd put on some bullshit charm with a man like Skip, knowing it's the easiest way to get someone like him to cooperate, but I'm not in a bullshit with a piece of shit like him kind of mood. Not when I know what he's trying to do behind the scenes and the kind of shady deals he makes.

"I'm sorry; you must be mistaken. Everything is all quiet here."

I notice he doesn't even glance in Serena's direction when he speaks. As far as he's concerned, I'm the only one on this front porch worth addressing.

"Someone called in a report of a woman screaming and a man yelling at this address. We would like to come in and speak with any other occupants of the house just to confirm all is well. If it's quiet, as you say it is, then this won't take long at all." Serena speaks up this time, projecting her voice in that no-nonsense, brooks no argument tone that can quell an entire frat house of drunk pledges. She doesn't take her laser focus off Skip, her dark, honey-gold eyes narrowed in a *try me, please* expression. She's not in the mood for bullshit either.

Skip finally cuts his gaze toward Serena, his smile faltering at her icy stare. If looks could kill, Skip would be in dire need of emergency resuscitation. He blinks, taking his time responding, calculating his odds of Serena backing down. He must realize they're not in his favor. Nodding curtly, he steps to the side and gestures for us to enter.

Serena takes point and enters first, her keen eyes scanning the environment, looking for any signs of an altercation. I follow her, keeping my attention trained on Skip, watching for any tells.

"Is your wife home?" Serena turns attention to Skip, her expression warning him that she will not tolerate any lies.

"She's in the bedroom, lying down. She has a headache." Skip does a good job of keeping his expression neutral, but I can see how his shoulders tighten. Hear how his voice loses all of the previously affected charm.

"I would like to speak with her. Where is the bedroom?"

"I'll show yo—" Skip moves to lead us to the room, but Serena steps in his path, blocking his way.

"You'll wait here with Officer Wilcox. Tell me where the room is." I can tell Skip wants to protest by the way his jaw clenches. He doesn't want Serena to talk to his wife alone.

"It's upstairs, third door on the right." Now his voice is cold. Irritated. Not nervous though. It's like he's angrier about being inconvenienced than he is worried about what she will find. Serena swings her uncompromising stare my way, and I see why Skip decided against arguing with her. When she has that look on her face, you know you're in the presence of an unyielding, uncompromising, individual. How she's managed to master this attitude by the ripe old age of twenty-four has a lot to do with why Dominick Reeves is in prison. She is not a woman willing to back down in the face of adversity or scorn. She is battle-hardened and unfortunately far too educated in the school of patriarchal bullshit. Between Dominick using his position of power to abuse her, and her being a woman in a male dominated field—full of men like Dominick—Serena has developed an almost bulletproof level of armor when it comes to men.

"Keep an eye on him. I don't want him coming up the stairs unless his wife says it's okay."

I nod, acknowledging her command. She might be a rookie but I am completely fine with her taking the lead here. I want Skip to know I accept her as an equal, not some silly woman playing cop.

Serena turns and jogs up the stairs. As soon as she's out of sight, Skip turns to me, hands up in a placating manner.

"Look, Dane. It's nothing. Veronica had too much wine, got mad about something stupid and threw a wine glass. She's sleeping off the wine now. Can you please call your partner off?"

Narrowing my eyes at Skip, I shake my head and speak slowly, so he doesn't misunderstand my words.

"My partner will determine if it's no big deal. If your wife gives her the same story, then you have nothing to worry about." Not a threat, just letting him know I'm not the cop to come to if he wants something swept under the rug.

He doesn't try to push his luck with me. Smart man. Instead we stand in the foyer, in a silent stare-off. Eventually Serena comes back downstairs, frustration etched on her face, her lips turned downward in a frown. She's not happy about what just happened.

She stops in front of Skip, her face a mask of barely contained rage.

"According to your wife, she had too much wine and dropped a glass, and it scared her. She apologized for worrying the neighbors."

Skip's lips twitch, threatening to smile. Unfortunately he's smart enough to stop it before giving Serena a well justified reason to punch him.

"It's no trouble, Officer Roberts." Skip lets his eyes linger on her badge, making a show of acknowledging her name in some misguided attempt at intimidation. "I'll be sure to let Captain Rogan know how diligent you are when responding to a call."

We leave without acknowledging the implied threat to his words. Back in the car, I turn to Serena. "How was Veronica? You look pissed."

"She was definitely drunk and had a cut on her hand she claimed was from the wine glass. I also noticed another, fainter bruise on her arm. I don't think that happened today. I'm not buying the accident thing at all, but she wouldn't give me anything." Serena blows out a breath in a frustrated huff. She knows better than most how hard it is to get a woman to leave an abusive relationship. Especially when her husband holds some sort of power or higher position.

"We'll keep an eye on her. Maybe we can get her to trust us or we can catch Skip slipping."

Serena gives me a flat stare, completely aware of how unlikely either of those situations are. At least of them happening before it's too late. Men like Skip get away with far too many transgressions against women entirely too often.

Instead of focusing on the futility of the situation, she decides to change the topic. "So you and Everly, huh? Care to start from the beginning and catch me up?"

And so I do, because I know, if anyone will relate to Everly's situation, it will be Serena.

CHAPTER 27
EVERLY

I can't do this. I don't know why I thought I could. Day after day of pretending to be the happy, doting wife while simultaneously trying to snoop around Bryce's study, trying to find…something? Evidence? A smoking gun? A confession? I'm not even sure what I expect to find. It doesn't help that Bryce has been surprisingly affectionate and considerate of my needs since the day after the fundraiser. I see glimmers of the man I fell in love with all those years ago. It's almost enough for me to question everything. To feel guilty for sleeping with Dane, for invading his inner sanctum. But at night when I'm asleep, the nightmares come.

Slow dragging footsteps. Heavy knocks on the front door. Gasping, pained cries of someone begging for help. Not someone. Jake. When I open the door, there he stands. Skin gray and

sallow. White, vacant eyes. Blood dripping from a large gash on the side of his head. In the dream I always stand there, frozen in horror at the specter in front of me. His plea is always the same.

"Why did you lie? Why won't you help me?" When I cry and try to tell him how sorry I am, he just shakes his head, his disappointment covering me like a shroud. Then he turns and shuffles away, one leg dragging with each step, a large gaping wound on the back of his head, pink brain matter peeking through the red, matted hair.

THE FIRST NIGHT I had the nightmare I bolted upright, convinced it was real. I had to rush to the bathroom to empty the contents of my stomach, the gruesome memory of his injuries my brain had conjured up more than I could handle.

I had nightmares before, when the accident had just happened and the responsibility of keeping Bryce's secret was a cross I bore in solitude. They weren't this dark though. I think sleeping with Dane has broken something in me. It's shattered the dam of flimsy excuses and rationale that kept me from telling the truth about Jake's death. Now the guilt has morphed into something raging and overwhelming, threatening to unravel my psyche if I don't find a way to make it right. Is that even a possibility at this point?

How did I think I could manage to keep up appearances of the dutiful, loving wife while planning to betray my husband? All the while developing feelings for his brother?

His brother who will rightfully hate me if he ever finds out I knew the truth. I'm in over my head, and I'm drowning.

Sighing, I put down the paintbrush I had been holding. I've been sitting in front of this canvas for so long my hand is cramping and my back is screaming in protest. Scooting off the stool, I cast one more look at the painting in front of me. The setting sun streams through the window, casting a red glow over the ghoulish face of nightmare Jake staring back at me. I flip the canvas over so I don't have to stare at the visual representation of my guilt.

Instead, I torture myself by picking up my phone and opening the text thread with Dane. I've kept him at a distance since returning home. After realizing how easily I could see myself falling for him, I knew I *had* to keep my distance. I won't go back on what I told him I would do. I will find something he can use to shut down Bryce's corruption. But I can't allow myself to fall further for Dane. Not when I know heartbreak is the only thing that lies ahead for us.

DANE

You ok?

This message was sent the day I went back home. I didn't respond, shame over what had transpired between me and Bryce staying my hand.

Two days later, Dane texted again.

DANE

Just checking in. Serena was wondering if you'll be at game night.

> By Serena, I mean me.

I bite my lower lip, fighting a smile at his playful
message.

DANE

> Just…let me know you're doing okay.
> Please?

That last message was sent this morning. I should
respond. Let him know I'm fine. Tell him not to message
me. Tell him to forget about me. That this won't work
between us. My fingers have a life of their own, however.

ME

> Can't do game night. Have to go have
> dinner with the Harringtons with Bryce. I'll
> try to make it next week. Send Serena my
> regrets.

> And by Serena, I mean you. I miss you.

Shit. I immediately regret sending that text, but before I
can undo it, it shows as read, and three bouncing dots
appear on the screen, letting me know Dane is responding.

DANE

> There you are. I was starting to get worried
> I'd have to show up and spend time with
> my dickhead brother just to see you.

I can't stop the smile his words brings to my face. Dane
just has this way of making me feel seen and cherished. I
used to get that feeling from Bryce. But it's been so long

since he's looked at me as anything other than a trophy. Even the glimpses I've gotten of the former Bryce this week have been shallow imitations of the genuine affection that radiates from Dane.

ME

No need to subject yourself to such torment. I'm fine. Promise. Just…taking things day by day.

IN THE BACK of my mind, a voice says I should tell Dane not to text me. Not to leave a digital trail, in case Bryce gets suspicious. We are playing a dangerous game, and Bryce is a suspicious man by nature. It's his job to sniff out lies and half truths. I need his trust, his defenses lowered, if I'm going to find anything we can use against him.

DANE

Can I see you?

Dane's request causes my stomach to flip, setting off dozens of butterflies in my belly from excitement and fear. Seeing him is dangerous. I know I won't be able to resist him if he gets within touching distance. I'm a flawed, broken woman who can't seem to do what's morally right. Only what feels right. And being with Dane feels so damn right.

Shaking my head, I do my best to let my rational side steer this ship away from the iceberg of bad ideas looming ahead.

There. It's not even a lie. It really isn't a good idea. The more we see each other, the higher our chances of getting caught are. My resolve is weak though. I know it. My body longs to be held by Dane again. To be kissed by him. To eat breakfast in bed and laugh with him. To be fucked by him. If he asks again, I don't know if I can say no.

The sound of the garage door opening startles me from the fantasy my mind has conjured. Blowing out a heavy sigh, I swipe, closing the text thread. Nothing good will come from letting my mind wander down that path. I don't deserve to dream of such a happy ending for myself.

I find Bryce in the kitchen, sipping from a glass of whiskey. The top two buttons of his shirt are undone, his sleeves rolled up to the elbow revealing his tan, muscular forearms. A sight that used to cause my heart to stutter and wetness to pool between my thighs.

Now it leaves me with a viscous feeling of dread slithering through my stomach. Dreading the next time he wants to be intimate.

After having sex the day I came home, I found myself retching in the bathroom, the combined shame of how my body responded to him plus the memory of what Dane and I did... That's the night Jake started haunting me in my dreams. I've kept him at arm's length for the last few days claiming I had a migraine, but my time is running out. I saw the way he watched me this morning as I stepped out of the shower. If he hadn't been running late for a court case, he would've bent me over the vanity right then and there. I just know it.

Bryce tilts his head, taking in my appearance, an expression surprisingly similar to concern crossing his face. "You feeling okay, babe? You look..."

"Rough?" I finish his sentence, wincing from his scrutiny. I know I look like hell. I have circles under my eyes so dark they look like bruises. My hair hangs limply on my shoulders. The lack of sleep is getting to me, and Bryce has noticed. My heart begins to pound, wondering if he can sense the guilt wafting from me. I am so enmeshed with it; it could be a visible aura surrounding me.

Bryce nods his head slowly, like he's trying not look like an asshole for noticing. I shrug, and force a smile, trying to downplay the fact that I look like the walking dead.

"I guess that migraine and lack of sleep just did a number on me." I duck my head and walk past him to get a glass of water. He stops me with a hand on my shoulder, and I fight to keep my body from tensing in revulsion from his touch.

"I have to go out of town this weekend for a conference. Chuck sprung this on me last minute."

My stomach flips in excitement at the thought of him being gone for three days. It would give me so much time to thoroughly search his study and go through his computer. I'm already mentally thinking about potential passwords he might use when he gives my arm a shake, startling me. "Everly, are you listening? Do you want to?"

Shaking my head, I realize I completely missed what he

just asked me. "Uh, sorry, I think that migraine is coming back."

"I said, do you want to come? It's in New York." It takes a moment for me to process his words. It's been a long, long time since he's invited me on a work trip. Is this bad timing? Is he suffering from a guilty conscience too? Or is he afraid to leave me alone? I desperately do not want to go on this trip with him. This is too good of an opportunity.

"I don't know, darling." The endearment tastes bitter on my tongue. "I feel like I might be coming down with something. I think that's what triggered the migraine. I think I'll just stay home and rest." I let my body sway slightly, forcing him to steady me. The briefest flash of something crosses his expression. Annoyance? Relief? Suspicion? It's gone before I can decipher it. "I was just going to lay down. Let's talk about it tomorrow if I'm feeling better."

"Of course." Bryce nods and pulls away, the concern that I thought I'd seen moments ago, gone without a trace.

There he is. The detached, work obsessed, callous bastard that my husband has evolved into. I let my lips turn up slightly in a demure *thanks for understanding* expression before making my escape to our bedroom, my mind thinking of ways to look sicker tomorrow, so he will buy my excuse when I ask to stay home.

CHAPTER 28
EVERLY

The problem with snooping through my husband's office and work files for evidence of criminal activity is that I'm not exactly sure what I'm looking for, or what will be enough of a smoking gun to put him away.

Bryce has powerful friends who owe him favors. It's how he's moved through life, elevating his status and position. He does someone a favor—gets their son out of a DUI charge, makes a rape accusation go away, pleads down a potential career-ruining felony to a misdemeanor. In turn, they introduce him to the governor or recommend him to a wealthy client, let him be the attorney on retainer for the millionaire owner of the local strip-mining company.

I've spent a lot of time this week reflecting on our life together, his career trajectory and his biggest cases. I can't believe I was so fucking oblivious to never notice how ruthless his ambition was. Even that first Thanksgiving we spent together, when I had hearts in my eyes, excited to finally bring a boy home the Honorable Judge Strauss would approve of, he was using his charm to ingratiate himself to my dad.

Not just because he wanted to be with me. But because of what being in my father's orbit could do for him and his career.

A fresh wave of bitter resentment makes my stomach flip, as I wonder if Bryce ever truly loved me. For now, I force myself to believe that he did. That at one point we truly were in love. Because the thought that I gave the better part of two decades, the best years of my life, to a man who never really loved me is devastating in a way that can drive a person to self-harm. And with nightmares of Jake plaguing me already, I don't think I can handle that level of heartbreak.

So instead, I choose to think Bryce lost himself along the way. Does it excuse him? No. But if he's truly been horrible the entirety of our relationship, what does that say about me? Wouldn't that mean I'm complicit? Because I benefit from his cutthroat ambition? Is this why I am trying to find something for Dane to use against him? To prove I'm a better person? So when the truth about his father's death inevitably comes out, I can pray this is enough to earn his forgiveness?

Thanks to the near constant state of moral crisis I've been in since losing my mind and sleeping with Dane, it wasn't difficult to fake illness when Bryce asked me about the trip again. I had spent the night fighting sleep and forcing myself to stay awake, hoping the exhaustion would make me look more like death in the morning. My plan worked, and Bryce left this morning. Now I have the next three days to search.

I've spent the last three hours combing through the files in his desk. Many of them were old case files, from the early days of his career. But there are a few newer ones as well. I don't know why he would choose to hold on to some in his personal home office. If there is a connecting thread or pattern for these cases, I don't see it.

Getting frustrated with how little I understand about his job and how the sociopolitical machinations of Birch Falls works, I reluctantly come to the conclusion that I'll need Dane's help in finding the evidence that we need. I had hoped I could do this without spending more time with him and falling further into this fucked up web of lies. I keep telling myself it's because I am protecting his heart for when he finds out the truth about his father's death and that I knew. That I don't want him to hurt. But the truth is, I can't stand the idea of seeing the look of betrayal in his eyes. Not after the way he looked at me like I was the sunset, as we lay in bed together, basking in the morning sunrise. Like I was precious and important to him. I don't deserve to have him look at me that way.

But, in order to get justice for Jake, I'm going to have to bring Dane in and risk breaking both of our hearts.

CHAPTER 29
DANE

My palms are sweaty, and my knees feel weak as I pound my fist on the front door of Everly and Bryce's house.

She called me today as my shift was ending, her voice timid and uneasy, so soft I almost couldn't hear her. I had to cover my free ear and stop walking to hear her when she asked me if I could come over tonight.

She said Bryce had left for the weekend to attend a conference. The prospect of having three days alone with Everly made my heart soar, but the caginess in her tone had me worried Bryce had done something. Something I might have to kill him for. The fact that I even had that thought and how little apprehension it gives me, should be a blaring alarm that my head is in a completely fucked up place and I should take some time off from work. That or go see a psychologist.

When Everly opens the door, my heart falls. She's pale, dark circles rimming her bloodshot eyes. Her hair is piled in a messy bun on top of her head. She's in an oversized sweater, a dark hunter green that makes her eyes deepen so much they resemble a coniferous forest at night. She looks…broken.

"Shit, baby, what's wrong. What'd he do?" I rush in, cupping Everly's face in my palms, kicking the door closed behind me. Her eyes widen in surprise, her hands come up and clasp mine but don't move, like she's uncertain if she wants to hold them closer or pull out of my grasp.

I thread my fingers into her silky hair, tightening my grasp on her ever so slightly so she doesn't try to pull away. I've been dying for her touch and out of my mind with worry for the last week as she's held me at a distance. My eyes scan every inch of her face, looking for any evidence or even a hint of physical harm.

"I'm okay, Dane. I'm fine. I'm fine. I'm fine." It takes a few torturously long seconds for her words to register.

"You're okay? Are you sure? Did he—"

Everly puts a hand over my mouth to stop me.

She narrows her eyes at me, and her voice hardens. "I said I'm fine. Please, let go."

I'm so stunned by her coldness, she slips out of my fingers when she takes a step back. I immediately feel cold as she moves away from my touch.

She must feel the same way. She wraps her arms around her waist and hunches her shoulders like she misses the heat of my body as much as I miss hers.

"I, uh, don't know exactly what I'm looking for. I've been hunting through Bryce's office and digging through old files all day, but I don't know if I've found anything useful. I need your help." She bites the corner of her plump bottom lip nervously, as if calling me for help is a failure on her part. "I tried to do it on my own. God, Dane, I didn't want to have to pull you into this." She's beginning to ramble, a sure sign of an impending anxiety attack, so I reach out and grab her again by the shoulders.

"Hey. Don't apologize. I'm here. I want to help. I was dying to see you." I move forward to kiss her, but she pulls back again, turning her cheek to me. Once again, I'm stunned into letting her go. Is she regretting what happened between us?

"Ever—"

"Don't, Dane." She steps back, shooting me a pleading look, her eyes softening at the rejection that must be written all over my face. "Let's just look for evidence. Okay? We have three days to find something while Bryce is out of town. We need to make the most of it."

I nod and follow her to the study. She's right—we need to make the most of this time. But I have a feeling her most and my most are vastly different.

Everly sits at Bryce's obnoxiously large and shiny bespoke desk, files strewn in front of her in various piles that seem to be chaotically organized. Everly struggles with organization thanks to her ADHD, but fortunately for me, I suffer from the same chaos brain. I just hope we can get these back into whatever order Bryce had them in.

I lean over Everly's shoulder, listening to her explain what she's found so far, but I find myself getting distracted by the sweet scent of her jasmine shampoo. It's not as intoxicating as when she smelled like me after showering at my place, with my soap, but my dick takes notice anyway. I rest my hands on the desk on either side of her, caging her in with my body, my body unable to resist the magnetic pull of hers.

"...so I put these files in this pile because they're all from ten years ago. I don't know how they link together, but it seems weird that he would hold on to them for this long, right? And this pile is for cases with names that are linked to local important people. Including your ex-part-ner, Dominick Reeves."

Hearing Dominick's name brings my mind out of the gutter, and I start paying attention to what Everly is saying. She had a point earlier; we need to take advantage of this opportunity we have. Fucking can wait until we have a reason to celebrate.

"Let's start with these," I say, pulling the pile of folders that holds Dominick's file toward me. Glancing through it, I see she's right. Each name seems to be linked to someone important in Birch Falls, or in our state. I notice the last name of our current attorney general in the stack. Interest-ing. I flip the yellow manila folder open and see a mugshot of a young white college-age man with a sullen look on his face. Brad Hopper. The douche who tried to assault Serena, and the one link tying Dominick to the murder of his buddy Todd. No wonder he got such a sweet deal for coop-erating; he's related to the AG. I take pictures of the infor-mation with my phone, saving it for later.

In the stack we also find Todd's file, with his rap sheet of petty misdemeanors, bar fights, and a few cases of sexual assault handled by the campus police that got swept under the rug. Apparently, Dom did do the world a favor when he killed Todd. Too bad it was so he could isolate and trap Serena in an abusive relationship.

There's one more name in the stack that I'm vaguely familiar with. Andrew Jameson. It doesn't appear that he was ever charged with anything, but he was arrested and questioned in the disappearance of a young college coed, Cassidy Grainger. Ultimately, he was released because there was no evidence to hold him. Knowing what I know about Dom, Brad, and Todd, I'm not inclined to believe that this Andrew character is an innocent victim of wrong place, wrong time. But what is the link between them?

We pore over the information in front of us for hours. Quietly reading, making notes, and calling out important seeming details when we find them. When I look up from the search I'm doing on my phone, trying to dig up more information on Jameson, I find Everly looking at me with a longing sadness that casts shadows in her eyes. When she realizes I've caught her staring, she clears her throat, looking back down at the paper in front of her.

Rising from my seat across from her, I round the desk and lean down, wrapping my arms around her shoulders, burying my face in her neck. Inhaling her scent, I brush my lips against the soft skin of her neck, causing her to stiffen and let out a quiet gasp. Her hand comes up to clutch my forearm, but she doesn't pull it away like I expect her to. Instead, she melts into my hold, letting her head tilt to the side to rest on my shoulder, giving my mouth better access to her tender flesh.

I plant open-mouthed kisses up the column of her

throat, along her jaw, until I reach her mouth. Using my fingers, I turn her head until our lips meet, my mouth capturing hers in a drugging kiss. I swallow her needy whimpers as she lets me plunder her sweet mouth with my tongue. Slowly I pull her up from her seat, never breaking our kiss, until I have her pinned flush against me, trapped between the desk and my body. Her hands roam my body greedily, like she's letting herself indulge in in the feel of my body. I have one hand wrapped around the back of her neck, tangled in the silky strands of her hair, while the other slides under her sweater and skates up her body until I am cupping her bare breast in my palm. No bra? I give her nipple a giddy tweak, drawing another whimper out of her. The need that had been a low banked fire of glowing coals between us ignites into an inferno.

Picking her up, I slide her onto the desk, wedging myself between her thighs until I can feel the heat emanating from her center. She opens for me, granting me the closeness I crave.

"Dane—" She pulls back, looking at me, her green eyes shimmering with conflict. She wants this as much as I do, but she's trying to stop whatever this is between us. I see the protest forming on her lips, so I lean in and kiss her again, pressing my rigid erection against her core, the thin material of her leggings doing nothing to hide her desire for me.

I thrust, grinding my dick against her clit, as I pinch her nipple again. This seems to crack the last of whatever resolve she has. Her hands come up, wrapping around my neck, pulling me deeper into our kiss.

I press my advantage and lean forward until I have her flat on her back on top of my brother's desk, writhing under my body with desperate need. I am going to fuck her on this desk as a fuck you to my shithead brother, and after everything I've read tonight about the people he makes a living defending, I'm not going to feel even a little bad about it.

CHAPTER 30
EVERLY

Dane has me pinned flat against the desk, his erection pressing into my center. The dark gray joggers he's wearing do nothing to cushion the hardness of his cock as he thrusts his hips against me, his mouth devouring mine. I'm vaguely aware of his papers shifting under my back; the clatter of several folders hitting the floor barely registers in my mind. My senses are so completely consumed by Dane. By his touch. His heat. His possessive kisses. The longer he kisses me, the harder is it to remember why we shouldn't be doing this. I tried so hard to be good and stay away from him, but the moment he kissed my neck, he shattered the defenses I had hastily cobbled together out of shame and guilt.

The way his touch is carnal but possessive, like he wants to crawl into my skin, undoes all of my good intentions. This is why I didn't want to involve him. I knew I would be too weak to resist him.

Dane's rough stubble scrapes along my neck as he

kisses his way down. His hands drag my sweater torturously slowly up my body, until I feel the chill of the air caress the bare skin of my breasts. I let out a lusty moan when he catches one of my sensitive nipples in his mouth, while his hands are busy pulling the sweater over my head. When my arms are free from the garment, my hands clutch his head to my breast, fingers gripping into his hair so tightly he nips at my nipple, grazing it with his teeth before grinning up at me. Our eyes lock, and the devilish gleam in his sends a surge of arousal coursing through my body. He wants this even more than I do. I'm not strong enough to fight this battle for the both of us, even if it only ends in heartbreak.

"God, Dane." His name is a prayer on my lips as his lips begin to journey further south, while his rough hands slide under the waistband of my leggings. He gives my hips a rough tug, forcing them up enough for him to pull down my leggings and underwear. I am bare before him, panting, flushed with a feverish desire, and he is standing there, devouring me with the most predatory gaze. Like he is *really* going to eat me.

"You are so fucking beautiful, Ever. You are perfect." His eyes trace over every inch of my skin, and I swear I can feel his gaze like it's a physical touch. My skin erupts in goose bumps as his tongue slowly runs over his bottom lip while his eyes finish their journey. I watch as his eyes widen when he sees how wet I am for him. I know my pussy has to be glistening. My panties were embarrassingly damp when he removed them. I had nearly come apart just from dry humping him. Slowly, like he has all the time in the world, he reaches into his joggers and gives his dick a leisurely stroke while he studies me.

"You are so fucking sexy. I love those gorgeous thighs and I can't wait to be buried between them." His praise lights me up from the inside. I know I don't look the same as I did when Bryce and I first began dating, but knowing this stupidly gorgeous twenty-something finds me irresistible still, this close to forty, does wonders for undoing the damage Bryce's neglect has caused. He leans forward and plants open-mouthed kisses on my stomach, slowly making his way to my aching pussy. He takes his time, nipping, kissing, sucking, and licking my flesh until I'm a needy, pleading mess.

"God, Dane. Please. Fuck me." My fingers thread into his hair again, and I push his head down to where I want him. No, *need* him. I feel his hot breath against my clit as he lets out a low chuckle. Then he dives in, his tongue lapping greedily at my clit, causing the air to rush out of my lungs. He pins my hips to the desk with one muscular forearm while his free hand moves between my legs, his fingers teasing my achingly empty cunt with the promise of being filled. I let out a needy whimper when I realize I can't thrust my trapped hips to get the relief I am desperate for. He continues to tease me with the most featherlight of touches and I realize he's doing this on purpose. Acting like a brat. Is this my punishment for brushing off his kiss earlier?

Just when I think I can't handle any more teasing, he plunges two thick fingers into my center, pulling a low, throaty moan from me. He curls his fingers just so, sending my back arching as I tried to escape the intense pleasure. He is relentless with his assault, his mouth worshipping my clit as his fingers graze my G-spot. An orgasm rocks through me, causing my muscles to seize, locking him into place. It feels like an eternity before I'm able to relax my thighs from his head. When I look down at him, I find him gazing up at me with triumph in his eyes and a lazy, satisfied grin tilting his lips up. I watch, mesmerized as he licks his lips, looking like a dangerous jungle cat.

"I'm going to fuck you now, Everly. Do you want that?" He crawls up my body until he's hovering over me, face to face, our lips millimeters from touching. I nod, still unable to function well enough to speak. Dane shakes his head, side to side, his eyes darkening with a dangerous admonishment. "Words, Everly. I want your words."

Fuck, how did he go from bratty to daddy so fast?

A pitiful *yes* is the most I can muster, but Dane shakes his head again, his eyes narrowing in warning.

"Yes, what, Everly?"

"Yes, I want you to fuck me."

"Yes, ma'am." Dane flashes a feral smile that temporarily stuns me with its beauty before he thrusts his hips, shunting himself into me to the hilt. My fingers claw into his arms in surprise from the intrusion. I hadn't even realized he had taken his pants off. Sitting up, I pull his mouth to mine, fighting for some sense of control as he thrusts into me at a punishing rhythm. At this angle he's so deep, he's pounding directly on that spot that will completely destroy me. I'm clinging onto him for dear life as the first wave crashes into me, but he does not relent. He fucks me through my orgasm until it builds into another one. This one has me digging my nails into his skin so hard I know I'm leaving marks, but it only seems to spur him on.

I'm afraid I'm going to pass out from lack of oxygen as I gasp through the pleasure, forgetting how to breathe. He finally breaks our kiss and bites down on my neck as his body goes rigid, his cock pulsing in me as he comes. He holds me for what feels like an eternity while our hearts slowly come back down to a normal pace. He peppers sweet kisses delicately on my face, like I'm something precious that should be cared for. The slick feeling of shame slithers under my skin as remorse, that I once again failed to protect his heart, sets in.

CHAPTER 31
EVERLY

Desperate for a moment of solitude, I excuse myself abruptly from Dane's hold, so he won't see exactly how close I am to the edge of having a mental breakdown. His stunned look of rejection is a stab in my heart, and causes my stomach to churn with the urge to vomit thanks to the crushing wave of guilt. Once in the bathroom, I splash cold water on my face, but it doesn't do much to hide the anguish churning inside of me. Anguish not from having once again cheated on my husband, surprisingly enough. As I study my reflection in the mirror, eyes red-rimmed and glassy, I realize I don't feel anything but hollowness when I think of Bryce. No, the sorrow I feel is from knowing I don't deserve for Dane to look at me like I am something precious, worth protecting. Worthy of being cherished by him. If he only knew the truth… The only option I have now is to make sure we find a way to make Bryce pay for his crimes.

When I'm finally calm enough to go back to the office, I

find all the papers that had fallen on the floor once again neatly stacked on the desk. Dane sits in Bryce's chair, shuffling one last folder back into order. When he hears my approach, he looks up from his work, his face softening from determined concentration to something far more affectionate as he drinks me in. Guilt still churns in my gut, but it is at war with my newfound determination. I will not let myself wallow in self-pity and doubt. Not when it's still within my power to right this wrong.

Dane rises from his seat and strides over to me, "Are you okay, Ever? I'm sorry if I pushed too hard. I just... I can't be near you and not be with you. Not after finally having you. There is no going back for me. Not now. I hope you understand that." His words wrap around my heart, binding it more securely to him. I can't help but lean into his touch when he puts his arms around me, savoring this brief moment of security. Whatever happens between us in the future, I will forever cherish these memories of the way he made *me* feel treasured. It's been so long since Bryce made me feel loved. Valued. Adored. I will not continue to live this half life of being his show pony he trots out when it is convenient for him or his career. I am done compromising on my morals for his ambition.

"I'm fine. I just needed a minute." I force a reassuring smile that doesn't reach my eyes. "We should get back to work." I try to move past Dane, but he wraps his muscular arms around me, enveloping me in a bear hug. I feel him press a kiss to the top of my head, and that gentle sign of affection has me melting into his body.

"Talk to me, Ever. Tell me what's going on in that beautiful head of yours." He runs one rough hand up my back to the nape of my neck and begins massaging out the tension that has been building in my muscles for the last week. With every press of his skillful fingers, my body relaxes, molding against his. Dane's compassion feels so foreign to me right now, I can't help but lower my defenses.

"I'm sad, Dane. The man I married isn't who I thought he was, and I'm stupid for not noticing it sooner. I've blithely lived this pampered life, willfully ignoring the red flags as they multiplied. Looking back, the signs were all there, and I just…ignored them. I let myself believe the lie that he was more good than bad. That he was still the man that rescued me from being assaulted and not just another manipulative, power hungry sycophant. Someone willing to trade justice for favors. I am complicit because I went along with it. Never questioning if it was worth the black mark on my soul. I feel sick over it."

I give him as much of my truth as I can. The urge to confess everything is strong. So fucking strong. But I don't dare. I don't want to bring it up unless I know for sure we can find a way to prove Bryce's guilt beyond a shadow of reasonable doubt. I don't want to risk telling Dane the truth and not being able to prove it, allowing Bryce to remain free. If I only get one chance at making this right, I do not want to fuck it up. Silent tears slide down my cheeks, dampening the fabric of the threadbare navy BFPD T-shirt he is wearing, making it look almost black.

"Shh, listen to me, Ever." The hand that was kneading my neck moves up to gently stroke my hair, making me want to purr like a kitten. "You are not responsible for

Bryce's actions. Bryce's choices are his own. He chose his career. He chose the path of arguing for the damned instead of helping the victims. That's not on you."

"But—"

"No buts, Everly. It's. Not. On. You. It's not on you anymore than it's on me, or our mom. I know she didn't raise him to put his desires and wants ahead of what is right. And I've known he's a dick for years now. He used your love for him as a shield and kept you blind to what was really going on behind the scenes. Now you've seen how the sausage gets made, and you know it's wrong. The only thing you can control now is what you do with that information now that you know. There are so many men out there like Bryce, doing the same thing, day in and day out. We can't stop them all, but maybe we can stop Bryce."

Dane's words worm their way under my skin and into my head, gnawing at the broken pieces of my conscience. The burden of guilt that's been hanging around my neck like an albatross seems to grow heavier at forgiveness I don't deserve but greedily drink in anyway. I can't find the words to express how much I needed to hear him tell me it's not my fault, that maybe there is a chance of real forgiveness in my future, so I just tighten my hold around his waist, holding on to this feeling, praying he will still feel this way when he knows the full extent of the damage Bryce has done.

"Come on; let's eat some dinner, then we can get back to work, okay?"

At his suggestion, my stomach lets out an embarrassing rumble, reminding me that I skipped breakfast in my haste to begin my search of Bryce's office, meaning I haven't eaten all day. My ADHD has a way of making me forget everything, including basic needs like eating, until my body starts to shut down in protest. That explains the lack of focus I had while combing through those files for the last hour. It wasn't because Dane is ridiculously attractive when he's in investigation mode. Well, not *just* because he's ridiculously attractive. Dane lets out a low chuckle that makes his chest rumble against my cheek, and the sensation causes butterflies to erupt in my stomach. I need to get some distance between us before I am tempted to go for round two and wind up passing out embarrassingly from hunger.

"Good idea. I'll make us some grilled cheese sandwiches."

Dane follows me into the kitchen, trailing so close behind me I can still feel the heat from his body. He immediately gets to work pulling the pan down from the hanging rack above our kitchen island, while I dig through the fridge looking for ingredients. When he sees me turn from the refrigerator, both hands laden with multiple types of cheese, his eyes go wide in surprise.

"What? I like cheese, okay?" My cheeks heat with embarrassment as I dump the, admittedly ridiculous, number of dairy products on the quartz countertop before diving back in for the butter and other ingredients.

"Umm..." Dane looks baffled by the spread in front of him. There are at least five kinds of cheese, prosciutto, fig jam, mustard, spinach, apple slices, pre-cooked bacon, pesto, and tomatoes. "Are you putting all of that on the sandwich?"

Laughing, I start dividing the pile of ingredients into different options. Brie with fig jam and prosciutto. Cheddar with apple slices. Mozzarella with tomato and pesto. Provolone with shaved roast beef. And of course, American cheese with bacon.

"I wind up eating a lot of dinners alone, so when I know Bryce won't be home, I usually just make a grilled cheese. I experiment a lot, and these are some of my favorite combinations."

Dane laughs as he comes up behind me and wraps his arms around my waist, resting his head gently against mine.

"Well then, I think I'm gonna need you to school me on the art of melted cheese and bread, because I've only ever done white bread with Kraft singles and butter."

And so I do. I make one of each, using a loaf of crusty bread from my favorite bakery, showing him my preferred method for buttering the bread, layering each ingredient, explaining how each cheese pairs with something salty or sweet. As I assemble, he grills the sandwiches in the pan. It's so wonderfully, blissfully domestic cooking together, I can't help but daydream what our life would be like if he was the brother I married.

CHAPTER 32
DANE

Eating grilled cheese with Everly feels like a dream. The way her face lights up in delight and amusement when the cheese from her sandwich makes a gooey trail from the toasty bread to her gorgeous mouth makes my stomach flip. She looks so light and happy in this moment, which is a stark contrast from the sullen, withdrawn women who answered the door. The way her eyes crinkle in the corners when she laughs is joy personified. I must be staring, because she stops mid-chew and looks self-conscious.

"Is there still cheese on my face?" She swipes at her chin, but I catch her hand in mine, grazing my lips against her palm.

"Just admiring the dramatic effect my dick had on your attitude." Her lips pop open in a surprised O at my comment, before she tosses the crust of her sandwich at me.

Before she can respond, I lean forward, capturing her

lips with mine, silencing any protest. Something shifted in her fundamentally between the time I got here and now, and I will fight to hang on to this feeling for as long as possible. I was terrified when Everly rebuffed me when I got here. I was sure she was going to end things between us. Say *sorry, Dane. I can't do it. I love Bryce* or *Dane, that was a mistake.* The way she had retreated into herself scared the shit out of me. But when I saw the way she was looking at me, like I was the air she needed to breathe—to live—I knew that wasn't the case. Because that's how I look at *her*, and I *know* she's the air I breathe.

I don't blame her for having conflicting feelings about this situation. I know it's fucked up beyond belief. But I also know it's the most right I have felt about anything in my life, and I will not let my shitbag of a brother or her guilty conscience diminish what this is between us.

When I pull away, there is a faraway, glassy look in her eyes, like she just woke up from a dream, and I know she is feeling the same way I do.

Before I get the chance to reignite the flames that were burning between us in the office, her phone buzzes on the kitchen table. Bryce's smug face lights up her screen, and Everly jerks back violently like she's been burned. Nerves and fear flash in her eyes as she stares at her phone like it's a snake poised to strike.

"Shit. I should get this. Umm… I'll be right back." Snatching her phone, I hear her voice chime out with a frazzled sounding "Hey, hon," as she ducks out of the kitchen. I debate whether I should follow her, listen in on her conversation, but I assume if she wanted me to hear, she would've stayed put. I don't want to make her more nervous and give Bryce any reason to suspect anything, so instead I clear our plates from the table, load them into the dishwasher, and put away the remaining food.

After finishing cleaning up, I go back to the office, careful to listen for Everly as I walk through the house, wondering what she and Bryce could be talking about. Is she pretending she misses him? Barely paying attention to his self-absorbed recounting of his day? When I reach the door to the office, I hear her muffled voice coming from her studio just down the hall. I know I shouldn't eavesdrop, but I want to make sure he's not saying anything to upset her.

Creeping closer to the studio door that's been left partially ajar, I hear Everly let out an exasperated sigh at something Bryce is saying. "...look I don't know what you expect me to do about it. Even if you think he had some sort of crush on me, or grudge against you, I don't think Dane is going to compromise on his morals. It's not like I can just bat my eye lashes at him and he'll do whatever I say."

My ears burn at the mention of my name. Why are they talking about me?

"We had one pleasant evening chatting while he was waiting for you. It's not like we're friends. Before that, the last time I spent any time with him was when I was having therapy sessions with your mom. I know this case is important to Skip, but maybe this is one you should just leave alone. That Dominick guy sounds like a real piece of work. Why would you want to help someone like him?"

Her words cut into the tender part of my heart that already wonders if there is an expiration date on what is going on between us. That I'm some sort of exciting rebound to make her feel good again after Bryce destroyed her self-esteem. My brain—known to be more rational and logical, thanks to my years on the force—knows she has to downplay our relationship to Bryce. She's doing the right thing. That doesn't take the sting out of her words, though.

She lets out another irritated sigh at whatever Bryce's response is. "Fine. I'll see what I can do. When will you be back?"

Everly crosses the room, and I see her through the crack in the door. She's biting her nails on one hand, her shoulders slumped forward. I've seen this body language so many times in my line of work. I've seen it on my partner, Serena. This is the body language of a woman who has been beaten down, emotionally, if not physically, by a man that she loves and who is supposed to love her back, and it kills me to see the effect he has on her. I want to take her away from this. Away from him. I don't know why she is so hesitant to leave him and make a clean break, but maybe I can use our time together this weekend to show her how safe she will be with me if she does.

Her conversation sounds like it's wrapping up, so I back away, careful to not alert her to my presence. I'll wait for her in the office and see if she brings up what Bryce wants her to do. I want to know if she fully trusts me enough to tell me his plans.

When Everly returns to the office, her body language is still off. She's closed in on herself again, like a flower closing its petals when the sun goes down. *Nyctinasty.* The word floats through my brain, resurfacing from a memory of me as a young child when I asked my mom why some of the flowers in her garden would close up at night. We were outside at dusk, watering the plants, and I noticed some of the petals furling in on themselves.

"Momma, why do the flowers all close up when the sun is gone?"

"It's called nyctinasty, sweetie."

"Nick-ti-nasty?

"Nyctinasty."

"Flowers go to bed too. When the sun goes down, their petals close up, tucking the warmth and the pollen inside where it will be safe for the bees to find in the morning. It's just like when your dad and I tuck you into bed at night and make you all warm and cozy and safe until morning."

Seeing Everly furled up and afraid makes me want become the sun so I can help her open back up and reveal her beauty to the world again.

CHAPTER 33
DANE

"Is everything okay?" I pull Everly into a hug, tucking her head under my chin and she instantly melts into me. She doesn't say anything for a long moment, but I'm a patient man, and I know what kind of mental gymnastics my brother is capable of pulling, so I wait for her to talk first. I just rub her back, letting her take whatever comfort she needs from me before she tells me about her conversation with Bryce.

"He's going to call you and tell you to come check on me while he's out of town."

"Oh, is he now?" I can't help but chuckle.

"Yeah, and then I'm supposed to sweet talk you into helping him with Dominick's case. He seems to think you have a crush on me and would be willing to do something if I ask you to do it." I can hear the smirk in Everly's voice. When she looks up at me, mischief is gleaming in her eyes.

"Oh…really?" I drawl, intrigued. "And how exactly

would you do that, Everly? I'm not the kind of man who would hit on his brother's happily married wife."

Everly matches my smirk with one of her own.

"I guess it's a good thing I'm not happily married then. It makes it easier to do something like this to help convince you." She tilts her head up, rising on her tiptoes so she can brush her lips again mine in a seductive ghost of a kiss that goes straight to my dick.

Reaching both of my hands around, I grab her ass, holding her body hostage against mine so she can feel the effect she has on me. "Hmm… I dunno. I might need some more convincing," I whisper against her mouth, before sweeping my tongue against her lips, beckoning her to let me in. She grants me entry and our tongues tangle, and I am lost in the taste of her again. We kiss like time has ceased ticking forward. I'm seconds away from pushing her down on the leather Chesterfield and claiming her on another piece of Bryce's pretentious office furniture when my phone begins to buzz in my back pocket.

"Fuck. Hold that thought." Pulling away, I check my phone and see Bryce's name on the screen. I flick a bemused glance at Everly, who is biting her lower lip, looking up at me with wide, innocent eyes. *Fuuuuck.* "Just a moment, babe. I think my brother has a very important favor to ask me." I hit answer, bringing the phone to my ear, turning away from Everly. I don't think I can look at her and talk to him at the same time. Not without letting him hear in my voice just how fucked I am.

"Bryce." There isn't an ounce of brotherly love in my greeting. I'm done with the pretense that we are capable of a civil relationship. That ship sailed the moment he used our mom in an attempt to blackmail me into helping him.

"Is that how you greet your brother?" Bryce's voice is so smug it almost makes me lose my erection. I would love nothing more than to be able to punch his douchey face through the phone.

"It is when your brother threatens to make your mother homeless. What do you want?"

Bryce huffs out a frustrated sigh at my barb. There is no question where we stand with each other now.

"I am out of town, and I need you to check on Everly for me. She's been acting…off lately, and I am worried about her." Bryce actually sounds almost convincing in his delivery. If I were at home, where I should be, and if we were on better terms, I could see myself giving in to his request. It turns my stomach to think how easily he can turn on the charm and manifest such believable lies. He does this for a living every day, helping bad guys walk free.

"You want me to check on Everly?" I sink as much dubiousness into my voice as I can, knowing he expects me to turn down his request.

This time when he sighs, he sounds resigned and a little worried. "Yeah, I-I think she's depressed or something. I tried to get her to come with me on this trip, but she refused. Can you please just go by and check on her? You know how she's my whole world." Turning around, I find Everly standing in front of me, pupils dilated so much there is only a thin ring of green left in her iris. Slowly, she sinks to her knees, and I lose the ability to understand English.

"Uh-huh…" is the best I can muster as I watch her tug down my pants, letting my cock bob free. She's so close it bounces against her lips, and the soft gasp she sucks in forces me to bite my lower lip to fight back a groan.

"She's been off since our fight last week, and I've noticed she's been drinking more than usual lately. It's not like her, and I think she's using alcohol to cope with something. I've been finding empty wine bottles in the recycling that I know I didn't help her drink. I know you think I'm an asshole, but you're still a cop. Consider this me asking for a welfare check on her."

"Riiiight…and what am I supposed to say to her when she asks why I'm stopping by while you're out of town?" I can't believe I managed to form a complete sentence while taking in the sight before me.

Slowly her tongue slips out, sliding against the base of my shaft. The hand holding my phone clenches so hard I'm sure it will crack. Bryce drones on, but now as I watch the dark-haired goddess in front of me swirls her tongue around the head of my cock. Bryce's droning has turned into *wah-wah-wah*, like an adult from a Charlie Brown cartoon, as I watch Everly worship my cock.

Everly bobs her head forward, taking me down her throat, swallowing when the head of my dick hits the back of her throat, just as Bryce barks out my name.

"*Dane!* Are you listening?" The false concern that had been shading Bryce's words is gone now, replaced with irritation. Oops.

"Yeah, fine, I'll check on Everly. I'll take care of her." I wink down at Everly, staring up at me with tears shining in her eyes from how deep she has me.

I thread the fingers of my free hand through her hair and hold her in place, forcing her to swallow around my dick again because it feels fucking amazing. *Fuuuuck.* My balls tighten as the urge to come builds. I thrust shallowly, slowly, pulling out hardly at all before pushing back in, choking her with my dick. I'm so focused on the gorgeous woman in front of me, I barely catch what Bryce says to me.

"I appreciate your help, Dane. Just let me know how she is." Everly rakes her nails against my inner thighs, sending chills up my spine, begging for more. I begin thrusting faster, giving her a chance to breathe before shunting myself back down her throat. Her mouth is heaven. My breathing is starting to become erratic with how close I am to coming. I'm tempted to stay on the line and make Bryce listen to me spill my load down his wife's throat, but I'm not a complete animal.

"Will do. Gotta go." I hang up, unable to hold back the growl ready to break free. I grasp Everly's face in my hand and wipe away a tear as it trickles down her cheek. "I'm close baby, God, you feel so good." When she doesn't move to pull away, I begin muttering praise to her like a prayer. *"So good. Fuck yes. You're perfect. Goddess."* When she lets out a low hum, that is the end of me. The vibration triggering my release, I come explosively. She swallows my release with relaxed, fluid motions that almost cause my knees to buckle.

When she pulls off my dick, I sink to my knees in front of her, and cup her face in my hands. Pressing a kiss to her lips, I taste myself on her. "Fuck, Ever. You're perfect."

CHAPTER 34
EVERLY

It was hard saying goodnight to Dane when he finally left around 10:00 p.m., but I couldn't let him spend the night. The neighbors might notice his car in our driveway overnight, and while I can explain it away during the day, since Bryce did ask him to come check on me, I'm pretty sure Bryce didn't intend for us to have a sleepover complete with pillow fights.

Then again, maybe that's what he did expect, since he thinks I can somehow convince Dane to help him out. After the way he flaunted me in front of Shane like a prime cut of meat, I'm not so sure what line Bryce isn't willing to cross to get what he wants. Even if it destroys the sanctity of our marriage. Good thing I stopped living under that delusion.

He's supposed to come back today to help me go through some old file boxes Bryce has stored in the attic. If we can't find what we need there, we may have to find a way to get into his office and snoop around, which will be considerably more difficult.

I woke up early so I could go over the notes I made yesterday during our search. I've been staring at the paper for nearly an hour now, trying to figure out why one name in particular keeps scratching at my brain like it is the key to unlocking everything. Jacob Wheeler. His is just a thin file, from ten years ago. An eighteen-year-old high school student who was charged with a DUI. It feels like such a nothing case. Well below Bryce's usual pay grade, so why would he handle it? It's the last name that keeps tickling my brain, refusing to let me move on.

Deciding the quickest way to figure out the mystery is just to look up Jacob, I pull out my phone and do a quick internet search for Jacob Wheeler + Birch Falls. I have to wade through a few pages of irrelevant Jacob Wheelers before finding a result about the Jacob Wheeler I am looking for. It's a newspaper article about the Birch Falls High football team and their undefeated season in 2012. Jacob was their quarterback and had been offered a full ride scholarship to Notre Dame. There is a picture of a smiling Jacob holding up a Notre Dame jersey, flanked by his proud parents on one side and his coach on the other. I read the caption under the photo. *Jacob— pictured with his parents, Adam and Heather Wheeler, along with Coach John Spence—officially accepting Notre Dame's offer.*

Adam Wheeler. Adam Wheeler. Adam Wheeler… Why is that name even more familiar? I don't recognize his face, but I *know* I've heard that name before. Opening a new tab, I put Adam Wheeler into the search bar, biting my lip while I scroll through the results. A picture of him wearing a white doctor's coat and a stethoscope draped around his neck stops me mid scroll. He is the medical examiner. I've heard Bryce mention him several times in passing in reference to difference cases he's needed to testify for. I quickly scan a few different articles, adrenaline rushing through my veins. I feel like I'm on the verge of unlocking something major.

A news article from the Birch Falls Gazette circa 2010 contains the answer I'm looking for. The article is a humanitarian piece about the previous M.E., John Graham, retiring after nearly thirty years in the position so he could care for his wife, who suffered from Alzheimer's. After several paragraphs listing his work history and homicide cases his meticulous work helped solve, Adam is mentioned as being appointed his replacement. Doing the math in my head, I realize Adam would have been the medical examiner when Jake died.

Jumping up from the desk, I begin pacing, trying to make the pieces fit together. Bryce has a DUI file for Jacob Wheeler. But when I googled Jacob there was no record of the DUI that popped up. Adam Wheeler was the medical examiner at the time of Jake's death... Bryce routinely works in favors and back scratching to get the outcomes he wants... Did he do Adam a favor by making Jacob's DUI disappear? Did Adam owe him a favor in return?

A knock at the door stops me in my tracks. Glancing at the obnoxiously pretentious grandfather clock, I see it's almost noon. Shit, that's got to be Dane. I hastily shove Jacob Wheeler's file into one of Bryce's desk drawers, not quite ready to open that can of worms in front of Dane. I want Bryce to pay for what happened to Jake, but I don't want to reopen that wound for Dane unless I am sure I can prove what he did. Right now it's still my word against Bryce's, and I know I'm not the one who will win that argument if it gets put in front of a court of law.

Opening the door, I find Dane standing on the porch wearing a fitted black tee that clings to his shoulders in a way that makes my mouth water. The way his thin, light gray athletic pants hug his thighs is obscene. His stubble is almost a full beard at this point, and the memory of it rubbing against my thighs when he went down on me yesterday flashes through my mind. After we fucked on Bryce's desk and I blew him while he was on the phone with him, I've given up all pretense of pretending this isn't happening. I know it is only going to end tragically, but I've decided to enjoy the ride before my whole life goes down in a fiery explosion. Bryce has taken too much happiness from me. I won't let him take this from me. It might be the last good thing I get to enjoy before the truth comes out. I don't know if this is a lie or the truth, but it helps quiet the lingering guilt lurking in the recesses of my mind.

Dane holds up a white bag of takeout food sporting the logo from my favorite Thai restaurant. A place we had dinner at together, with Bryce and their mother, for my birthday one year. The delicious scent of coconut and lime leaves from the Panang curry, and Pad Thai, momentarily distracts me from mentally climbing Dane like a tree.

"I thought I could feed us today while we work." He flashes me a lazy half smile that makes him look somehow boyish and sexy at the same time. Like a young-twenty-year-old who hasn't quite transitioned fully from boy to man. Very Jensen Ackles in season one of Supernatural. "Digging up skeletons is hungry work." Dane shoots me a wink that sends a jolt of lust straight to my core.

I step aside, letting him in, desperate to get the door closed—blocking us from prying eyes—so I can kiss him. As soon as the door slams shut, he has me pushed against it, caging me in with his arms, resting on either side of my head while his body pins every inch of mine against the cool wood. The bag of food is forgotten on the floor behind him. I snake my hands under the hem of his shirt and trace the soft hair dusting his chest and stomach that narrows into a trail leading under his waistband.

Bryce goes to a waxer more often than I do, so he is smooth. I love how rugged and masculine Dane feels under my fingers. How I can grasp his chest hair to pull him into me, to let him know how desperate I am to climb into him. To be a part of him. I love how his muscles are thick, under a layer of softness that shows how strong he is, but that he isn't so vain he spends all his free time in a gym. I love how his palms are rough and calloused from the grip of his gun. Most of all I love how safe and protected I feel when he's near.

He licks into my mouth in languid, lazy strokes, like we have all the time in the world to memorize one another's taste. Slowly his hips grind against me, mimicking the movements I'm desperate to feel with no clothes between us. It's blissfully cruel torture. We kiss for what feels like an eternity before he pulls away to pepper kisses along my jaw and down my neck.

"Fuck, Ever. I missed you. I couldn't stop thinking about you last night after I left. It made me sick thinking of you in his bed." My heart clenches painfully at his earnest confession. A spiteful voice in the back of my mind reminds me I don't deserve his adoration.

Holding on to that harsh truth, I use it to pull me out of the fog of lust we are lost in. Gently, I push his shoulders, separating his lips from where they were suctioned to my neck, perilously close to leaving behind evidence I won't be able to hide.

"We don't have much time. We need to find what we are looking for before Bryce gets back. Digging first. Fucking second." Dane's eyes narrow like he's not entirely sure he likes my plan. I'll admit, I'm not sure I like it either, but we have to find a way to make Bryce pay. I *have* to find a way to make him pay for what he did to Jake. I will not give up until I find a way to make it right.

"HEY, I'm gonna go grab a bottle of wine. I can't handle reading about this level of douchebaggery while sober. It's too depressing." I stand up from the Chesterfield, lifting my arms up as I arch my back, stretching out the soreness that has settled in from sitting hunched over, scouring old case files. Dane flicks his gaze up to me, a playful smirk on his face.

"Is that how you survived being married to my brother for so long?" My expression flattens out at Dane's jab.

"You know, he wasn't always a douche," I bite out, feeling defensive. Not necessarily for Bryce's sake, but for mine. I feel like I need to defend my choice to marry him in the first place. Dane raises a skeptical eyebrow at me.

"You do realize I've known him my whole life, right? He's always been a douche." Dane's expression flattens out, matching my own.

I can feel my cheeks heating up, flushing with irritation. I don't even know why I'm mad at Dane right now. I open my mouth to say something, anything, to prove him wrong. I want to argue with him, even if it makes no sense. I know Bryce is a bastard and always has been toward Dane. I saw it years ago, but I chose to overlook it because Bryce was good to *me*. I just assumed it was run-of-the-mill sibling rivalry and they would find their way to a brotherly relationship once Dane was older.

Now I can see how blind and foolish I was about what kind of man Bryce is, and it makes me feel like shit. If I could fall in love with a man like Bryce, what does that say about me? Dane looks at me, challenge in his eyes, his large hands resting on the desk, clenched into fists, daring me to defend my husband. This must be the side of him that comes out when he is on duty, because I wither under the intensity of his stare.

"He…he was good to me. He made me feel important. I

know you two weren't close but…he loved me in a way I had never felt before. We used to be happy."

Dane's eye soften at my confession. He shifts like he's going to stand, but I can't handle his pity right now. I don't deserve it. Instead, I turn on my heel and leave the office in search of some liquid fortification to help dull the gnawing guilt eating away at my insides.

Once in the kitchen, I lean on the counter, burying my face in my hands, trying to calm my racing thoughts. The longer this goes on, the harder it is to keep a handle on my warring emotions. The desperate need I have to fix what Bryce did and the guilt over letting Dane develop feelings for me crash over me like waves before a tropical storm hits land. Growing in intensity and frequency until they will inevitably wash over me, drowning me in ruin.

Grabbing a wine glass from the cabinet and the first bottle of wine my hand touches in the wine fridge, I set to work on opening the bottle. My hands tremble from nervous energy, and I struggle to get the opener to sit right on the bottle. Fuck, why can't we be normal and buy cheap wine with screw-top caps?

A buzzing sensation in my back pocket interrupts my battle with the wine opener. Slipping my phone out of my pocket, I see Bryce's face staring at me with an incoming FaceTime call. Fuck. Closing my eyes, I take a fortifying breath, attempting to soothe the anxious energy flowing through me. Bryce picks up on every tell, and I cannot let him know what I am up to. Not until I'm ready to take him down for good.

Plastering a placid, agreeable smile on my face, I hit the answer button and pray this conversation will be quick.

CHAPTER 35
DANE

Something is going on with Everly. The longer we go through Bryce's case files, the more distant and cagey she gets. It's as if she's searching for something specific, and the longer she goes without finding it, the more frantic she gets. Part of me wants to chalk it up to guilt over cheating on Bryce, but another part of me thinks it is bigger than that. What could be more guilt inducing than cheating on the person you promised your heart and life to?

While she's in the kitchen, I decide to poke around in Bryce's desk. See if he has any secrets stashed away in these drawers. Opening the top drawer, I find another file that looks like it was hastily put away, the papers halfway jutting out from the manila folder. I take a quick glance at it and see it's for some young college kid named Jacob Wheeler, busted for a DUI. I snap a few pictures of the first page so I can look up the details of the case when I'm back at work. Putting it back, I start riffling through the rest of

Bryce's desk. I feel a little like Nicholas Cage in *National Treasure* searching through the Resolute Desk looking for clues. Didn't that desk have hidden compartments? Bryce is definitely the kind of douche who would think he was important enough for hidden compartments.

Just as I tug open the middle drawer, it gets stuck. Something is preventing it from opening. I tug again, and it gives slightly but doesn't open all the way. Whatever preventing it from opening is flexible. Peering into the slight opening, I don't see the obstruction. Giving the drawer a wiggle and lift, careful to not damage it and leave behind evidence of our snooping, I manage to slowly work it open until something falls out from underneath it.

It's a thick envelope, slightly battered and wrinkled from being jammed under the drawer. My heart pounds at the possibility that this might be the smoking gun we are looking for. Bryce wouldn't take the time to hide something so carefully if it wasn't important.

Glancing up at the doorway, I wait to see if Everly is on her way back from the kitchen. I hear the muffled sounds of cabinets opening and closing. I can just barely make out her voice too. It sounds like she's on the phone. Did Bryce call again while I was busy prying the drawer open? I hesitate, wondering if I should wait for her to be here when I open it. But what if it is something truly heinous. Like evidence of an affair? The urge to protect her from more pain is visceral, and I rip open the envelope without another moment of hesitation.

Unfolding the contents of the envelope, it takes a long, confusing moment for my brain to parse what I am

looking at. It appears to be a medical examiner report for…
my dad? Ice runs through my veins as I frantically try to
make sense of the words in front of me. Why does my
fucking shitstain of a half brother have the M.E. report for
my dad? My mind whirls with possibilities as I scan the
document in front of me. Nausea swirls in my gut as grief
bubbles up, as fresh and all-consuming as it was the day he
died.

The words go blurry as my eyes sting with tears threatening to break free. Closing them, I take in a deep breath,
seeking the calm space in my mind. It's a trick the therapist
I started seeing after his death taught me. I was in a bad
way for a while after Dad died. Having your dad die unexpectedly is hard, but as a sixteen-year-old boy who thought
his dad hung the moon, it was fucking tragic. I nearly got
expelled for fighting two weeks after we buried him,
because some asshole made a joke about my dead dad.
That's when Mom signed us both up for therapy. It worked
pretty well for me, but she struggled for years, and she's
still not the same as she was before his death.

Once the wave of grief threatening to overwhelm me
subsides, I return my attention to the report. This report
doesn't make any sense. Why does it say he died from an
injury sustained to the back of his head? My dad died in a
car accident. His car went off the road, went down a steep
embankment, slammed into a tree, deploying the airbags,
and he died from the resulting injuries.

I remember vividly hearing the officer recount the
details to Bryce and Everly. They had gone into the kitchen
to talk while Mom and I were busy comforting one

another. I had gotten up to get more tissues for Mom and heard them talking. Bryce asked if he had died on impact. The officer said that was likely, as he was dead when they got on the scene.

I remember the brief flash of relief, knowing he didn't suffer, before it subsided and the anger took over. The anger over how unfair it was for my dad to die. For my mom to lose him. That was the feeling I held on to when I went back to Mom, tissues in hand. That was the emotion that landed me in therapy after punching Chad Thompson for making a shitty joke about my dad dying. I can feel it still lurking under my skin, like a long dormant monster that's been in hibernation. It doesn't matter how much time passes, I will always be a sixteen-year-old boy that had to go through his most formative years without his father.

I'm so preoccupied with making sense of what I'm reading that I don't hear Everly return. I'm so confounded by how he could've gotten an injury like that, I jump when she speaks. Her voice, cautious and hesitant, interrupts the cold dread creeping up my spine as my brain finally processes what the report says.

"Did you find something?"

My heart leaps at her question. Oh, I found something alright. I just don't know what it means. Did Bryce think something was weird with the report from the M.E. too? Why didn't he ever say anything? Why is he hiding it? My intuition tells me I need to tie all these puzzle pieces together to form a complete picture before saying anything to Everly. My gut tells me something is seriously wrong, and Bryce knows more about my dad's death than he's letting on. Hastily I shove the report back into the envelope and tuck it under one of the other files I was reading.

"What is it? Did you find what we need?" Something in the way she looks at me, with cautious hope, causes the dam to burst and the tears to finally fall freely. The fresh wave of grief stirred up by reading the report washes over me in a tidal wave. Fuck. I bury my face in my hands, trying to fight back the sob threatening to burst free. *Get it together, shithead. You can't say anything yet.*

Everly lets out a surprised gasp, then I feel her delicate fingers running through my hair and down my face. She gently guides my head until it is resting against her chest. She murmurs soft reassurances while gently stroking her fingers through my hair, as my tears soak into the thin cotton of her T-shirt. I wrap my arms around her waist and cling to her, letting the grief pour out of me in a way I refused to allow when I was trying to be strong for Mom in the wake of his death.

Everly's heartbeat is a frantic staccato under my ear, and I realize I must be freaking her out with this sudden emotional outburst.

When I manage to get my shit together enough, I pull away from her and find her looking at me with tears making her hazel-green eyes vibrant with emotion. It's like she took all the grief I just poured out and is holding onto it for me.

"Dane, baby, talk to me. What did you find?" There is so much worry in her eyes. I debate for a moment if I should tell her the truth, but the lizard part of my brain, that gives me my best hunches while on the job, stops me. This means something. Something bigger than just getting frat bros and local politicians out of minor legal troubles. My gut tells me this is a secret that is going to change both of our lives, and I want to know what it is first.

Clearing my throat, I say, "I found a copy of my dad's obituary. I…I wasn't expecting it, and it just stirred up a lot of old grief." The lie spills out, not entirely untrue, but not the exact truth either. Her face crumples at my words, and she slides onto my lap, wrapping her arms around my neck in a crushing hug. The tears that were quietly waiting for their cue, escape from her in a sob she muffles by burying her face in my neck. She is saying something, but it takes me a minute to make out what the words are, thick with sadness.

"I'm so sorry. I'm so, so sorry. I'm so fucking sorry." She murmurs it on repeat, like if she says it enough, somehow she can take the pain away from me. I squeeze her against me, press my lips to the crown of her head, and inhale the scent of her jasmine shampoo. This woman cares so much for me that my grief has become her grief. Knowing she hurts so much when I hurt does something inside me. A feeling that has been hovering on the periphery of my consciousness finally clicks into place. I love her. I love her, and I never want to be the reason she hurts.

When we finally pull apart, our faces sport matching red splotches and red-rimmed eyes. We both let out a soft, embarrassed chuckle.

"Do you want to take a break?" She looks up at me, with cautious uncertainty wavering in her eyes. This emotional outburst took a lot out of us both, and whatever made her cagey and defensive earlier seems to have been a casualty of it. Right now I want nothing more than to keep holding her in my arms. Nodding, I press my lips to hers in a gentle, chaste kiss.

"Let's take a break." I shift my hold to under Everly's ass and stand, eliciting a surprised squeak from her as she locks her thighs around my waist in a crushing grip. Fuck, her thighs are thick and strong. My dick gives an interested twitch, which Everly must feel through the fabric of her black leggings, because her eyes widen in surprise. If she thinks I'm too sad to fuck, she's about to be surprised. The need to bury myself into her and under her skin is so visceral, it makes my skin itch.

"Where is your bedroom?" My voice is husky with need as I whisper against her throat gently ghosting my lips along the delicate skin of her neck. God, she smells so good. I inhale as I press my teeth into her tender flesh, putting just a small taste of the pressure it would take to mark her as mine the way I want to.

"Up the stairs, first door on the left." Her head falls back, granting me more access to her neck. I lick and press open-mouthed kisses on every exposed inch. Her skin is salty from her tears. My dick hardens in response to the knowledge that she cares so much. That I'm not just a consolatory fuck. That maybe…she loves me too.

CHAPTER 36
EVERLY

When my back hits the thick, tufted, goose down comforter on my king-size bed, Dane is immediately on top of me, pressing his erection against the seam of my leggings as his mouth continues to explore every inch of my skin. His hands slide under my T-shirt, pushing it up, exposing my breasts to him. I hadn't bothered with putting on a bra, and Dane is pleased with this discovery. I feel his lips curve into a smile between the kisses he keeps pressing into my skin.

He moves his body down mine until he can take one of my nipples into his mouth. I dig my fingers into his hair, holding him in place as he lavishes attention on my breast. Somewhere in the back of my mind, I know I shouldn't be doing this. That we should talk. I should check in with him. That I should stop being such a selfish cunt and just confess the truth to him, but when he looked at me after being hit with that fresh wave of grief and devastation, I couldn't bring myself to hurt him further. Not without a way to fix it. Knowing the truth and proving it are two entirely different things, and I am determined to be able to prove it in a court of law before Bryce knows what is coming at him.

All thoughts of redemption fly out of my head when he captures my nipple between his teeth and bites. Sending a jolt of sharp pain that shocks my system before softening into pleasure, causing whatever objections had been running through my mind to scatter, swept away from a wave of bliss.

"So good. You're so good, Dane. So good to me." I shower praise on him as I grind my center against his rigid length. He worships my breasts, alternating sides, licking, kissing, sucking, biting, until I am a panting, needy mess beneath him. Just when I'm seconds away from begging him to put his dick in me, he releases my breast with a pop —a bright red mark on the verge of going purple stands out against my pale skin.

"I need to be in you, Everly. I need you." There is a frantic sort of desperation in his eyes that dissolves any remaining shred of moral goodness I have inside of me. I can't say no to this man, and I will go to hell for it.

His lips capture mine in a kiss that feels as desperate as he looks. His lips are salty from tears. I lick them, trying to erase the evidence of his hurt. I would do anything to make sure he never goes through that kind of pain ever again. His hands pull my leggings down, and cool air greets the flushed, hot skin of my pussy. The wetness on my vulva only has a moment to cool before Dane shoves two fingers in me, curling them to my G-spot in one fluid motion. I'm so slick and ready for him, he hits his target, causing my hips to buck up, seeking more pressure.

"You're so ready for me, aren't you, baby? I'm going to fuck you until I'm under your skin. Until I'm your everything, like you are mine." Dane whispers his filthy vow directly into my ear as he curls his fingers into a come hither motion, detonating me. Wetness gushes from me as I bite on the fleshy part of my palm in an attempt to muffle my scream. Dane captures my wrist with the hand that just wrung every ounce of pleasure from me, leaving me empty and gasping for air.

"Don't you dare keep your screams from me. If I make you come, I want to hear it. I deserve to hear it." His words are so commanding, but there is an earnestness to them that wraps around my heart, binding it to his inextricably.

Dumbfounded and lust drunk, I nod my understanding while I lose myself in the forest green of his eyes. Then the thick head of his cock is pressing against my entrance. Somehow he got both of our pants off and made me come like some sort of sexual hat trick. Unwilling to wait for a second longer, he shunts his dick inside me with a forceful thrust, the desperate need to merge our bodies together radiating from him. "Need to be inside you. God, I need you."

His words are a quiet prayer whispered against my skin that I'm not sure he even knows he is uttering. I drag his shirt up so I can feel his skin against mine. We break apart only long enough to lose our shirts. With no more barriers between us, our movements become less frantic and more languid and intentional. He traces his fingers along the curve of my waist. I drag my fingernails up his back. His thrusts go from powerful and frantic to slow and methodical. His hips move in a fluid, languid rocking like the surf lapping at the beach.

I lose all sense of time as we kiss, our bodies undulating in a rhythm that only they know. We move together like we've done this a thousand times already. Pleasure builds in me slowly, like a fire catching from the smallest spark. Soon the heat builds to indescribable levels. I dig my fingers in his back, urging him to keep going, and Dane responds by kissing me harder, but continuing to fuck me like he's savoring it and in no hurry to come.

My orgasm is so close, but just out of reach. I lock my ankles around his hips, urging him to fuck me harder, and he responds by biting my lower lip.

"You want to come, Ever? You gonna let me hear this one?" His eyes darken at his question, and I know there is only one correct response.

"Yes. Please make me come."

The corner of his mouth lifts in a smirk before he snaps his hips, fucking me hard, just the way I need.

"Fuck, yes!" I don't hold back this time and rain praise down on him as he drives into me, unleashing another orgasm from me that causes me to clutch on to him so hard I know I draw blood. Dane doesn't miss a beat, and keeps fucking until I feel him thicken inside me as his own pleasure erupts. Our mouths find one another as he slowly lowers his body so we are pressed together—chest to chest, his dick still inside me, coated in our release as it softens. We are breathing each other's air as our kiss becomes slow and tender. I can feel our hearts crashing together where our skin touches. Dane did it. He is inside of me. He is part of me now. There is no going back for me now. No matter how wrong it is.

CHAPTER 37
DANE

This doesn't make any fucking sense. No fucking sense at all. Pacing in front of the small table in my kitchen, I run my fingers through my hair for the millionth time, trying to puzzle out the information in front of me.

I have the medical examiner's report spread out. I've read every line in it multiple times. The urge to vomit has been haunting me since I read each documented injury. There were plenty of injuries that could be explained by the impact between the car and the tree and the airbag deploying. But one in particular haunts me, because it makes no fucking sense.

The crush injury to the back of my dad's head. Described as central to the occipital bone, about four centimeters in diameter. His skull was smashed in, resulting in trauma to the occipital lobe. It is listed as the cause of death.

How in the hell did he wind up with a traumatic injury to the back of his skull in a forward collision?

I try to think back to the day we got the news. *Did the officers give Mom or Bryce any indication that dad's death was anything more than a tragic accident?* But my memory of that day is just a fog of grief. I refuse to ask Mom about it. She was doing so much better last time I saw her. More like the woman who raised me than she has been in a decade since losing Dad. I am not going to set her back just to sate my curiosity.

I also refuse to talk to Bryce about it. At least until I have a better idea of what the truth really is. I know how easily he lies and manipulates, and I want to be prepared with facts I can check him with.

Glancing at the clock on the stove, I see it is nearly midnight. I go on shift in the morning at seven. I make a plan to go into the station early to see if I can find the police report from Dad's accident, to see if anything unusual was noticed when they arrived on the scene.

I pull out my phone to see if Everly has texted me. Nothing. After making love to her, we both fell asleep, emotionally and physically drained. When I woke up nearly two hours later, the gnawing feeling that this is the key to unlocking everything would not leave me alone. It made me anxious, my body thrumming with renewed purpose. The need to have answers driving me away from the comfort of her embrace. She didn't rouse at all when I crawled out of bed. I left Everly sleeping, so beautiful and peaceful, so I could solve this mystery.

It felt like I was leaving a piece of my soul behind when I walked out of her bedroom. It also felt a lot like I was leaving her alone in a lion's den.

THE NEXT MORNING I arrive at work an hour earlier than usual. The skeleton crew that works the nightshift are sitting in the dimly lit room, quietly finishing up their paperwork from the night's events. Birch Falls at night is fairly quiet unless there is a big event on campus or it's rush week at BFU. Mostly DUIs, a few bar fights, sometimes an out of control college party. The crew that works this shift has been on it for years. It takes the right kind of person to work that shift. Most newbies can't hack it, too used to the normal biological circadian rhythm. But when someone clicks with it, they really click with it. Hugh Harvey is one of those people. He's been on the nightshift since I joined the academy six years ago. Probably even longer. I'm not sure when he moved to Birch Falls. All I know is he came from a bigger city a few hours away, with a much busier and more troublesome population. He said he moved to Birch Falls because he was getting too old for that shit. He's however not too old to be a night owl apparently.

"You're up early. You forget daylight savings isn't until next week?"

"I need to look something up. Figured now would be the best time to go digging into the file room before things get busy." I wave my thermos of coffee at him, not stopping my stride, not interested in small talk. Hugh grunts a dismissive goodbye in return. I take two steps before it dawns on me—Hugh might be exactly the person I need to talk to.

Turning on my heel, I head back over to Hugh's desk. "Hey, Hugh, when did you join the BFPD?"

Hugh had already buried his nose in his work so my question catches him off guard. Hugh sits back in his chair, causing it to creak from his substantial size. He's a big man. Nearly six-foot-five, probably 280 pounds on a good day. Night shift is hell on the body. I can tell Hugh used to be fit and formidable in his younger days, but the sedentary life-style is catching up to him. Still, though, when he knocks on your car window after pulling you over at two in the morning, you realize he is not a man to be trifled with.

"Winter of 2008, why?" Blood rushes to my head. That is six months before my dad's accident. Hugh would've definitely been one of the responding officers.

I take a seat on the metal chair next to his desk. "Can I ask you about a car accident you might have worked in 2009?"

Hugh's bushy eyebrows creep up in interest. "Sure, kid. This mind is a steel trap. I remember everything." He taps his temple, a serious, no-nonsense expression on his face.

I believe him. I've heard him recount arrests from early in his career nearly twenty years ago with a surprising amount of detail.

"My dad died in a car accident off of Route 19 in the summer of 2009. Went off the road and head first into a tree. Died on the scene. Were you one of the responding officers?" I pull on every ounce of training I have for deliv-ering bad news to next of kin. I keep my voice even, expression flat. I don't want him to think I think he did something wrong when investigating and put him on the defensive.

Hugh leans forward, resting his elbows on his desk. His expression goes soft as he realizes what I'm asking about. His face turns thoughtful, and I can see him searching his memory bank, recalling that night, getting the facts in order before responding.

"Yeah, I was there. O'Malley and I got the call. It was the only one we worked that night. Someone called in when they drove by and saw the old fence line broken. It had rained that night, so they thought maybe someone lost control going round the curve. I think his name was Smith?"

"Were they there when you got to the scene?" I lean forward too, resting my elbows on my knees, eager to hear more.

"Nah, they were long gone by the time we got there. I thought it was weird they wouldn't stick around to see if someone needed help. When O'Malley and I got there, we went down the embankment and found an truck smashed headfirst into an oak tree. Front end crumpled like a soda can. Must've been going way too fast around that give and went into a skid." He makes a face when he realizes he's talking to the victim's son. "Sorry, I—"

Shaking my head, I wave him off. "It's fine. Listen, do you remember anything else unusual about the scene? Anything that didn't add up or that made your spidey-sense tingle? Anything that indicated it *wasn't* an accident?"

Hugh's brows furrow as he considers my question. I can

tell he's mulling it over, going through all the facts in his head, before he responds. He knows I'm not asking just for curiosity's sake.

"Other than the lack of skid marks on the road and the missing good Samaritan who called it in?"

"There weren't any skid marks?"

"Nope. Not one. I looked myself that night and checked again when the sun came up. It was like he drove off that embankment on purpose. I thought maybe it was..." He trails off, not wanting to finish that sentence in respect for me.

A slick, nauseous feeling roils in my gut. My dad would not have killed himself. He and Mom were so happy. They had been planning a trip to Puerto Rico for their anniversary in October. Aside from Bryce being a dick to Dad and me, our lives were great. There is no fucking way Dad would've driven into that tree on purpose. So...who did?

Then it hits me. The memory of the last time I saw my dad alive. He had dropped me off to go to the game with Jason. He took me instead of Mom because he said he had to go see Bryce anyway.

Bryce was the last person to see him alive.

"Hey, kid, what's up? You look like you've seen a ghost." Hugh's gruff voice pulls me from the memory, and I know he can see the shock written all over my face.

"I found... I found the medical examiner's report for my dad when I was...looking through some stuff," I hedge, not willing to tip him off that I was hunting through Bryce's files in case Bryce paid Hugh off to help forge the police report. "The medical examiner said dad had a crush injury to the back of his skull. Does that make any sense based on how he was at the scene of the accident? Was his—" I pause, choking back the pain from discussing my own dad's death so plainly. "Was he thrown from the car?"

Hugh shakes his head immediately. "No. He was buckled in. Driver's seat. Slumped toward the passenger seat, but definitely mostly in place. Air bag deployed. Both actually, even though there wasn't anyone in the passenger seat." Hugh's brows furrow in confusion as he considers that fact. "What kind of car did your dad drive? Was it new or older?"

"It was new. I remember he bought it just a few months before he died. Why?"

"Newer cars, after 2007, were designed so the passenger airbag shouldn't deploy if no passenger is detected in the seat. Shit. I should've noticed that."

My blood runs cold at Hugh's words.

My dad wasn't alone in the car the night he died.

And I think I know who was with him.

CHAPTER 38
EVERLY

When I wake up, bright morning light streams in through the partially open curtains, casting a golden glow in the bedroom. As I blink my eyes open, exhaustion keeps my limbs heavy and pinned to the bed. Groggy and disoriented, I stretch my body, trying to remember what decade it is. I was having the most blissful dream about Dane doing the most obscene and filthy things to my body. Why am I even awake? I was sleeping the sleep of a well-fucked woman, and my brain hasn't come back online. I let one arm drift to the middle of the bed, searching for Dane, but my fingers only find cold sheets.

There is a loud buzz as my phone vibrates with an incoming call, causing it to clatter against the hard wood of the nightstand. Dane's name is on the screen, and I sit up, suddenly feeling very awake. Cool air caresses my skin as the comforter falls away, reminding me I must have fallen asleep naked after Dane and I fucked in my marriage bed.

Guilt prickles up my spine uncomfortably as I add to my tally of the unforgivable sins I've committed.

Cover for husband when he murders his stepdad? Check.

Lie about it for a decade so don't have to face the fact that you're married to a killer? Check.

Cheat on said husband with his brother, who also happens to be the murder victim's son? Check.

Let that brother develop feelings for you that you know he wouldn't even consider if he knew the truth? Check.

Comfort him with your magic vagina when he's sad about said dead dad? Double check.

"Hey, where are you? I just woke up." My voice is husky, thick with sleep, hopefully masking the crisis of conscience that is happening in my mind.

"I couldn't sleep so I went home to keep working on Bryce's files. I found something I wanted to look into at work—" Dane starts to talk, then cuts himself off, like he's debating what to say. "Ever, baby, we need to talk." There is an urgency in Dane's voice that has my pulse skyrocketing and goose bumps pebbling my skin.

"Is everything okay?" I ask, dread creeping up my spine, lifting the guilt of all of my sins like a rising tide.

"I'm on my way to your place. Can you pack up an overnight bag and be ready in twenty minutes? We can talk when I get there." I can hear road noise in the background, and I realize Dane is driving. Driving to me. To…talk? Pick me up? He doesn't sound like a man who just realized I've been harboring the biggest mind fuck of a secret ever kept. Maybe he wants to push me to leave Bryce for real? I can't do that. Not yet. Not until I find a way to get justice for Jake.

Just then, the chirp of the alarm system alerting the front door has been opened sounds through the house.

"Shit, I think Bryce just got home." I'm out of bed, my body moving without thought as I hunt frantically for clothes to put on before Bryce comes up the stairs.

"Everly, listen to me—"

"Everly, babe? You upstairs?" Bryce's smooth baritone drifts up the stairs just a moment before his footsteps follow.

"He's home. I have to go. Don't come over." I hiss out my warning before hanging up on Dane. The door to the bedroom opens just as I finish pulling on an oversized T-shirt, covering my nakedness and hopefully any marks Dane left on my body.

I turn around to face my husband. My hands grasp the dresser behind me with a death grip, desperately trying to hide the way my body is trembling with adrenaline. Bryce rakes his gaze over me. His eyes are dark with hunger and something more sinister.

"Did you just get out of bed, darling? It's almost noon." There is something in the tone of Bryce's voice that does nothing to abate the nervous energy thrumming through my veins right now. It's the tone he uses when cross-examining a witness, ready to catch them in a lie. That cool, aloof cadence that almost seems casually disarming but is really a trap ready to snap shut. His whole demeanor is cold, calculating, and assessing. He's not looking at me like his wife. He's looking at me like I'm on trial.

"Um, yeah, I, uh, guess that migraine really took it out of me." I fumble through the lie while simultaneously creeping away from Bryce toward the bathroom, hoping like hell I don't smell like sex, his brother's cologne, or some unholy combination of the two. My eyes drift to the unmade bed, scanning for any evidence of Dane while my mind races for ways to buy more time before Bryce tries to touch me. *Get to the bathroom! Claim you're still sick! Rip a big fart!* My brain screams for my body and mouth to do something. Anything to diffuse this situation.

"I-I thought you weren't coming home until tonight?" I stammer out, my body refusing to cooperate and listen to the alarms blaring in my skull. Bryce prowls closer, closing the distance between us slowly, methodically. I watch in terrified fascination as he begins unbuttoning the cuffs of his white dress shirt before moving on to the front buttons.

"What? A man not allowed to miss his wife?" The look he gives me is lascivious, and if he had been giving me this look a year ago, or even six months ago, my reaction would be very different. Instead of hot arousal coursing through my veins, there is only cold fear. I can't do this with him. Not again. Not after this weekend. Bryce reaches me, pinning me against the wall next to the bathroom door, halting my escape.

My breathing becomes rapid, shallow pants as panic truly begins to set in. Bryce leans in, breathing in my scent. He lets out a low, bitter sounding chuckle.

"You did it. I wasn't sure if you would actually go through with it."

I flinch, turning my face away from him as his warm

breath tickles my skin. "Did what? I don't know what you're talking about." I squeeze my eyes shut, trying to contain the tears threatening to form and give me away.

"Don't lie to me, wife. You smell like him."

Oh, fuck.

Bryce grips my chin, forcing me to look at him.

"I'm not mad, darling. You did exactly what I told you to do. Is he going to help me now? Did you convince him to adjust his moral compass with that delicious cunt of yours?"

I whimper in pain from the harshness of his grip. "Bryce. Stop. Please."

"Did the little simp just fall over himself to put his dick into you? I knew he always wanted to fuck you. He's been panting after you for years."

"Bryce! *Stop!*" I wedge my arms between us and shove, startling him enough that he stumbles back several steps. I keep my arms up in front of me in a pitiful attempt to ward him off.

"Fucking stop it! I can't do this anymore!" I lunge forward, shoving him back another few feet. "Fuck you, you selfish bastard! I'm done. I'm done lying for you. Covering for you. I am *done* with you!" I punctuate each exclamation with a furious pound of my fist against his chest.

The lustful hunger that darkened his gazes morphs into pure unadulterated fury.

"You're going to regret that." Bryce grabs me by the neck, spinning us until my back is slammed against the wall hard enough to knock the air from my lungs. Or it would've, if he wasn't closing off my windpipe.

"Let's get something straight, *darling*," Bryce spits the endearment at me with venom, his fingers digging into the tender flesh of my throat, cutting off my ability to breathe.

"You will never be done with me. If you think you can turn me in for what happened ten years ago and just walk away, you've got another thing coming. You aided and abetted. You *lied* for me for years. Do you really think you won't be drug into the shit too? Are you that fucking stupid? We go down *together*."

Just as my vision begins to darken and consciousness begins to slip away, the sound of the front door slamming open with a bang causes Bryce to jerk back in surprise, releasing my throat. I collapse to the carpet, gasping for air, the blood rushing to my head muffling the frantic shouts of Dane calling my name.

"Why the fuck is he here?" Bryce's question is a frustrated growl that I echo in my own mind, as I silently plead for Dane. I don't know if I'm praying for him to turn around and leave, to save me, or just to forgive me when the truth all comes out.

CHAPTER 39
DANE

"Shit, I think Bryce just got home." Everly's words make my blood run cold. Bryce is already home. That will make getting her away from him trickier, but I can't just leave her there with a murderer.

"Everly, listen to me—" I say, trying to warn her.

"He's home. I have to go. Don't come over." Her hissed whisper is the last thing I hear before she ends the call.

Don't come over? The hell I won't. Pressing down on the gas pedal, I speed through the streets of Birch Falls in a race to rescue the woman I love.

After my conversation with Hugh, I went back to all the notes I had taken while digging through Bryce's files and started putting the pieces together. The familiar names clicking into place as I realized the depth and breadth of Bryce's manipulation to keep his involvement in my dad's death a secret.

I knew Bryce wasn't above blackmail and currying favors to help his criminal buddies stay out of jail, but knowing he's capable of murder sent panic surging through me for Everly's safety.

Minutes later, I'm pulling into their driveway, Bryce's silver Mercedes parked out front like the most pretentious harbinger of bad tidings. Seeing the expensive new car mocking me as I climb out of the nearly two-decade-old Corolla my dad bought me when I got my first job reminds me just how much he stole from me. Not just my dad, but all the missed opportunities I could have had if my life had been different. Anger flares under my skin, hot and vicious.

I storm through their front door, letting it slam against the wall, my desperate fury guiding me. I don't know what I am going to do or say to Bryce. All I know is I can't leave her here with him. "Everly!" I scan the open foyer, looking for any sign of Bryce or Everly. I see Bryce's leather overnight bag sitting at the foot of the stairs. A muffled thump and pained whimper from the second floor sends me rushing up the stairs. "Everly, are you okay?"

Bryce meets me at the top of the stairs. His arms are crossed over his chest, a smug look on his face. "Little brother, what brings you—"

My fist slams into his face, sending him staggering back against the wall, cutting him off. The only words I want to hear out of his mouth are a confession.

"You killed him! You fucking killed him you son of a bitch!" I am on him, landing blow after blow on his stupid fucking lying face. My vision is red with anger. The only sound I hear is the thud of my fist slamming into his face.

Nothing exists right now except for my hatred for my brother. "Why? Why did you do it?"

"Dane!" Everly's startled cry reaches me the same time she does. I feel her soft hands wrap around the arm that is cocked back and ready to swing. "Dane, stop! Please!" She lands on her knees next to me on the plush carpet, forcing me to look at her. What I see does not lessen the urge to kill my brother pumping through my veins. Dark bruises are forming on her neck, her eyes red-rimmed and her face red from crying. Bryce groans under me, stunned and semi-unconscious from the beating I just gave him.

"Did he hurt you?" I cup her face gently, but my voice is a dangerous, low growl. I don't care if I go to jail for killing him. He doesn't deserve to live.

"Dane, you have to stop. You can't kill him. You're too good..." Her pleading softens something in me, breaking through the anger. Slowly I lower my arm and climb off Bryce's limp form on the ground. Focusing my attention on Everly, I scan her face looking for any more signs of injury.

"Are you okay, baby?" Her eyes widen at the endearment at the end of my question, like she's surprised I'm concerned for her.

She nods, but the way her face crumples and fresh tears shimmer in her eyes betrays the strength she's trying to broadcast. Tugging her into my chest, I stroke her hair gently, ignoring the throbbing ache in my hand from where I used it to punish Bryce.

"I was coming to get you. You can't stay here. He's

dangerous." Everly leans back so she can look at me, a confused wariness on her face. "He killed my dad."

Her eyes go wide in fear, and her mouth pops open in shock when she hears the last part. "H-how do you know that?" I can feel her body tremble, fear consuming her as she realizes how dangerous her husband truly is.

"I found the medical examiner's report in his desk. My dad died from an injury that couldn't have been caused by the accident, and Bryce was the last person to see him alive."

Another wet moan gurgles out of Bryce's limp form as his head lolls side to side weakly. "No proof..." The words are a barely audible mumble, but enough to let me know I haven't punished him nearly enough. My body tenses, ready to rain more hell down on him. I feel Everly go rigid in my arms as she processes the revelation.

"W-was with...Everly." Bryce lips part in a gruesome, bloody smile, mocking me. "Wasn't I, darling?" His hand slides across the carpet and grips her thigh, leaving a bloody hand print on her pale skin. Everly jerks at his touch and flings herself backward, out of my hold and crawling away from us both, a panic-stricken look on her face.

"She's my alibi..." Bryce makes like he's going to sit up so I lean over, pushing him back down, my hand wrapped around his throat. The urge to squeeze until I crush his trachea is almost too strong to ignore.

"If you touch her again, I will fucking end you." Bryce grips my hand, desperation flaring in his eyes when he realizes he can't budge my hold on his throat. His face turns a satisfying, deep shade of red, bordering on purple. I could just keep my hand here a little longer and put an end to all of this.

"Sheknew." The strangled words that slip past Bryce's lips make time stop. Everly lets out a gasp; my hold on Bryce's throat goes slack. The only sounds now are his desperate choked gasps for air, mixed with his dark, bitter chuckle.

My gaze finds Everly's. I stare at her, shock and disbelief holding my mind hostage. *She knew?* No…no…there is no way. Everly sits there, frozen in place as a flurry of emotions play across her beautiful face one by one. Shock, horror, resignation, until finally settling on remorse. Dread settles in the pit of my stomach when I realize Bryce is telling the truth.

"Is it true?" The question comes out in a choked whisper as I force the words out. The idea that she knew the truth this whole time… The betrayal cuts deep. So deep I can feel it physically. I press my aching hand against my chest, where it feels like my heart is cleaving in two.

Bryce shifts, rolling on to his side, his laugh morphing into a coughing fit that sends blood splattering on the carpet. He pushes up to his hands and knees, shooting a vicious stare in Everly's direction.

"I don't know what you think you can prove, little brother, but I promise you if you open that can of worms, I am not the only one that will pay the price for it. Do you really think you could turn my wife against me when she has as much to lose as I do? What do you think it will do to our poor mother if you accuse her son of murdering her husband?" Bryce wipes the blood dripping from his nose on his shirt sleeve, looking more annoyed than defensive about being accused of murder.

The mention of our mother gives me pause. Oh god... What would this truth do to her? She barely functioned for years after Dad died. If she found out her own son killed him...

Sensing my hesitation, Bryce presses on. "Dane, I thought you were smarter than this. A man like me does not get where he is in life without knowing how to pull some strings. I'm willing to forget this little incident if you are. You have no evidence supporting your ridiculous accusation, and you can't compel her to testify. Spousal privilege." I shoot him an incredulous look. He has truly lost it if he thinks I'm going to just drop this, even if it hurts to reveal the truth.

"He can't compel me to testify, but I can volunteer to willingly." Everly's voice is as cold and as sharp as the knife that feels lodged in my heart right now. "I don't care if I go to jail too. You manipulated me, and I am tired of carrying the weight of your crimes. If I have to go to jail so Dane can have his justice, then I am okay with that. I told you I was done with you. I meant it." Everly carefully gets to her feet, her body still trembling from the adrenaline surge of the confrontation, but her voice is strong. The look she gives Bryce is as cold and unyielding as steel. She shows no uncertainty in her decision.

"Dane, call the police. I want to report Bryce for assault and murder." She doesn't look at me at all. I don't know how to resolve the conflicting emotions warring inside of me right now.

"You backstabbing little bitch!" Bryce lunges from his position on the ground, tackling Everly to the ground. Her back knocks against a framed picture of them from their wedding on the way to the ground, sending the frame crashing down on top of them. Shattered glass crunches under them as Bryce pins Everly to the ground, his hands wrapped around her throat in a deadly grip. "You're going to pay for that!"

Bryce is lost to madness as he chokes her. Everly's hands flail around her, groping, searching for something to use as a weapon. My mind finally catches up to what is happening, and I jump into the fray, knocking Bryce off of her. We roll against the wall, my body pinned between it and Bryce as I hold on to him in a headlock with my legs around his waist. Out the corner of my eye, I see his arm rise up, with a long shard of glass clenched in his fist. Everly sees it too and rolls out the way of his strike just in time.

I do my best to hold on to Bryce, but he bucks and flails in my hold like an angry bull. His arm holding the glass shard swings wildly.

"Everly, run! Get away from him! Call for help!" I try to adjust my hold on Bryce to get better leverage to cut off his airway, but when I do, he swings his arm back, sinking the glass into my side, just under my ribs. Pain erupts where he stabbed me, causing my hold on him to go slack.

"Dane! No!" Everly's horrified cry cuts through the blood pounding in my ears, muffling my hearing. Bryce is up now, stalking after her as she frantically backs away from him. I try to get up, but when I move the pain lances through me, immobilizing me there on the floor. My side becomes wet and sticky from the blood pouring from the wound, and my vision darkens at the edges. I lose track of Bryce and Everly as I focus on holding pressure on the wound, trying to staunch the bleeding.

"I'm going to fucking kill you!"

"Go fuck yourself, Bryce! I am sick of your shit!" There is a loud thud, a grunt, and then the sound of something heavy rolling down the stairs. The last thing I see before I pass out is Everly's angelic face as she kneels next to me, her trembling hands pressing down on to hold pressure as my hand falls away limply.

"Don't you dare die, Dane. Stay with me. Please stay with me."

CHAPTER 40
EVERLY

"You backstabbing little bitch!" Bryce's face, bloody and battered from Dane's furious beating, morphs into a terrifying mask as he lunges for me. His body collides against mine, slamming me against the wall with force. There is a loud snap of glass cracking as my head smacks against the large framed wedding portrait of us hanging on the wall. Stars explode in my vision, and something sharp slices into my scalp. Our bodies tumble to the floor, the portrait coming loose from its place on the wall follow us, raining shattered glass down everywhere.

Bryce's hands are wrapped around my throat, squeezing so hard it feels like he is going to crush my trachea. "You're going to pay for that!" His outraged yell is muffled thanks to the blood pounding in my ears. My hands claw and scramble, searching for something, anything to use as a weapon to get him off of me.

His eyes are black with rage, his face twisted in

demonic fury that makes him unrecognizable from the man I married. From the man I once loved. Tears slide down my face as my vision darkens once more, and I think this time he might succeed in killing me. All I can think is that at least he won't be able to get away with my murder. Not with Dane here to witness it.

There is another furious roar and then Bryce's crushing weight is gone. I suck in some air and immediately begin coughing and choking as my lungs remember how to breathe.

Bryce and Dance roll away until their bodies crash against the other wall, where Dane has Bryce in a headlock. "Everly, run! Get away from him! Call for help!"

Gasping, I get on my hands and knees slowly, trying to follow Dane's orders. Then in terrifying slow motion, my eyes lock on Bryce's arm as it swings up wildly, holding a deadly looking shard of glass in his fist. Blood drips from his hand where the glass cuts into his flesh, but Bryce doesn't seem to notice. I watch, horrified, as his arm descends, plunging the shard into Dane.

"Dane! No!" I crawl backward, scrambling to my feet as Bryce staggers to his feet, Dane clutching the wound on his side as blood pours from it entirely too quickly. Oh, god. He's going to die.

"I'm going to fucking kill you!" Bryce lurches at me, his face unrecognizable, contorted by demonic fury. Gone is the man I used to love. Gone is the boy who saved me and made me feel safe. The young idealistic lawyer who charmed my dad and took me to Paris. The doting husband who carried me across the threshold of our first home is nowhere to be found. No trace of him remains in monster standing in front of me. I don't know if he ever truly existed.

When he lunges for me, I don't think. I only react.

"Go fuck yourself, Bryce! I am sick of your shit!"

Reaching for the closest thing I can find, my hand lands on a heavy ceramic vase I made him as a gift for our ten year anniversary. I painted scenes from our honeymoon in Italy on it, and suggested he take it to his office and put a plant in it. It has sat unused on this hallway table for the last five years. It's so heavy it jerks my arm down, pulling my shoulder, but I swing it anyway, aiming for Bryce's head.

The momentum of the swing sends my body turning away from him just as he reaches for me again. The heavy vase makes a sickening thud as it makes contact with the side of Bryce's head. He stumbles, eyes wide in surprise, then his body pitches forward as he runs out of hallway and meets the top of the stairs. My own momentum sends me crashing to the ground in the opposite direction, barely missing the same fate Bryce just met.

I don't wait to see if he gets up and comes back for me. I scramble over to Dane and press my hands against his side, now drenched in a catastrophic amount of blood. He's barely conscious, his arms going limp as I take over holding pressure

"Don't you dare die, Dane. Stay with me. Please stay with me. Staywithme." I can't see anything; my vision is so blurred with tears. Frantically I use one hand to pat at his pockets, praying he has his cell phone on him. I keep the other pressed against the wound, holding pressure best I can. I blink away tears, clearing my vision enough for my eyes to lock with his. I am unable to look away, paranoid if I do, he will close his eyes and I will lose him forever. His blood is hot and sticky, and it seeps between my fingers. Bile rises in my throat, but I swallow it back, forcing myself to hold it together long enough to get Dane help.

I nearly cry out in relief when my hand meets a hard rectangle in his back pocket. Pulling it out, I hit the emergency call button on the lock screen. The phone tries to slip through my blood-slick fingers, but I hold on to it as the screen lights up with the outgoing call. Dane's eyes take on a distant, glassy look, and his lip quirks up at the corner in an almost smile. Abject terror clutches my heart in its fist as his face takes on a serene expression.

"I love you, Everly." His words are so quiet, I'm not even sure I hear them at first, but his hand weakly squeezes my arm, letting me know they were real. Dane loses consciousness just as the call connects.

"9-1-1, what's your emergency?"

"I need help! He's been stabbed, and he's losing so much blood."

"Ma'am, who's been stabbed? Can you tell me where you are? Are you currently in danger?"

"Dane. He's stabbed Dane! 276 Vista Drive. Please send somebody. I can't stop it. I can't stop the bleeding. Please help me." I'm mindless with terror now, as Dane grows paler in front of my very eyes.

"Ma'am, did you say 276 Vista Drive?" The dispatcher's

voice sounds so far away as her question cuts through the fog of hysteria.

"Yes!" I'm sobbing now, in full on hysterics as I beg and plead for Dane to hold on. "Oh god, Dane don't die. Don't die. Don't die. I'm sorry. I'm so sorry."

The voice on the phone stays calm as she instructs me to keep holding pressure on the wound, assuring me that help is on the way. My mind clings to her words of comfort in a desperate bid to hold on to the last shred of my composure. I can't save Dane if I fall apart. My head throbs, eyes stinging from tears, and my arms ache from the amount of pressure I am putting on them to staunch the flow of blood.

I lose all sense of time as I kneel there, soaked in Dane's blood, begging him to live. Eventually, chaos erupts around me, as two large bodies kneel on either side of me. A third person pulls me from my position, and I jerk and fight with them, terrified to remove my hands from Dane.

"Ma'am, we've got him. Let us take over." A young man with blond hair and eyes the most serene shade of blue appears in front of me, stealing my focus as one of his partners scoots into the position he forced me to vacate.

My muscles—no longer rigid with purpose, their only job to keep Dane alive—go lax, forcing my body to go limp in his arms.

"Hey there, I've got you." He guides me gently back until I'm on the floor, the adrenaline that had kept me going flushed out of my system in one blink of a moment. The EMT leans over me, keeping my focus on him as he checks my pupils and rattles off my vitals to someone nearby that I can't see.

My brain gets sluggish, turning his words into muddled sounds I can't quite follow. I hear the word *bleeding* again, but it almost feels like he's talking about me. I think I should be concerned, but instead I just feel tired, and I close my eyes, letting the darkness take me.

CHAPTER 41
DANE

I'm cold. So fucking cold. That's the first thought that drifts through my mind as I slowly regain consciousness. I part my lips to say something, but my mouth is so dry it feels like it is glued shut. I try to open my eyes, but I'm so groggy and they're so heavy. They flutter shut again almost immediately. The only thing I glimpse is white sterile walls and harsh florescent lighting. A soft, rhythmic beeping is a metronome that prevents me from fully succumbing to the sleep that is beckoning. That and the pain that rolls through me every time I take a breath.

"Whhhterrr…" My throat burns when I try to speak, the words coming out an unintelligible mumble. Where am I? What happened?

"Dane! Hey, I'm here." A soft, warm hand finds mind under the scratchy blanket that is doing a pitiful job of containing my body heat. "You want some water?" I move my head in the barest hint of a nod, and I hope whoever is here with me saw it. Why does everything hurt so much?

"Here, open your mouth. I've got a cup with a straw."

Keeping my eyes shut from the harsh light, I follow the familiar voice's direction. I know who this is, but my mind won't tell me who it is. Cool water rushes into my mouth, soothing the parched feeling. I drink and drink, until the straw makes a gurgling sound as air is sucked into it. Releasing the straw, I let out a relieved sigh, feeling slightly better now that my mouth doesn't feel like it is stuffed full of cotton.

Slowly I blink my eyes open again, squinting to let in as little light as possible. Serena—with her halo of curls, gold eyes, and exhaustion etched onto her face—comes into view. She's wearing a BFPD hoodie and looks like she was dragged out of bed in the middle of the night.

"Hey you. Nice of you to decide to rejoin the land of the living." Her words are joking, but the tremor in her voice betrays how worried she is.

"Where—" I want to say *am I?* but exhaustion keeps me from forming a complete sentence.

"You're at Birch Falls Memorial. You were brought here yesterday. Do you remember anything about what happened?" Serena's tone is cautious, like she is afraid of revealing too much of the circumstance that brought me here.

Closing my eyes, I try to think about the last thing I remember. Everly. Everly was in danger. Bryce was hurting her. I remember punching him. Tackling him. Rolling on the ground. Pain. So much pain. Then Everly begging me to stay with her.

"Everly... Bryce...hurt her..."

"Yeah, you were at Everly and Bryce's house. It looks like there was some sort of confrontation, and you got hurt. You were stabbed." That explains the searing pain in my abdomen. Realizing I was injured and incapacitated, leaving Everly alone with Bryce, sends fear straight into my heart. The beeping of the heart monitor ticks up in rhythm in response.

"Everly…okay?"

"She's okay. She was checked out when she was brought in yesterday and discharged this morning. She's been taken to the station to give a statement." Serena hesitates, like she's unsure of how to continue. When she resumes speaking she's using the soft, sympathetic tone she uses when notifying next of kin of an accident.

"Dane… Bryce is dead. He was found at the bottom of the stairs. Everly said he fell down them during the struggle. He hit his head on the marble floor and died from a brain hemorrhage."

I didn't think it could be possible to feel colder than I do already, but it feels like someone injects ice water straight into my veins when I hear that my brother is dead. Not out of grief, but fear.

Memories come flooding back. Me smashing my fist into Bryce over and over again. I was so angry about something. Consumed by hate for him. Everly stopping me from killing him. The fear in her eyes and bruises on her neck. Bryce taunting me. Mocking me about something… His words drift away before I can remember what he said. Then Bryce was on top of Everly, screaming at her. Saying he was going to kill her. That's when I tackled him and got him in a chokehold. Then pain…and nothing. Shit.

Did Everly kill him? Did I? Is she being arrested? Then the memory of why I was so angry hits me. Bryce killed my father. Bryce killed my father, and according to him, Everly knew.

"Everly called 911 at approximately 12:47 p.m. yesterday. She was in hysterics trying to get help for you. She said you were bleeding out, and she couldn't get it to stop. She stayed on the line the ten minutes it took the ambulance to arrive. She held pressure the whole time, begging you to stay conscious." Serena's words mingle with the memory of Everly begging me not to die.

Wetness trickles down my cheek and my vision blurs with stinging tears. Pain unlike anything I've ever known grips my chest as her betrayal and sacrifice slices through me.

"You know what she didn't do during that ten minute phone call?"

I shake my head, eyes squeezed shut, like it can protect me from what Serena says next.

"She didn't mention Bryce at all."

CHAPTER 42
EVERLY

The interrogation room at the police station is cold. So cold I keep my hands wedged between my thighs in a futile effort to keep them warm. If they lowered the temperature a degree or two, I wouldn't be surprised to see my breath misting in the air. My jaw aches from how hard I'm clenching it to keep my teeth from chattering, but I can't blame my uncontrollable shivers on the frigid temperature of the room. I haven't been able to stop shaking since I woke up in the hospital and realized I killed my husband.

The moment Bryce stabbed Dane with that broken piece of glass, I lost all sense of reason. The only thought in my head when I saw the crimson stain spreading over his clothing was *no. Not him too.* Everything after that is a blur. The only thing that stands in sharp relief is the memory of how hot and slippery the blood coating my hands was until it cooled and grew sticky on my skin. *That* memory will never leave me. I've showered and washed my hands dozens of times, and I can still feel Dane's blood coating my skin. Now I understand why Lady Macbeth was driven to madness. I stare at my dry, cracked hands, raw from being scrubbed so harshly, wondering if anyone is ever going to come take my statement, or if they're letting me sit here in misery until I confess to something.

When I woke up, groggy from the anesthesia they gave me to stitch up the cut on my head, I kept crying out, asking "Where is he?" The abject terror I had been experiencing at the thought of losing Dane before passing out came roaring back as soon as I regained consciousness. The poor nurse who was taking care of me thought I was asking for my husband. She told me tearfully that there was nothing they could do for him. He had a massive head injury in the fall and was unresponsive when the first responders arrived. My body began quaking as the realization of what I had done hit me, and it hasn't stopped since.

My eyes begin to droop as I sit there, exhaustion from the last twenty-four hours pressing down on me. My head aches from the concussion Bryce gave me during our fight. The nurses kept waking me up every two hours last night to check on my vitals. There is a bald patch on the back of my head; they had to shave it to put in stitches where the glass from the picture frame cut my scalp. Briefly I think about how Bryce will hate the fact that I'll have to cut the rest of my hair short to make it look okay, but then I remember Bryce won't be around to care. He's dead now. The fact that I forgot that almost makes me break out in hysterical giggles. The lack of sleep and emotional whiplash I've been experiencing is beginning to wear on my tenuous grip of my sanity.

The sound of the door opening snaps me out of the delirious path my mind is starting to wander down. I raise my bleary gaze up to find Serena standing there, out of uniform, a wary look on her face. Last I saw her, she was at the hospital, waiting for Dane to wake up from surgery. She had stopped by my room to make sure I was okay, but two officers had already arrived to take me down to the station for *questioning*. I made her promise to stay with Dane and contact his mom as soon as he woke up. She tried to argue with her fellow officers about bringing me in, but the guilt clutching my heart in its unrelenting fist would not allow me to get her involved. Too many innocent people had been hurt already because of Bryce and his lies, and I didn't want her to get swept up in my mess. I just needed her to stay there and make sure he was going to be okay.

I rise to my feet, tears stinging the backs of my eyes, afraid she's here to give me bad news about Dane.

"Is he…" My words trails off, unable to voice my greatest fear.

"He's awake. He's okay." Serena gives me a sympathetic smile, and my knees go weak, causing me to collapse back onto the cold, hard steel chair behind me.

"Oh, thank fuck." I sob, burying my face in my hands, unable to hold back the relief I feel.

Serena's arm snakes around my shoulders, pulling me into a hug as I weep, soaking her soft gray hoodie with my tears. I don't know how long she holds me, letting me sob on her, as the exhaustion, adrenaline, and fear that has been building up inside of me finally pours out.

When it feels like I've been wrung dry, we finally pull apart. I expect to see judgement or pity on her face, sure she's here to give me bad news about my situation. I know we are friends, but she's also a cop, and I killed a man. There is no getting out of this for me. Dane will likely tell them about how I helped Bryce cover up the murder of his father, and I'll be charged with something, I'm sure. I don't expect anything less. I don't deserve anything less. I know he said he loved me before losing consciousness, but I can't expect him to be okay with my lies. No matter if I let Bryce manipulate me into believing they were justified.

"Why are you here? I thought I was supposed to be making a statement or being questioned or something..."

"Dane told me to come here and make sure you're okay. He told me to make sure you don't talk to anyone without a lawyer present."

My mouth falls open in surprise at Serena's words. "D-Dane said that?"

She nods solemnly. "Keep your mouth shut." Her words are low, so only I can hear them, but there is a gravity behind them I can't ignore. "Do you have someone you can call? A lawyer?" I let out a small, incredulous huff of a laugh at her question. Lawyers are the one thing I have too much of in my life.

"I can call my dad. He's a judge, but he knows people. He has plenty of friends he can call on."

"Good, then call him and tell him you need a lawyer. Do

not talk to anyone until they get here. Do you understand me?" For the first time since Bryce stormed into our bedroom, I feel the faintest flicker of hope.

"I understand."

"Okay, good. I'll get you a phone and make sure no one comes to take your statement until your lawyer gets here."

I watch Serena leave the room, trying and failing to keep the hope that this means Dane forgives me for my part in keeping the truth from him from bubbling up. I don't dare to hope that we still have a future together. Not after everything I've done.

Serena returns a few minutes later with a phone I can use. I call my father and wait for him to pick up. My stomach is in knots with anxiety. Logically I know he won't leave me high and dry, and me being arrested will be almost as bad for him as it will be for me, but I still can't push away the thought that maybe he would've rather had Bryce still here instead of me. When his rich baritone voice comes through the line, it opens the flood gates, and I am once again a young girl who needs her daddy.

"Daddy, it's me. I need your help."

SERENA SITS with me for the next hour while we wait for my lawyer arrive. When I explained to my dad I was at the police station waiting to be questioned about Bryce's death, the silence that met me was so complete I thought he had hung up on me. After a long moment, when he finally spoke, I was surprised by the concern that laced his words. All he said was, "Don't say a word. I'll have Jessica there in an hour." His tone was that of the concerned, loving father I hadn't seen in nearly twenty years. The fact that he was calling Jessica meant he understood exactly how seriously he was taking my situation.

She was a junior associate at my dad's law firm before he became a judge, and was one of his star employees. When he left, she rocketed to the top of the firm, becoming the youngest partner there. She was on track to become a senior partner there and take on a more managerial role, until ten years ago when her sister was arrested for the murder of her husband, a prominent local politician on track to run for congress. Jessica dropped everything to handle her defense and managed to prove her sister had been acting in self-defense.

The trial was a circus, and the police botched the investigation, causing the tide of public opinion to turn against her sister, but Jessica managed to build a strong case in spite of that. Her experience defending her sister highlighted a need for more strong, competent female attorneys defending other women from a system rigged to diminish their fears and support their abusers. Jessica moved and switched to focus solely on criminal defense, and is now the lead defense attorney at the bigger firm in Richmond.

As far as I know, she only takes high profile cases after thoroughly vetting her clients, and her rates are astronomical, but she is very good at her job. She uses the salary from those cases to enable her to take on pro bono cases for women without the financial means to hire her. I don't know if he is only doing this so that this doesn't get out of hand and ruin his reputation, or if he truly cares about me, but I will gladly take the lifeline he is throwing me. I can worry about fixing our relationship after Jessica makes sure I'm not arrested for Bryce's murder.

CHAPTER 43
DANE

I'm lying in bed, fisting the scratchy, stiff hospital blanket as I attempt to sit up. The nurse won't let me out of the bed unassisted yet, stating I'm a "fall risk" after losing nearly two liters of blood from where Bryce stabbed me. She's probably not wrong, but I'm tired of having a tube up my dick so I can pee. I'd like to prove I can get up so they will let me go to the bathroom. Pain lances through me as my abdominal muscles flex and strain, putting pressure on the stitches snaking up my side. A cold sweat breaks out on my forehead, and halfway to sitting up, I give up and flop back against the pillow.

"Fuck!"

I feel so fucking helpless lying in this bed. When Serena left, she promised to go to the station to check on Everly before stopping by Mom's house to pick her up and bring her here. I wasn't entirely lucid thanks to the painkillers and brain fog from the anesthesia, but I knew I had to be the one to tell my mother that her son is dead.

I've been debating for hours now how to break the news to her. Never mind the fact that he's a piece of shit wife beater. Oh, and that he killed her husband. If losing my dad in an accident put her in such a depression she couldn't work, what will this news do to her? I want to be angry at Everly for keeping Bryce's secret. Scratch that. I am angry. She helped him get away with murder. But when I think about telling my mom the truth, my stomach sours thinking about how devastated she will be. Bryce is dead now. He'll never be punished for what he did. Is it worth shattering my mom's entire worldview just so the world will know what an evil shit he is?

The answer to my moral quandary comes when the door to my room opens and Mom rushes in with red eyes and her face puffy from crying. Serena stands behind her, an apologetic look on her face as she watches Mom rush across the room to wrap me up in her embrace.

"Oh god, baby. Are you okay? Serena said you were stabbed!" Mom sits on the side of the bed and cups my face in her hands, scanning me like she's looking for evidence that I'm truly okay and not actually dying. I flinch when her leg bumps against my stitches, causing her face to crumple in slow motion when she sees I'm in pain. "Oh baby, I'm sorry. Did I hurt you?" She nearly smothers me, cradling my face against her shoulder.

I pat her arm until she lets up and lets me pull away from her. Taking her hands in mine, I try to reassure her before giving her the worst news. "I'm okay, Mom. I promise." I glance in Serena's direction, hoping she will stick around. I'm afraid Mom will need more support than I can physically give her once she learns her other son is dead. She gives me a nod—a silent communication, letting me know she's here to stay.

"The doctor said I should be okay to go home tomorrow. None of my major organs were injured. I'll just have to take it easy while I heal. I lost a lot of blood." Mom's face pales at my words, so I give her hand a reassuring squeeze. "I'm okay." I speak the words slowly, giving them a chance to sink in. When the worry in her face relaxes a fraction, I suck in a deep breath before preparing to telling her the rest.

"How did this happen, Dane? Did you get stabbed on the job? Did they get the person who did it?" She glances back at Serena, firing off more questions in her direction. "Were you there? Did you see it?"

"Mom, look at me." Squeezing her hand again, I wait for her to turn her attention back to me. My throat feels thick with emotion as I try to get the next words out. Slowly her eyes drift back to meet mine. "Bryce is the one who stabbed me. He was hurting Everly, and I stopped him. We fought; he stabbed me; he went after Everly… I'm not sure what happened, but he's dead, Mom. Bryce is dead." I don't want to say too much about what happened. Not while Everly is being questioned. I'm not sure what she will say, if anything, but I don't want our stories to conflict. Not until I get a chance to talk to her myself.

The progression of emotions that cross over my mother's face as I tell her what happened nearly rips my heart out. The way her mouth drops open in shock as the color drains from her face tells me any further bad news is going to be more than she can handle. She raises one trembling hand, covering her mouth as a horrified sob escapes her throat.

"B-Bryce..." Trailing off, her eyes fill with more tears as she processes everything I just told her. "No...no... That can't be right. Not my Bryce..." She tries to move away, but I tighten the grip I have on her hand.

"Mom, listen to me. He was abusing Everly. She called me for help. When I got there, he was choking her. I had to stop him before he killed her."

Serena comes up behind my mom, placing a supportive hand on her shoulder. The gut-wrenching wail that leaves my mother comes from a place only a parent who has experienced the death of a child knows. I watch as Serena gently holds my mom, as the weight of grief crushes her spirit completely. Mom buries her face in her hands, muttering denials between hiccupping sobs, refusing to believe what I've told her. I can't even blame her. Who would want to believe one of their children is capable of trying to kill the other?

I decide then that the truth about the worst of Bryce's crimes will die with him, because my mother doesn't deserve to know any pain greater than this.

CHAPTER 44
EVERLY

When I finally walk out of the police station, it's dark outside. Jessica arrived forty minutes after I got off the phone with Dad, resting bitch face and power suit in place. We had a brief chat before the investigating officers came in to do their questioning. I will forever be grateful for her presence. Between the nerves, concussion, fatigue, and oppressive guilt weighing on me, I don't think I would have gotten through the interrogation without winding up in jail. She interjected when needed and kept me from saying anything that would make the officers inclined to think what happened was more than a case of self-defense gone tragically wrong.

There is a chill in the brisk fall air as the wind blows, but I don't mind it as much now that I'm outside. The fresh air helps revive me some after being trapped in the interrogation room, with the stagnant air and stale smell of burnt coffee in the air, for hours on end.

"Do you have somewhere to stay? Your dad told me to

make sure you're taken care of before I head back into the city. I can book a hotel room for you on my corporate card until your house is no longer considered a crime scene."

I stop in my tracks, turning to face Jessica. She's looking down at her phone, scrolling through a hotel booking website, already looking for a place.

"I can't go home?" I'm honestly not sure if I want to go home, but it hadn't occurred to me that I wouldn't even have the option.

"I can take you by to pick up some clothes and necessities, but it's still considered a crime scene until the investigation is completed, so you can't stay there. It shouldn't take more than a few days, but then there will be clean up needed. Sounds like it might've gotten bloody." Jessica doesn't look up when she responds; she just taps on her phone more. In the last few hours I've learned she is a no-bullshit kind of person. She doesn't coddle, she doesn't let men steam roll over her, and she doesn't mince words. She can be abrasive, but I can already tell her attitude is the exact reason why she is good at her job. She doesn't let emotion rule her. She doesn't let anything get under her skin.

"I've got you three nights booked at the Magnolia. That will give you enough time to figure out what you want to do next. Hopefully they'll have the investigation wrapped up by then, but we can reassess in a few days."

My stomach turns at the thought of staying at the Magnolia. It holds painful memories of the moment I truly realized how fucking depraved my husband is—was—but it's still better than going home and seeing where Dane almost bled out thanks to Bryce.

"D-do you think they'll arrest me? Bryce had a lot of powerful friends. Do you think they'll make trouble for me?" A gust of wind blows, causing goose bumps to erupt over my skin, reminding me I'm still wearing flimsy hospital scrubs. This question catches Jessica's attention, and she finally looks up from her phone.

"Not if I have anything to do with it. We have a solid case for self-defense with your documented injuries. It's obvious Bryce was out of control and would've killed you if given the chance. Plus he went after Dane, and the boys in blue look after their own. Sometimes a little too well. I don't think you have anything to worry about." Her warm brown eyes soften with empathy, reassuring me just enough to let the tension out of my shoulders.

I nod, blinking back the fresh tears threatening to fall. Whether they're from relief, exhaustion, or just being overwhelmed, I'm not sure. All I know is I want to take a hot bath and sleep for the next three days.

I open my mouth to say something else, but she puts up a finger, stopping me.

"Don't say anything else until we are somewhere private. Let's go get your stuff, and I'll drop you off at the Magnolia. We will meet for breakfast in the morning and go over everything, okay? You need to rest." She gently takes me by the elbow and guides me to the sleek black Audi parked a few feet away. Once I'm in the passenger seat, my body cradled by the supple leather, Jessica turns on the heater, and I find myself unable to fight the urge to close my eyes, letting exhaustion pull me under. I fall asleep to the soft, soothing voice of a NPR correspondent reading off the day's headlines.

AFTER JESSICA GETS me checked into a suite at the Magnolia, assuring me all of the expenses are being covered by my dad, I take a long, hot bath before collapsing into bed. I fall into the deepest sleep I've ever experienced—the full body shutdown after an adrenaline crash is not to be underestimated.

THE NEXT MORNING, I wake up, disoriented and confused by the unfamiliar surroundings but feeling slightly less like run over roadkill. My head still aches, and my vision is still blurry from the concussion, but the bone-deep exhaustion is finally gone. The clock on the night stand reads 9:08 a.m. I slept for twelve straight hours. No wonder I have no fucking clue where I am. Groggily, I fumble around for my phone, to see if there are any messages waiting for me. I was so tired last night, I forgot to call my dad to let him know I had been released. I hate myself for even daring to hope that there is a message from Dane waiting for me. My heart clenches painfully when I see the only thing waiting for me is a text from Jessica. Not even a missed call from my dad checking in? I guess that answers the question of if it was me or his reputation he was more worried about.

JESSICA

I'll be at the hotel by 10. I'll bring pastries
and coffee.

Tea is normally my preferred morning beverage—caffeine makes me feel anxious—but I have a feeling this conversation is going to require something with a bit more oomph to it. I wonder briefly if I could convince her to stop by the liquor store so we can make those coffees Irish. Then there is sharp throb at my temple reminding me I'm concussed and alcohol is probably a bad idea.

I pop a few extra strength Tylenol before brushing my teeth and splashing water on my face, readying myself for the day. Looking in the mirror, I can still see dark circles shadowing my eyes, and the hair on the back of my head is thinner where the hospital staff shaved a patch in order to stitch up the gash I received during the struggle with Bryce. There are dark purple smudges on my neck where Bryce wrapped his hands around it, and there is a tender raised place on the side of my head. Cuts from the broken glass dot along my arms in a gruesome pattern. How many scars will I be left with to remind me of the worst day of my life?

Jessica's sharp, efficient knock brings me out of the whirlpool of sorrow threatening to pull me under. Right. I have to keep my shit together. When I open the door,

Jessica waltzes in, a box of pastries and two coffees balanced in one hand while her other pulls her rolling briefcase behind her. Her expression is all business; her stride so smooth the coffees don't even shake as she crosses the room. I have a feeling this is only half the amount of bad bitch energy she commands in the courtroom, and that puts me at ease.

She wastes no time in setting up her laptop and getting out a camera. I'm puzzled about why she has a camera, but I don't say anything. Instead I eye the box of pastries sitting on the table, and my stomach lets out an obscenely loud rumble, reminding me I haven't eaten in nearly twenty-four hours.

"Borborygmus."

"I'm sorry, what?" I shake my head at the nonsensical word Jessica just casually dropped while typing on her laptop.

"Borborygmus. It's the word for the sound your stomach makes when it growls."

"Oookaay…" I'm not sure how to respond to the non-sequitur, so I just pluck a scone from the box and take a bite. It's cranberry-orange, my favorite. Closing my eyes, I take a moment to savor the citrusy-sweet confection.

"Sorry, I'm not good at small talk. If you haven't noticed from the RBF, I'm not exactly a people person. I've been told little known facts or trivia can be a good icebreaker."

I blink, staring at Jessica's impassive face, and realize she is one hundred percent serious. Okay, at least now I know what I'm working with.

"Right. Well, we're good. You brought me sugar and

carbs, and I'm currently not sitting in a jail cell, so you're my favorite person at the moment." I flash her a grateful smile before taking another bite of scone.

She gives me a tight smile before adjusting the camera on the tripod. "I want to document your injuries and record our version of events while it's still fresh. So far I haven't heard of any official charges being brought against you, but I want to go ahead and establish our case for self-defense and head it off at the pass if we can. You have a very strong case already, and combined with Dane's statement, I think you'll be in good shape. Even if Bryce had friends in high places, I doubt they'd be willing to tarnish their reputation to defend a wife beater once your story comes out."

"Comes out?" I blink as my brain slowly processes Jessica's rapid-fire stream of words.

"We will tell the world what kind of monster Bryce was and how he hurt you. We will make him look like the biggest POS since Scott Peterson. You get public sympathy on your side early, and they won't dream of bringing up charges."

I think about her words, and it's not the getting away with murder part that kindles a spark of excitement in my chest. It's the telling the world what kind of person Bryce Carmichael really was part that ignites a fire inside of me. He may not have to pay for what he did to Jake, but maybe if I shine a light on his willingness to tamper with witnesses and evidence, I can help other victims of his corruption get justice.

"Let's do it."

JESSICA LEAVES after the most grueling six hours of my life. She makes me recount every instance of manipulation, coercion, gaslighting and abuse that Bryce put me through. She has me tell her about the night of the gala, when he tried to dangle me in front of Shane as a bribe for making a backroom deal for one of his clients. She makes me recall everything in vivid detail—going back, repeating details, lining up timelines, confirming facts as she's able when I give dates and times. She is not leaving any openings for someone to weasel in and discredit my version of events. She photographs the blotchy purple bruises on my neck and arms and the stitches on my head. When she leaves the hotel room, I am wrung out and hollow. My face is red and puffy from crying, but now I am empty. Empty of tears. Of feelings. I poured out every bit of resentment, guilt, fear, anger, sadness, and hurt into telling my story.

I hope it's enough.

Enough to destroy whatever reputation and goodwill Bryce ever had. He doesn't deserve to be remembered as a good man. He doesn't deserve to be mourned. I know if Caroline hears all this she will be devastated, but this is the least I can do for Dane. I can show him I'm on his side.

I know there is still a distinct possibility of Dane opening an investigation into his father's death, and if he does, I won't fight it. As my last act of contrition, I decide to write Dane a letter, letting him know the ball is in his court now.

When I finish with the letter, I send Serena a text asking if she'd be willing to deliver it to Dane for me. I know a letter is the coward's way out, but I can't face him and see the hate he must have for me in his eyes. I want to remember what we had before it all went to shit. It's selfish of me, but it's all I have left at this point.

CHAPTER 45
DANE

Three days later, I am finally discharged from the hospital. The doctors have been dragging their feet on signing off on my discharge, but after I threatened to leave AMA, Dr. Oleander finally relented and signed off. Three long days of staring at white walls, listening to beeping monitors and overhead hospital pages, and barely sleeping thanks to the multiple nightly check ins from nurses doing their rounds. Three agonizing days of simmering in anger, confusion, and guilt. I refused to take the narcotics the doctor prescribed for the pain. When they tried to administer the dose through my IV after I fully woke up, I ripped the IV catheter out of my arm, forcing the nurse to agree to stick to over the counter pain relief.

The physical pain is the only thing that rivals the hurt of betrayal I've been wrestling with since learning the truth of Dad's death. It's the only thing that keeps me from falling into a bottomless pit of despair over how fucking foolish I was. Everly pushed me away time and time again, but I wouldn't listen. I had to have her, and now look. Both of our lives are in ruins. Old wounds have been ripped open, left gaping and oozing to the elements, while fresh wounds bleed us dry. How do we even come back from something like this?

Now I am waiting for Mom to pick me up so I can go home and wrestle with my demons in silence. That and hopefully sleep for a week straight. I know it won't happen. There's going to be statements to make, paperwork to fill out so I can take leave from work, and I'll have to figure out how to help Mom afford the rent on her house now that Bryce isn't paying for it, but a guy can dream, can't he?

A knock on the door interrupts my thoughts. "Come in." I expect for either Mom or one of the nurses who have been hovering over me non-stop to come in, but it's Serena who enters the room. "Hey, what are you doing here?"

I'm surprised to see Serena. She normally gives me a heads up before her daily check in. Not that I've been great company. I mostly sit in silence while she updates me on what's going on at the station and if there is any progress on the investigation of Bryce's death. She has to keep the details vague since I'm considered a part of that investigation, but from what I've gathered, Everly's lawyer has been laying groundwork on showing a history of abuse from Bryce, effectively squashing any motivation to really dig into the circumstances of his death. As angry as I am at Everly, I don't think she deserves to be tried for his murder. He was an evil fuck, and the world is better off with him gone.

Serena comes over and tosses a white envelope on my lap. "Everly asked me to drop this off for you. She said she hopes you read it, and she'll go along with whatever you decide to do."

I look up at her, brows pinched in confusion. She just shrugs her shoulders, before slumping down into the green vinyl "recliner" next to the bed. She watches me, a keen interest in her eyes letting me know she's not going to let me get out of this conversation by being a grumpy asshole.

"Look, I've been where Everly is. I know what it's like to survive an abusive relationship. I know you're a good man, Dane, even if your brother was a piece of shit. But there is more going on here than you're telling me, and I want to know what it is. A woman like Everly doesn't deserve to go to jail for stopping her abuser, and I want to make sure she's not confessing to something stupid out of some misplaced sense of loyalty or guilt. If she's trying to protect you because Bryce caught you dipping your dick into his cookie jar, I will have to step up and say something. I like you, Dane. I do. But as a woman, I will stand by Everly. I won't let her go down to protect a man. Even if it's you. That is not why I became a cop." Serena levels me with her no-bullshit stare, and I don't argue with her. I know better than to pick a fight I won't win. Instead I pick up the letter and read it.

Dane,

I'm writing this letter to you not to ask your forgiveness or make excuses for my actions, but to give you the power to get justice for your father's death.

That night ten years ago, when Bryce came home shaken up, scared, and broken, he was still the man I loved. The man who I built a life with. The man who saved me. Held me. Took me to Paris. The man I had promised my heart to. He was still good. At least, I thought he was.

He sobbed while I held him, devastated because of the death of his own father and scared because his emotional outburst has caused Jake's death. At least, that's the story he spun for me. And I, a woman blinded by love, swallowed my own doubts and questions and agreed to keep his secret. I kept it because I believed he truly was remorseful. I also kept it for your mother's sake. I believed him when he told me telling the truth would destroy her. He made me believe if she knew the truth of Jake's death, then she would be losing both her husband and her son, and I just couldn't do that to her. This isn't an excuse. I know it was wrong, but I hope it at least helps you understand my motives were pure, even if my actions weren't.

The weight of that secret has been an albatross hanging around my neck for the last ten years. It's been slowly killing me, watching the man I thought I loved disappear. Replaced by some twisted, corrupt version that looked like my husband but wasn't him. Now I wonder if maybe the version I married wasn't real. Just a mirage, shiny and beautiful enough to seduce me into believing in it.

When you came back into my life, showing me empathy and kindness, my lonely heart craved it, but the guilt wouldn't let me believe I deserved it. This is why I kept pushing you away, and god, I am so sorry that I wasn't strong enough to keep pushing. I never should have let things between us go as far as they did. I was too selfish to fight the way you made me feel, even knowing if you ever learned the truth you would hate me and I would deserve every bit of it. This is why I was so hellbent on proving Bryce's corruption. I thought maybe if I could find evidence of something, he would finally suffer some kind of consequences. I just wanted to do something to make it right for you.

If you want to open an investigation into your father's death, I will cooperate. I will tell them everything I know about that night. Consider this letter my confession.

I regret every day not going to the cops the night he confessed, but I can't bring myself to

regret those stolen moments of happiness with you,
even if I had no right to them. Thank you for
showing me what true happiness really looks like.
Everly

MY HEART CLENCHES PAINFULLY as I read her letter. I feel the anger that had been simmering in my veins fizzle out as her words soak in. Did I not come to the same conclusion when I told Mom Bryce was dead and chose to keep his secret? Do I have any right to hold on to my anger at her when we both made the same choice? She did try to push me away. She tried to do the right thing, and I'm the one who pursued her. I pursued her knowing full well she was married. I am not blameless in this situation.

Serena watches me as I wrestle with my conscience, all the pent-up anger from the last few days slowly ebbing out of me like the tide flowing back out to sea. Looking at my friend, I give her a reassuring nod.

"You don't have to worry about Everly. I won't do anything that will implicate her in Bryce's death." Serena's brows furrow, like she doesn't fully believe me.

"This is about something else. Something that happened a long time ago. It's not worth dragging up now. It can't be changed, and it will only lead to more people getting hurt. She just…wanted to apologize. Look, I'll talk to her when I get home. I've been discharged, and I'm just waiting for Mom to pick me up." Serena's face relaxes at my reassurance.

"Good. Look, I don't know what she has to apologize for, but I hope you know that woman deserves to have a peaceful life now. I saw the recorded statement she made for her lawyer, and your brother deserved worse than what he got. Do not fuck up her path to healing. You understand?" Serena's fierceness when it comes to defending domestic abuse survivors is exactly why she is needed in the force. Not enough cops believe women when they come forward asking for help, and I'm proud to call her my partner.

I nod my understanding. "I won't. I promise. Just...let me know if the investigation takes a turn in the wrong direction, okay?"

"I don't think it will. Not after seeing that video. I don't recommend watching it unless you want to get in the mood to piss on your brother's corpse and light it on fire."

The anger that flashes in her eyes terrifies me briefly, reminding me exactly why I don't want to be on her bad side.

Just then, Mom arrives, cutting our discussion short. Serena stands up, taking the opportunity to leave.

"I'll come by and see you when you're settled. Take it easy, D. Mrs. Wilcox." Serena gives Mom a brief goodbye hug before making her escape.

Mom looks confused about Serena leaving so abruptly, but she is gone before Mom can protest. Mom looks like hell, her face pale and her eyes shadowed by exhaustion. She's been at the hospital with me as long as visiting hours would allow her, but I can tell it's taking a toll on her. She went home to take a nap and freshen up while I was waiting to be discharged, but it is clear she wasn't able to rest at all.

We haven't spoken much about Bryce. She cried for what seemed like hours after I told her what happened that night at Everly's. She just kept saying she was sorry, like all of this was somehow her fault. Then she kept vigil at my bedside, doting and fussing over me, making sure I didn't want for anything, like somehow, maybe she could make it up to me. We don't say much as I take a seat in the wheelchair she pushes into the room, and she does one last sweep, looking for any personal items I might be forgetting. Not that I came with much, considering how unexpected my stay was. I just have the clothes I'm wearing, my phone, and now the letter that I keep clutched in my fist. She wheels me outside, and for the first time in days, I'm able to breathe in fresh, not-hospital air.

"ARE you sure you don't want to stay at my house for a few nights? You've got those steep stairs to get up to your loft, and I worry you'll pull your stitches." Mom shoots me another worried glance as she pulls away from the front entrance of the BFH. Her small sedan creeps through the parking lot at a snail's pace. Mom doesn't drive much these days, and it shows. She is white-knuckling the steering wheel while driving ten under, and I'm not sure if she's more worried about other drivers or jostling my injuries by hitting a speed bump too fast.

"I just really want to sleep in my bed, Mom. I've been kept awake by nurses poking and prodding me all hours of the night, my side hurts like a bitch, and I'm tired as fuck. I promise all I will do when I get home is sleep." I shoot her what I hope is a reassuring smile, but it feels forced. I'm not lying. I am exhausted. I'm also desperate to be alone so I can call Everly and talk to her. After reading the letter, I have to let her know I am not going to hold her accountable for Bryce's crimes. Serena is right. Everly deserves the chance to find peace now.

We haven't spoken since the altercation with Bryce, and I have no idea how she's doing. Hopefully Serena is right about the video testimony being enough to shut down any further investigation into Bryce's death. Between that and the statement I gave to Officers Brady and Vaughn while lying in a hospital bed recovering from that fucking stab wound Bryce gave me, we'll ensure it is. I was very adamant in letting them know he was dangerous and violent. I may have left out the part where I took the first swing but considering everything, I don't feel even a little bad about it.

Mom lets out an unhappy huff at my response, but when she reaches the parking lot exit, she turns in the direction leading to my apartment and not her house. Along with the burning need to talk to Everly, to let her know I read her letter, I just need some time alone to process the maelstrom of feelings I've been experiencing after learning the truth of Dad's death. Without Mom hovering nearby, looking like she's on the verge of a nervous breakdown.

Seeing Mom return to that dark emotional pit she buried herself in after Dad's death is one of my biggest fears. It's not like he can be punished for it now, so what is the point of telling anyone? He's dead. His reputation is trashed. Depending on the extent of the backroom deals and blackmail he did to win cases, some of his may be reopened. The only thing bringing that truth to light will accomplish is destroying what's left of my mother's grieving heart. Knowing her son died as an abuser is a tough enough pill to swallow.

Twenty minutes later, Mom follows me through the front door, hovering behind me like I'm learning to walk for the first time and she's going to catch me if I fall.

"Do you want me to make you some lunch? Dinner? I can cook some meals that you can just reheat so you don't have to be up cooking. The doctor said you need to limit your activity so you don't pull your stitches. You're still anemic from blood loss. They said it will take a few weeks to get your energy back. I can come by and help with your laundry."

We make it as far as my couch before I'm overwhelmed by exhaustion and Mom's suffocating mothering. This is the exact opposite of the husk of a woman who left me to fend for myself during my most volatile adolescent years. I should be grateful that she's throwing her grief into concern over me and not despair over her dead son. I'll take being smothered over her losing the will to live again.

"Thanks, Mom. That'd be great." I try to hide my

grimace as I slowly settle onto the couch in a comfortable position so she can stop hovering. I guess calling Everly will have to wait. While Mom busies herself in the kitchen, I reread Everly's letter, desperate to feel connected to her again now that the anger poisoning me is gone.

Two hours, three BLTs, one crockpot full of chicken tortilla soup, and five forehead checks later, Mom leaves. She only relented when I promised my only plan for the rest of the day was crawling into bed and sleeping. I'm not sure exactly what it is she expects me to get into, but it became clear as time wore on and her worrying didn't decrease that maybe she's not coping as well as I thought. I make a mental note to talk to her about touching base with her therapist ASAP.

I decide to take a quick shower to wash the hospital off before crashing. In the bathroom, under the obnoxiously bright vanity light, I examine the angry red scar marring my left oblique. It's about three inches wide. Jesus, how big was that piece of glass? I try to remember if the doctor said anything about getting the wound wet, but I'm too tired to think. Looking in the mirror, I see the exhaustion etched onto my face. My eyes are bloodshot and my skin pale under my facial hair, which is now more closely resembling a beard than my usual stubble. Fuck it. Shaving can wait.

After the world's hottest shower, I'm lying in bed, staring at my phone, finger hovering over the call button. Everly's face, a profile picture linked to some social media account, stares at me, her mouth split into dazzling smile with the wind blowing her hair wildly around her face, framed by a bright blue ocean behind her. I need to call her. I need to talk to her. I need to let her know I forgive her. I need her to know that before she decides to come clean about something she can't take back. Before she decides to take my silence as condemnation and writes another letter of confession to give to the cops.

Pressing call, I inhale a steadying breath and wait for her to answer. After one ring, my call goes to voicemail and my heart clenches.

"Hi, this is Everly. I can't answer your call. Please don't leave a message. I won't listen to it. Text like a normal person instead."

Dammit, Everly. I don't want to leave a voicemail or send an incriminating text while there is an open investigation. We don't need to raise suspicion about our relationship and cast doubt on Everly's case for self-defense.

Instead I send a link to the song "Dig" by Incubus and hope she gets the message.

CHAPTER 46
DANE

Seven days, one very lengthy phone call to my mom reassuring her I am fine and that she doesn't need to come over and cook for me *again,* and more unanswered calls and texts to Everly than I care to admit to, I am stir-crazy enough to leave my apartment. The pain from my stab wound is down to a dull ache, and thanks to the hearty food and iron supplements Mom has been forcing me to consume, I finally feel strong enough to venture out on my own.

Serena has been my only connection to what is happening with Everly and the investigation. She has assured me that it doesn't look like anyone is going to press charges against Everly and that she's probably keeping her distance until that is certain, but that doesn't change the fact that it feels like she's absconded with a piece of my heart.

I've spent the last few days playing out the conversation I want to have with her in my head. I want her to know that I don't think any of this is her fault, and I don't blame her for keeping Bryce's secret. After seeing my mom's carefully constructed facade of being okay come crumbling down again, I have no doubt that knowing Bryce was the reason for her husband's death would have been more than she could bear. She resisted my suggestion to call her therapist at first, throwing herself into caring for me, to the detriment of her own well-being. It wasn't until I caught her sleeping in her car after she supposedly left my place, exhaustion from grief finally overcoming her, that I got her to agree to call and make an appointment.

I brought her back into my apartment and held her while she cried for the son she thought she knew. It was difficult, watching her heartbreak all over again in real time, and as much as I hate Bryce for what he did, I can't begrudge my mother from mourning him. She doesn't know how twisted and black his soul really was. As far as she is concerned, Bryce became possessive and jealous over Everly and thought she was cheating on him, and he was more like his father than any of us realized. Letting Brian's fucked up genes take the blame for what went wrong with Bryce is a kindness I am granting to my mother—it has nothing to do with protecting his legacy.

But I have to talk to Everly. There is an urgent need inside me to let her know she doesn't have to hate herself for what she did and to make sure she doesn't try to sacrifice herself to balance some moral scale. I want her to know we can just let him go and move on with our lives.

I swipe my car keys off the hook by the front door and open it, finding it as gloomy and bleak outside as it is inside my mind. Heavy gray clouds hang in the sky, looming over the trees, threatening to unleash a torrential downpour at any moment. I hesitate, wondering if this is an ominous sign I should heed, but the ache in my chest is worse than the one in my side now, and I have to do something about it.

When I pull up in front of her house, there is a Coming Soon sign from a local realtor swaying gently in the breeze in the front yard. The police caution tape that was up during the investigation is gone. There is no sign of the bloody confrontation that happened in this quiet, gated community. My skin prickles at the thought that maybe Everly has left me completely. That she chose to run away from me. From us.

I park my car in their obnoxious circular driveway and jog up to the front door, pounding it with my fist. The wound in my side protests at the vigorous movement, but I ignore it. My heart is hammering in my chest, fear that I'm going to find an empty house and no Everly sending me into a panic. *Please be here.* I send up a silent prayer, hoping I haven't missed my chance to let her know how I feel.

An intolerable amount of time passes before I hear footsteps on the other side of the door. "Everly!" I pound on the door again, relishing in the pain as I hit it harder than I should with my fist. The pain is a momentary distraction from the anxiety building inside of me. That foreboding sense of being too late is thrumming through every synapse.

Pressing my forehead to the door, I plead with her

again. "It's Dane, Ever. Please open the door. We need to talk."

There is quiet shuffling on the other side of the door. Furtive movements like she's struggling with what to do. Then I hear a soft sigh and the turn of the deadbolt. When the door swings open, there she stands, fragile and broken. Her hair has been cut short, in an asymmetric bob that shows off the angry, red gash on her scalp. Her face is pale and eyes bloodshot. From tears or lack of sleep, I have no idea. Her body is covered completely in a chunky sweater with an oversized collar but I can see splotches of purple, green and yellow marring the creamy skin of her neck, and it sends a fresh wave of hatred toward my brother coursing through me. He did this. He broke her, and I have to fix it.

"Dane, why are you here?" Her voice is soft. Timid. She glances past me to the driveway, like she's worried someone will see us. Her body language is closed off, and I can tell I'm going to have an uphill battle getting her to listen to me.

"We need to talk. Can I come in?" As much as every instinct in my body is screaming to go to her and pull her into my arms, I hold back. I will not be like my brother. I will not take away her choices or manipulate her. I watch as she bites nervously on her bottom lip, considering my request before slowly nodding and stepping aside to let me in.

Entering the foyer, I see cardboard boxes against the wall. The smell of bleach and cleaning products is thick in the air. I guess that means the crime scene cleanup crew has been out here already.

She watches me as I cast my eyes around the space, taking in the bare walls that used to hold framed photos of her and Bryce, documenting their make believe fairy-tale romance.

"You're moving?" The question is painfully dumb based on how obvious the answer is, but I'm not sure how to begin now that I have her in front of me. The connection that flowed between us the last time we made love, tethering my soul to hers, feels brittle and fragile. I'm afraid if I say the wrong thing it will shatter into a million pieces, causing me to lose her forever.

"I can't stay here. Not after everything. This life was built on lies. I don't want it." She turns, leading me to the living room where open boxes sit, half packed with a myriad of books and pictures, waiting to be filled. I follow her like a puppy, unable to be apart from her for one second. The bleach smell is strongest at the bottom of the stairs as we pass them, the only sign that this is where Bryce died.

"Where are you going to go?"

"I don't know yet. My friend Ana has a guest house, so I'm going to stay with her until this house sells. Then…I'm not sure. I just know I can't stand to be in this house any longer. It was never mine to begin with. This house was Bryce's dream. I thought it was mine too, but now that he's gone I don't feel like I belong here." She turns to face me, her lips set in a thin, determined line. "Why are you here, Dane?"

"I've been trying to get in touch with you, but you

haven't been returning my calls." I reach out to grab her hand, but she steps back, out of my reach.

"My lawyer advised me it would be a good idea for us to keep our distance until the case is officially closed." She averts her eyes when she says those words, and I have a feeling it's more her idea than her lawyer's. That realization stabs me in the heart.

"Does she know? About us?" Everly shakes her head, causing the longer half of her hair to shift, curtaining one of her eyes. She bites her bottom lip again, and I can see where she's worried it so much it looks chapped and raw.

"No. I told her he wanted me to convince you to help him with a case and he became paranoid that we were having an affair behind his back, but I haven't told her the full truth. She just thought it would be a good idea for us to not give the police any reason to pull on that thread and look deeper. If…if you want to tell her *everything*, you can. I won't deny it. I meant what I said that night. I will take the blame for hiding the truth of Jake's—"

I cut her off with a kiss. It's gentle, barely more than a brush of my lips against hers, but it does the trick. She lets out a soft gasp and looks at me with bewilderment dancing in her hazel eyes.

"Listen to me, Everly." I cup her face in my hands, directing her gaze to my face so she can't hide from what I'm about to say. I will not leave without telling her how I feel. If she can't be with me after that, I'll accept it, but I have to let her know. I won't let her linger in this hellish purgatory full of guilt and self-loathing. Not when I know her heart is so good.

"I forgive you." Her lower lip trembles at those words, so I press on, making sure I make myself abundantly clear.

"I forgive you. I understand why you didn't say anything. I know you were trying to do what you thought was right. Bryce is the one I hate. Not you. Never you."

Tears shimmer in her eyes as she lets my words sink in. It takes a long, long moment for them to seep through the layers of remorse, shame, and culpability I know she's buried herself in. She tries to look away, but I hold her face firmly, making her hold my gaze.

"I love you. I know we have some epic, fucked up baggage we are going to have to work through, but you're it for me, Everly, and I need you to know that. I don't blame you. You're a victim of his fucked up manipulation. Do not let Bryce's darkness diminish the light inside of you, Everly." Silent tears trickle down her cheek, and I brush them away with my thumb. I see the shadows that have been haunting her flicker and fade out as the tears come pouring out of her, cleansing what I hope is the last of the guilt burdening her soul.

I wrap Everly in my arms, clutching her delicately to my chest, letting her pour her grief into me, praying this is the moment we can begin again anew.

CHAPTER 47
EVERLY

Dane's arms wrapped around my shoulders—locking my body against his in the safety of his embrace, while I finally let my grief out—feels more right than any of the previous years of my marriage to his brother. The soft, worn cotton of his T-shirt dampens from my tears as sobs rack through my body, expelling all the grief I held back over Bryce's death.

I haven't let myself mourn properly or process Bryce's death, too busy trying to right his wrongs and make up for the complicity of my silence. I haven't mourned the boy I married. The man I loved. The husband I thought I knew. The lie I lived. I've become a shark, forcing myself to keep moving, afraid if I stop I'll sink into the abyss and not be able to find my way back out. As soon as I got the okay to go home, I immediately began dismantling the charade that was our perfect life, unwilling to play along with the farce any longer.

The last few days have been full of long, grueling

hours of packing away a life built on lies and dealing with all the paperwork involved with Bryce's passing. I donated his suits to a local nonprofit that helps the unhoused get back on their feet and find jobs. I've packed away photos, mementos of a life that I'm not even sure was real. Donated the clothes I barely wore because I hated dressing like a stepford wife when Bryce trotted me out at events like a show dog. The longer I worked at deconstructing the life we had together, the more I realized how much I hated it. Hated how little of me there is in this house. How little of my dreams I got to follow. I threw myself into the work of closing this chapter so maybe one day I can live the life I once imagined having, as a hopeful young girl who had dreams of helping others.

Dane isn't the only person whose calls I haven't returned.

I've ignored calls from his business associates and our "friends", their proffered condolences little more than thinly veiled attempts at getting more information for the rumor mill. I've seen news vans parked in front of our house and reporters going door to door interviewing the neighbors. When something bloody and violent rocks a quiet, posh community like this, they love to try to come up with a reason why. An explanation. Some sort of anomaly. A deviation from the status quo that would lead to such a tragedy so they can point and say, "Oh, that was just an outlier, that could never happen again. Not here. Not in our neighborhood." Instead of looking inward to see how they too could fall to such ruin, they look for our faults so they can assign blame and sleep better at night tucked safe in their beds.

I don't know how long we stand there, entwined, as Dane absorbs my pain, my anger, my guilt. He takes it all and doesn't say a word. He just holds me, gently running his hand through my hair, giving me more comfort than I deserve, considering the role I played. The fact that he can forgive me after everything is testament to how much better he is than his brother, and he deserves so much more than what I can give him.

When I finally pull away from him, it is with great reluctance. I know once I leave his arms, I won't allow myself the privilege of his embrace again. When our eyes meet, there is worry in his. He knows what's coming next. He doesn't want it. Truthfully, I don't either, but I don't see any other way forward for us. How can there be with such a gulf of fucked uppedness between us?

"Everly—"

I cut him off this time, with a gentle finger to his lips. I don't dare let mine touch his again, afraid if I do, I won't have the strength to do what is right. Instead I take his hand and lead him to the couch, where we sit, facing one another. I try to put space between us, determined to do the right thing, but Dane scoots close enough that our knees touch, refusing to break the connection between us. There's resignation in his eyes, but also a steely determination. Like he knows what I'm going to say and is ready to make a counter argument.

"Listen to me, Dane. Your forgiveness is more than I deserve, and I will cherish it and do my best to earn it. I promise. But whatever this is"—I motion between us—"it can't happen. Not…not right now. I am not okay, and I need to find a way to be okay on my own. It's been so long since I've been *me*, and I need to figure out who I am now."

Dane's handsome face becomes a blank mask as he tries to hide how much my words are hurting him. Even now, he's trying to make sure he protects me, even from the consequences of my own choice. I try to lighten the mood, hoping he will see this is what I need more than anything.

"I need time. Time and a metric fuckton of therapy. Besides, I don't think your mom would be cool with me shacking up with one son after killing the other…"

The corner of Dane's mouth twitches, the barest hint of a smile, letting me know he knows I'm right.

"You made me realize how much I was missing out on. How much I had settled for. At one point I thought Bryce was everything I could ever want. Ever need. But then life became about fulfilling his goals. Making his dreams come true. Making sure his star was always rising. I thought once he got to where he wanted to be, then I could follow my dreams…but it was never enough for Bryce. There was always a bigger case, a higher position, another favor to curry. It was a never-ending pursuit for more fueled by ambition, and my dreams were just one of the casualties." As I speak, it feels like a weight is lifting from my shoulders. It wasn't just the weight of guilt crushing me before, I realize now, but the weight of everything I gave up for him. For a man who only saw me as tool to use for his own personal gain. I see how Dane's leaf-green eyes soften at my vulnerability, understanding dawning on him that I'm not pushing him away because he's not enough for me. But because I need to be enough for me.

"I need to figure out how to live for me. How to find my own happiness. You understand that, don't you?" I grasp one of his hands, noting the fading yellow bruise left behind from the IV he must have had in the hospital. It matches my own slowly fading bruise on my wrist. I move to pull away, but his warm hand closes around mine, stalling my retreat. Delaying this break between us.

"Can I ask one favor, Ever?" Dane looks at me with such earnestness that I would give him anything he asks for. Pushing him away is already the hardest thing I've ever done. I don't know how much longer my resolve to do the right thing will last.

"Sure, Dane. Anything."

"Promise me you won't cut me out. Let me still be your friend. I'll give you all the time you need, just don't disappear on me. I want to see your light shine."

I nod, unable to speak, my composure on the brink of crumbling again. I have to get through this. I have to let him go. He must sense how fragile my grip is on my emotions. Leaning in, Dane places one last kiss on my forehead before standing and backing away slowly toward the door.

"Take care, Ever. I'll be here when you figure out who you are." He winks playfully, trying to keep moment from becoming too melodramatic. I love him for that.

Just as he reaches the door, I spot the brown package on the coffee table that I had been steadfastly ignoring for the last two days.

"Oh! Dane, wait!" I grab the box and meet him at the front door. "Umm…these are Bryce's ashes. I had him cremated per the instructions in his will. I wasn't planning on holding a service because…well, because, but I wanted your mom to have them so she can do something. I'm so sorry I didn't get these to her sooner, but I was waiting until the investigation was officially closed and…honestly I don't know what to say to her…" I trail off, letting my guilt simmer between us. Facing the mother of my husband after taking his life feels like more than I can bear right now. Dane looks at the nondescript container holding what's left of his brother, his face now a mix of confusion, repulsion, and sadness. The exact slurry of emotional turmoil I felt when I picked it up from the funeral home.

A long moment passes between us while he wrestles with his conscience over taking it. Eventually he nods and takes the box from me, tucking it under his arm.

"Thanks, Ever. I'll make sure this gets to Mom."

Then he's gone. One second he's there and then I'm alone again. This time though, I'm alone because I chose to be. Not because I was forgotten about. And that makes all the difference.

CHAPTER 48
EVERLY

It's been three weeks since the police officially closed the investigation into Bryce's death. It was ruled self-defense during a domestic dispute once all the evidence was examined, and I had to recount the events of the alter-cation so many times I thought I was being forced to relive it as some sort of hellish Groundhog Day-esque punish-ment to atone for my part in things.

Despite the brave face I put on for Dane the day I said goodbye to him, I'm a wreck. Falling apart at the seams, held together only by sheer force of will not to let Bryce win. Sleep has been hard to come by. The nightmares of a ghoulish zombie Jake begging me to tell the truth have been replaced with Bryce straddling my chest, choking the life out of me with dark eyes burning with anger. I wake up sweat-soaked, heart trying to burst through my chest, adrenaline pumping through my veins almost every night. The first time I had the nightmare, I vomited on the carpet next to the bed, then wound up curled in a fetal position, sobbing until exhaustion forced my eyes to close, letting me drift off into a mercifully dreamless sleep.

That was the last time I slept in the house I shared with Bryce. I finished packing up the rest of my belongings, hired an auction company to handle the sale of the rest of Bryce's estate, and moved into Ana's guest house. Nightmare Bryce still haunts me, but waking up in the chic, airy space of the minimalist but somehow trendy guesthouse makes it easier for me to remind myself that it isn't real. That he can't hurt me any longer. I can more easily fall back to sleep. Every day it gets incrementally better. I have hopes by the time I turn forty I might actually be sleeping through the night again.

I'm bleary-eyed, waiting for my chai latte at Brewed Awakening, when I hear a familiar voice call out my name. I look up, expecting to find the barista holding my to-go cup, but they're still busy frothing milk behind the counter.

"Everly? Is that you?" A tentative voice floats toward me from the front of the cafe. Turning, I see Caroline standing at the entrance, looking as pale and as broken as I am. Dark circles ring her bloodshot eyes. She looks like she's sleeping as well as I am. I freeze, unsure of how to respond. Does she hate me for killing her son? For not talking to her after? Is she going to yell at me? Scream curses at me for being so callous and not checking on her? I took the coward's way out in giving Dane Bryce's remains to pass on to his mother, but what does one say to a woman grieving the loss of her child, when that child tried to kill them?

"Caroline…I…umm…" My mouth opens and closes, as my brain fails to come up with the appropriate greeting.

"Hi, good to see you. Sorry about killing your son?"

"Hey, sorry I've been MIA, but your son was a piece of shit, and I didn't know how to act around his grieving mother."

"I'd say I'm sorry but…"

Instead, when the barista calls my name, I take the escape route offered and turn away from her to grab my latte, praying she isn't about to announce to the crowded coffee shop that I'm the callous monster who killed her son and doesn't even have the decency to apologize for it. When I turn back around, she's still there, between me and the exit, looking sad. Tired. Broken. But not angry. There isn't a hint of anger in her expression.

"Can we talk, Everly?" Her question is hesitant, like she's fully expecting me to tell her no. To continue to ignore her pain and sorrow so I can avoid the tsunami of guilt I should feel for killing her child.

I inhale a fortifying breath, girding myself for the conversation I don't think I'm ready to have. That I'll never be ready to have. "Sure, Caroline." I nod and force my face into an expression that I hope resembles something sincere and empathetic, not the pained grimace it feels like.

She leads us to a table for two in a small alcove hidden by shelves full of books and plants. Brewed Awakening's mismatched, eclectic style creates lots of little nooks and privacy for their patrons so they can work in peace during busy hours. Right now I'm grateful we won't have an audience for what is about to be the hardest conversation I've ever been forced to have. We sit, silence stretching between us for what seems an eternity. I stare down at the paper cup in my hands, focusing on the little sticker featuring a cartoon fox drinking a coffee that covers the opening of the lid. I feel the tell-tale burn of tears threatening and I close my eyes in a futile attempt to fight them off. If anyone deserves to cry right now, it's Caroline, not me.

Soft, warm fingers wrap around mine, prying them away from the death grip they have on the paper cup that is perilously close to being crushed and spilling hot chai everywhere. "Dane told me what happened. I'm so sorry, Everly."

My head snaps up at her words, bewildered by her apology.

"Why are you sorry? I'm the one who should be sorry, Caroline—"

"I'm sorry for who Bryce turned out to be. I tried so hard to raise him to be a good man but he still turned into his father." Now I see the tears shining in her eyes, shame written all over her face, like somehow this was all her fault. That she was a failure as a mother. Knowing how Dane turned out, I know nothing could be further from the truth.

"Caroline." I want to say something, to tell her it isn't her fault, but she shakes her head, cutting me off again.

"Brian used to cheat on me. He traveled for work a lot and had mistresses in multiple cities. When I found out, he apologized and begged me to stay. I did, because we had Bryce. I was young, only worked part-time, and was scared of supporting the two of us on my own."

My heart cracks at Caroline's confession, knowing exactly how cold and alone she must have felt then.

"Things were okay for a while, but eventually I discovered another affair. When I tried to leave with Bryce, Brian called in a favor with some buddies in the PD and had me arrested for parental abduction. He threatened to take Bryce away from me if I ever tried to leave him. Brian had a lot of powerful friends in the right places in town, and I knew he could carry out his threat."

There is a damp heat on my cheeks, and I realize I'm crying. Not for myself or my shame, but for Caroline and the misery she must have endured, being trapped in a marriage like that. I only knew a fraction of the suffering she must have felt being trapped *with* a child.

"Then Jake came along and…things got better." A small smile ghosts her lips for the briefest of moments. "We fell in love. Dane came along. Brian left." I can see the shadow of happier memories flicker across her face. I know she's leaving a lot out, but I won't push her for the more painful details.

"Bryce had a hard time with his father leaving. Brian just abandoned us when he found out Dane wasn't his. I tried so hard to be everything Bryce would ever need. Mother and father. Jake did his best to treat Bryce as his own, but the wall was erected the moment Brian left without so much as a goodbye to us. To him, Dane was born, Jake showed up, and he didn't have a dad any longer. He was twelve years old. An awful time for a boy to lose a parent."

My lower lip trembles, my heart breaking for the boy

Bryce used to be. Knowing the full truth behind his childhood and dislike for Dane and Jake finally makes everything click into place. I feel the mental picture I have of him morph and shift like one of those terrible before and after plastic surgery transitions and realize just how long he was manipulating me. My blood runs cold, causing goose bumps to erupt over my skin. Was any of it true? Did he ever love me? He acted like his mom cheated on his dad, causing him to lose his loving and doting father. The news of his dad being an abusive manipulator rocks me to my core. Did he know? Surely he remembered his mom getting arrested? Did he know and still make Jake and Caroline out to be the guilty party?

"I had no idea, Caroline. I knew Bryce had a strained relationship with Jake, but he always implied it was because of the affair you had."

Caroline nods, like she expected my response. "I never told Bryce how his father treated me. We pretended to be a happy family for a while after the arrest. I took all the blame for that; maybe that was my mistake. Not letting Bryce know the truth about what kind of man his father was."

This time I grab her hand and squeeze. "No, you were trying to protect your boy. You were doing what you thought was best."

"I'm heartbroken that things ended for Bryce the way they did. I tried so hard to love him enough, to love the hurt and anger and abandonment away, but there was something broken in him that couldn't be fixed. I'm so, so sad for the boy I raised. I just want you to know, I don't blame you. Please don't blame yourself. I'm doing my best to do the same. My therapist has been helping me work through it. It's been rough, but...it's helping. If...if you need someone to talk to, you should call them." She pulls a business card out of her purse and pushes it into my hand.

My lips press together in a thin line as I bite back the urge to full on sob now. "I need to go, I'm going to be late for my appointment with Dr. Perkins. Everly, please take care of yourself. I still consider you my daughter." She gives my hand one final squeeze and vacates the table, leaving me to process this emotional tsunami building in me in private.

CHAPTER 49
EVERLY

"Knock, knock." A soft rapping at my door announces Serena's presence as she pokes her head into my new office in the creative wing of Whispering Grove's main building. "You ready to go? I had a hell of a day, and I need a glass of wine." Serena leans against the door frame, arms crossed, a furrow creasing her brow—a subtle indication of the kind of day she's had.

"Sure, rough day?" I ask, as I grab my purse and slip on my favorite faded denim jacket to ward off the chill of the spring evening as I follow Serena out to our cars. My wardrobe has become considerably more casual since being on my own. Bethany doesn't mind what I wear to work, knowing I'll wind up covered in paint or clay during the day. The feeling of finally doing what I love, what I studied for, while helping others, has honestly been the biggest piece of the puzzle in figuring out who Everly Carmichael is now.

I've been in my new position for almost three months now, and Serena and I have had a standing weekly girls' date since I started working here. She comes to visit her mom on Wednesdays, then stops by my office when she's done. We then usually go to a cute little bistro down the street that specializes in wine and cheese plates for a "girl dinner" and catch up.

I haven't been coming to game nights—I'm still trying to limit the amount of time I am around Dane while I am getting my shit figured out—but Serena refused to let me push her away. She still invites me to game night every week, even though I always come up with an excuse to skip it. She knows I'm not ready to be around Dane, so she doesn't push, but her invitations are a constant reminder that he's still there. Still waiting for me.

It's not like I've shut him out completely since that day when I said goodbye to him and told him I needed to figure out who I am. We text back and forth a few times a week. It's usually light conversation—mostly funny memes, interesting articles, general encouragement, or just quick hellos—but Dane is diligent about not letting the tether between us break. He doesn't push for more; he just patiently waits for me to decide when I'm ready to take the next step.

We've even run into each other in the wild a couple of times. It was awkward at first, me not sure how to act after telling him I needed time, despite the metric fuckton of baggage between us, but that man never lets it be weird. He always has a genuine smile for me, even if there is a hint of longing in his eyes when he looks at me. Even if there is more than a hint of longing for him in my heart. He'll ask me how I'm doing, listen intently when I talk, then gives me the briefest hug before saying goodbye.

One morning, when we bumped into each other at Brewed Awakening, he surprised me by telling me he saw the article in the Birch Falls Gazette about my new position as director of the Art Therapy program at Whispering Pines. The pride shining in his eyes was almost enough to break my resolve to keep him at arm's length and let him back in. But that was only three months after everything went down, and I still had a boatload of therapy to go to.

I was in the middle of rebuilding my life, establishing new boundaries with my dad, exploring my deep-seated daddy issues and working through my trauma with my new therapist, Dr. Perkins, while figuring out my new role at Whispering Pines. Inviting Dane and the swirling vortex of emotions and lust he stirs within me back into my life was not a good idea at the time. It's still not a good idea, but every day that passes leaving me feeling more firmly on my feet and more confident in who I am, makes me a little more inclined to throw caution to the wind.

As I follow Serena out of the building, she regales me with her afternoon filled with dealing with a crazy Karen who was convinced the neighbor's landscaper was casing her house to rob her. "He *owns* the company, Ever. They have four locations in the surrounding area. The house he owns in twice the size of hers. He was just stopping by to pick up some piece of equipment left behind by someone on his crew, and since this lady had never seen him before, she was convinced he was planning on breaking in to her house."

"Let me guess. Was it Mrs. Greene?"

Serena raises a surprised eyebrow at me over the top of her car, as we prepare to head to the bistro.

"How'd you know?"

"She lived two houses down from us before we moved to McMansion hell, and she was innately distrustful of anyone born after the Vietnam War. She used to yell at Bryce when he would go jogging past her house. Come to think of it, she might have been on to something..."

Serena lets out a very unladylike snort at the dig at my husband. She has been my rock these past few months, having been where I was, processing the realization of being a survivor of abuse.

It was a tough pill to swallow as I confronted all the red flags and signs I ignored while married to Bryce. How deeply I buried my head in the sand so I could pretend everything was fine. When, during my third appointment with Dr. Perkins, she told me I was a victim too, not just an accomplice, and she listed out all the subtle ways Bryce manipulated, controlled, and managed my life to the point I was isolated in his orbit with no life of my own. My mouth fell open at that particular truth bomb, and it was like one of those movie montages where the puzzle is solved and the world is saved.

Our entire relationship flashed before my eyes, and suddenly the red flags were everywhere. I upped my appointments from weekly to bi-weekly so I could work through that mindfuck. Serena having been through a similar relationship before Kai has been a godsend in helping me process all of this. Her irreverent, dry sense of humor allows me the freedom to be as snide and mean as I need to be as I work through my anger at my dead husband. Laughing through the pain is a million times better than simmering in anger and falling into depression.

When we are seated at our table at The Wine Thief, glasses of Riesling in hand, a mischievous look comes over Serena's face, erasing the annoyed tension that was there previously. "So when are you coming back to game night?"

Serena asks me this every couple of weeks. Outside of my therapist, she's the only person who knows the truth about my relationship with Dane. She knows why I am keeping my distance from him, but that doesn't stop her from tapping her foot impatiently, waiting for me to get my shit together so we can "get on with the inevitable", in her words. When I told her the full story of our relationship and depth of my betrayal, she said there was no way we would go through that kind of hell and not wind up together. I'm not as confident as her about her ability to manifest a romance novel-level happy ever after. Real life doesn't work like that.

My grasp on happiness is tenuous at best as I settle into the new version of my life, and I don't know if I could handle realizing the gulf of secrecy and guilt between us is too far to overcome and I lose him completely. No, I have to have my feet planted more firmly on the side of *mentally stable, emotionally independent* and *has fewer daddy issues* life before attempting to navigate that minefield of a relationship. I know happiness after surviving a situation like that is possible—I see it with Serena and Kai every day—but I also know how fragile that ground can be in the beginning. I can't take that step until I know I am one hundred percent not still punishing myself for what Bryce did.

I bite my lower lip, thinking of everything I still need to accomplish. After settling Bryce's estate, I gave the majority of it to Caroline, keeping only enough of the proceeds from the house sale to use as a down payment for a future home of my own and my art and studio equipment. If anyone should benefit from this entire fucked up situation, it should be Caroline. I've been house hunting recently, tiring of the commute from Ana's guest house. There's a cute little Craftsman with a "she-shed" that would make a perfect studio in the backyard that I have my eye on, two streets over from Serena. I don't mention it though, not willing to jinx my plans.

Instead I shrug and say, "I'm not ready, yet."

Serena just gives me an understanding smile at my response.

"Naomi brought one of her girlfriends to game night last week. She thought maybe Dane and Carmen would hit it off."

My stomach clenches, and I flinch at the thought of Dane hitting it off with someone else. I take a long drink of wine to try and hide the jealous knee-jerk reaction, but Serena catches it with her keen eyes.

"Oh?" I try to keep the jealousy out of my voice.

Serena quirks an eyebrow, not missing it, however.

"She might as well have been an interesting house plant

as far as Dane was concerned. When she asked him out at the end of the night, he managed to let her down so gently she still gave him a hug as she walked out the door."

The grip I have on the wine glass relaxes. She watches me for a long moment, cataloging all of my micro expressions. This is what makes Serena so good at her job and why one day I know she'll make detective.

"He's still waiting for you. I think he's always been waiting for you." Serena's reassuring words settle over me like a weighted blanket. Warm and comforting, settling my nerves, giving me the confidence to keep traveling the road I am on.

CHAPTER 50
DANE

I pull up to Serena's house, five minutes early for game night. I grab the six-pack of beer and bottle of Moscato I brought to share, but am nearly knocked down on the sidewalk by a very large, very furry, brown and white… muppet?

A horrified, familiar voice calls out, "Ulysses! No!"

Ulysses, the oversized teddy bear, pushes me against the side of my car, pinning me in place with his front paws while he assaults my face with his tongue. My hands are full of booze, and my only defense is to crane my neck back, trying to keep my face out of the danger zone. Ulysses is nearly as tall as I am, so he just licks my neck, which unfortunately for me, is the most action I've had in almost nine months.

"Oh my god; I'm so sorry." Ulysses' owner comes and pulls him off of me, recusing me from accidentally going to second base with a dog. "Bad dog, Uly! We don't jump!"

When I get my bearings, I realize the woman crouched

in front of me, scolding the dog-sized woolly mammoth, is Everly.

"Ever?" She jerks her head up, eyes wide with shock, just as surprised as I am. Why is she in front of Serena's house? Why does she have a dog the size of a small pony?

We haven't talked in a few weeks. Our texting relationship has drifted apart, replies becoming more sporadic and infrequent. I assumed that she was pulling back because she realized I wasn't who she wanted after all. To keep my mind off of that prospect, I threw myself into work. Serena and I have had our hands full with a new case, and I started teaching self-defense classes twice a week to college students.

"Dane, hey. Sorry about that; we are still learning our manners. Aren't we, Uly?" Everly's face lights up with a genuine smile, and I'm momentarily stunned by how beautiful she is. She still has the asymmetric bob, but the shorter side has grown out enough to cover her scar. It's also dyed a bright magenta. A color I know Bryce never would've approved of.

I'm speechless as I take her in. She's a little softer-looking now, less hollowed out, like she's finally getting a chance to enjoy life and indulge in her favorite treats. There's a flushed glow to her cheeks that reminds me so much of how beautiful she looks when she's coming around my cock. I have to look away before I get a boner and she thinks it's for the dog.

I'm not sure what to say next. It doesn't look like she's upset to run into me, or in a hurry to leave. It seems like she's genuinely excited to see me. "Uly? You got a dog?" I throw out the most neutral thing that comes to mind, instead of what my heart is dying to scream out to her. *I miss you. I'm drowning without you. Please come back to me.*

"One of the residents who just moved into Whispering Pines adopted him a few months ago, thinking he was going to be a mini version of a Bernedoodle. Uly is over the pet size limit for the apartments, so they had to re-home him. I offered to take him, since I know what being re-homed is like. I thought maybe Uly and I could be good for one another." Her lips turn up in a half smile, and my heart swells with pride at how well she seems to be doing. Then my brain remembers the other half of the equation that was confusing me.

"What brings you and Uly here? You coming to game night?" I try to mask the hope bubbling up. I don't want to assume this is more than it is.

"Oh, Uly and I were just on a walk… I, uh…" She trails off, her eyes glancing down to the ground, like she's guilty of something. "I live two streets over now."

Oh god, did she meet someone? Is she living with him now? Is that why she stopped texting? I swallow, trying to fight the bile rising in my throat. I only want Everly to be happy, and if she found someone else that does that… I honestly didn't think a future where we weren't together was possible. The thought of her with another man is like a gut punch. When she looks back up at me, her eyes go wide in horror, like she can see the devastation written all over my face.

"I bought a house! Two months ago. It's just me and Uly." She rushes these facts out so fast it takes my brain a solid thirty seconds to process them. *She bought the house. It's just her and the dog.* I blow out a slow breath, trying my best to calm my racing heart. Her soft hand cups my cheeks as she forces me to look her in the eyes.

"Dane, are you okay?"

"You…you didn't tell me. I thought maybe you decided it was better to move on." *Forget about me. Find a man who won't remind you of your dead husband.*

She grants me a sad smile as she shakes her head. "No—well, yes. It was time to move on. That's why I bought a house. I was ready to finally start my life for real. I wanted to make sure I was fully happy with my life. With myself. I wanted to know I could do it on my own. I had to know I was capable of being all I would ever need. I can't ever let myself get back to a place where I rely solely on a man."

Her words sting, being lumped in the same category as Bryce, but I know she's got every right to set that standard for herself. It isn't about me; it's about her knowing what she's capable of.

"I'm sorry; I should have said something, but I was afraid of giving you false hope for something that might never happen, and I didn't want you to feel like you had to keep waiting for me. You deserve to be happy, Dane. You didn't deserve to have your life put on hold while I worked through my shit. I thought if we were meant to be, we deserved to have a fresh start on the universe's terms."

"Are you?" The question comes out in a raspy whisper, my heart racing now for an entirely different reason.

"Am I?" Everly tilts her head to the side, brows

furrowed in confusion. She looks adorable, and I can't fight the grin that wants to break free.

"Happy?"

Her face breaks into a smile that mirrors my own.

"Yeah, I am happy."

It feels like there are fireworks going off in my chest.

"Well then, I think Uly here is the universe giving us our fresh start." At the sound of his name, Uly jumps up and once again assaults me with his tongue. Everly bursts into laughter and leaves me to my fate, but I'm okay with it, because I have a feeling there are going to be a lot more sloppy dog kisses in my future. Hopefully a few from Everly as well.

"Do you and Uly want to join us for game night? He can play with Archie in the backyard." I know Serena has been inviting Everly to every game night, so she won't mind. In fact, it might piss her off that I'm the one who finally brings Everly back into the fold, and the thought of being able to hold that over her head is delicious.

Everly only thinks on it for a moment before bobbing her head in an enthusiastic nod.

"Yeah, we'd like that." She hooks one hand into my offered elbow, and we let Uly drag us up the sidewalk to Serena's front door.

CHAPTER 51
EVERLY

The clatter of metal hitting tile causes my whole body to jerk in surprise just as I am applying one last swipe of mascara. The mascara wand jabs my eyeball, and it immediately begins to well up with tears. "Shit!" Within seconds, my left eye is a watery mess. Red and irritated with black running down my face, making me look like a sad clown.

Dane is coming over for dinner tonight. It's the first time I've invited him to my house. He's only made it to the front porch so far, only because he insists on walking Uly and me home after game night. We've been taking it slow the last several weeks, getting reacquainted with one another in a slow, careful, non-trauma bonded way. We've been attending game nights together, letting a new friendship bloom with the buffer of our friends there to help maintain the boundaries I've been hesitant to dissolve.

Dane has followed my lead and allowed me to set the pace for how things progress between us. Game nights, hikes with Uly, meeting for coffee before work. Casual, no pressure situations that allow me to slowly filter through the feelings I have been harboring for Dane, trying to suss out if they are real or simply a result of my desperate need to be loved and cherished by someone.

Therapy has done wonders for my abandonment and daddy issues, and I have decided that yes, they are real. Everything I feel for Dane, every spike in my heart rate, every breath of air that gets sucked from my lungs when seeing him, every blush that creeps up my cheeks when I catch him staring at me like I'm the brightest star in the sky…it's all real. And tonight is supposed to be the night I tell him that. Tell him that I want more. Tell him that he doesn't have to keep waiting.

I'm terrified that maybe I've made him wait too long and that maybe I've misread everything and he really is just my friend, but I won't let that fear hold me back from speaking my truth to him. I'm done letting the fear of chasing after my own happiness hold me back from living my life. After almost two decades of living the life Bryce wanted for us, I'm living for myself now.

More clattering comes from the kitchen, and I realize with horror that Uly must have gone counter surfing. "Fuck, fuck, fuck." I grab a washcloth, run cold water over it and press it to my face as I rush out of the bathroom to see the damage.

I find Uly happily slurping up the remnants of the pasta salad I made to go with dinner. He's so engrossed in finishing the job he doesn't even look up when I let out a frustrated yell. "Uly! No! Bad dog!" My heart plummets when a knock at the door comes, announcing Dane's arrival. "Ugh." I let out a frustrated groan at the situation, hoping Dane won't mind that dinner is missing half its main course.

I shoot one last reproachful glare at Uly as I mutter under my breath, "That's it. You're going to doggy boot-camp buddy. I'm signing you up tomorrow." Uly finally looks up at me, his tongue busily licking the dressing from the pasta salad that is still stuck to his fur. "You better hope nothing in that will make you sick. If I have to clean up doggy diarrhea tonight, you won't get any treats for a week." Another knock at the door causes Uly's ears to perk up, and he lets out a low *woof* before running to the front door to investigate our visitor.

When I pull open the door, Uly shoves past me, jumping up to greet Dane first. Dane laughs as he's forced back a step by the not-at-all miniature Bernedoodle.

"Hey there, big fella, yes, I missed you too."

My heart melts a little watching Dane with Uly, quickly causing my frustration with the muppet dog to dissipate.

"Down!" He barks out a sharp command, and Uly drops to his haunches instantly, the pup sitting at attention, staring up at Dane like he hung the moon.

"Why does he listen to you? It's not fair!"

The smile on Dane's face falls quickly when he finally moves his attention from the traitorous, date-ruining dog to my face. I must look like a mess, standing there half dressed, wet, dripping wash-cloth pressed to my face, effectively ruining my makeup. His expression quickly shifts to concern.

"Are you okay? What happened?" He pushes past the devil dog and cups my face in his warm hands, his eyes tracing over me with frantic concern that has me melting into his touch.

"I'm okay. I was in the bathroom finishing up my makeup when *someone*"—I cut an annoyed glare at the betrayer who is skulking off to his doggy bed by the couch —"decided he wanted to try the pasta salad I had prepared. The sound startled me, and I stabbed myself in the eye with a mascara wand." I pull away the washcloth and show Dane my raccoon eye. He presses his lips into a tight line, biting back a smile.

"It's fine; you can laugh. I know I look ridiculous." Dane just shakes his head and pulls me into a hug, tucking my head under his chin. My arms wrap around his waist, my body molding to his like two puzzle pieces meant to fit together. This is the closest we've been since the day I told him I needed time, and a dulcet feeling of felicitousness settles over me as I let myself settle into the embrace.

When we break apart, he presses a kiss to the top of my head. "Go fix your face, Krusty, I'll have a talk with your unruly son."

My eyes narrow in a playful glare at the jab.

"Watch it, mister, or I'll revoke your invitation for dinner." A wicked grin causes Dane's lips to curl up.

"That's fine by me. I'm okay with skipping straight to dessert." I'm caught off guard when he steps into me again and brushes my lips with his in a delicate tease of a kiss. I catch myself chasing after his mouth, desperate for more than just the hint he gave me, as he pulls away.

The air between us is charged. Electric. I'm torn between following my original plan of pouring my heart out to him over a homemade dinner, and saying *fuck it* and dragging him by his collar into my bedroom so he can make love to me. My need for him is suddenly so all-consuming and desperate, it's discombobulating. Nodding, I take a reluctant step back, my body fighting every step, like he's a magnet and I can't help but be drawn to him. He shoos me away with a wink, and I retreat to the bathroom to wash the ruined makeup off.

In the bathroom, I stare at my reflection in the mirror. Face now clean from all traces of makeup, my left eye only slightly red and angry looking. I glance at the dress hanging from the hook on the door that I had planned on wearing, then back at the threadbare T-shirt and tiny boy shorts I have on. Tonight was supposed to be special. I was going to light candles and pour wine. I was going to dress up, play soft music, and confess that I love him. That I never stopped loving him. I wanted tonight to be the beginning of our new forever, and I wanted to make it memorable.

The sound of pans clattering and the refrigerator door opening and closing pulls me from my rumination, and I wander back out into the main part of my small but homey 1920s craftsman to find Dane in the kitchen, his face pinched in concentration as he carefully butters bread and tops it with cheese before putting it in a pan. A tea towel is draped over one shoulder, the cuffs of the white linen shirt he's wearing rolled up, exposing his forearms, and I don't think I've ever seen a more attractive sight in my life.

I can't help it. I stand there, silently taking it all in. How perfect he looks in my kitchen. How at home he is, here in my space. How *right* this feels. I notice an open bottle of beer on the island, waiting for me, as he finally notices me and beckons me over with a tilt of his head. All of my carefully constructed plans for a romantic date night melt away as I realize that this is so perfectly us. I forget about the dress. I forget about the steaks sitting in the fridge, seasoned and ready to grill. I forget about the expensive wine and the carefully curated playlist. Instead, I slide onto the bar stool across from Dane as he flips the golden, melty sandwich in the pan, take a sip of the dark, rich, chocolatey stout he opened for me, and watch him prepare our dinner.

When he plates the sandwiches, he walks around the counter island and grabs the back of my stool, spinning it so I'm turned to face him. He steps between my legs, closing the space between us, until the only thing I feel is the heat from his body and the only thing I see is the brilliant verdant green of his eyes. My heart begins to race in my chest at his proximity, as the exciting realization hits me that tonight means the same thing to him as it does to me.

"You didn't have to do that." My protest is weak and unnecessary. Dane shakes his head as his eyes crinkles with a secret smile.

"I know. I wanted to. I want to take care of you, Everly. That's all I've wanted to do for so long." My throat constricts from the emotions his confession stirs up inside of me. There is no duplicity in his expression. Only pure, unadulterated truth, longing and need.

"Will you let me? Take care of you? Now and forever?" Dane's face becomes a blur as tears well in my eyes, as he cracks open my chest and takes my heart as his own. I can only nod, afraid if I open my mouth to speak I'll ruin the moment with my newfound inability to keep my composure around him. Instead, I reach up and pull his face down, capturing his mouth with mine. The kiss is salty from my tears, but the way his tongue sweeps into my mouth, as his hands cradle my face like I'm his most precious possession, makes my body light up like the sky on the Fourth of July and soon the only thought I have room for in my head is how badly I need him inside me.

CHAPTER 52
DANE

Heaven. This is what heaven feels like. It has to be. Nothing has ever felt so perfect and so *right* in my whole damn life, as Everly does, legs wrapped around my waist, my hands cupping her ass, our tongues dancing together in a rhythm only they know. I carry her up the stairs, as our kiss grows more and more passionate. Frenetic energy builds between us, so charged and heated it feels like we will combust if we don't come together right this second.

"First door on the right." Her words are little more than a gasp between swipes of her tongue but it's enough to get me to our destination. I steer us into her bedroom and kick the door shut behind me so we don't wind up with an uninvited four-legged guest interrupting us. When my shins meet her bed, I drop Everly on the soft, colorful bedding. She looks like an angel, framed by stained glass, the riotous colors of the pillows and blankets surrounding her are so...*her*.

Her cheeks are flushed with the prettiest shade of pink, her lips swollen and a little raw from my beard. The way her chest heaves as she stares up at me, breathless, anticipating, desperate, goes straight to my dick. My god, this woman is perfect. I stand there, just staring at her, almost unable to believe this is real. That we really are here. Together. Just us. No secrets, no shame, no guilt.

"Ever, you are so fucking perfect. I hope you know that." Her eyes widen at my compliment, but I have to make sure she knows this is so much more to me than just sex. This is it. My forever. I want nothing else in this life but this woman in my arms. By my side. Under my skin. In my lungs. Running through my veins.

When she doesn't say anything, I lean over her, forcing her back on her elbows as I cage her in with my arms on either side of her body. I run my nose along her neck, trace my lips against the shell of her ear, and she leans into the touch, a silent plea for more.

"Tell me."

"Tell you what?" Her words are a little whiny, a little frustrated, and I can't help but let out a low husky chuckle that causes her to shiver.

"Tell me that you know you're fucking perfect. Tell me you understand how absolutely fucking magnificent you are to me." Her breath hitches, and I can tell she's not used to being adored like this. A brief flash of anger erupts inside me at my brother and how fucking foolish he was, but it's quickly doused by the realization that *I* will get to be the one to show Everly her worth. I will be the one who gets to adore her. Cherish her. Love her. Until my heart gives out and stops beating. It will be my only purpose in life.

I pepper teasing, featherlight kisses along her jaw and down her neck. She arches into them, thrusting her breasts into my face, trying to distract me from what I want her to do.

Pulling back, I let out a disappointed tsk. "Nu-uh, gorgeous, I'm not going any further until you give me what I want." I have to fight the smirk that wants to break free when she looks up at me, lips turned down in such an adorable pout. I'm torturing myself at this point, but I'm having too much fun watching her squirm, desperate and needy for my dick.

"I'm perfect." She mumbles the words then reaches up to pull my shirt off, but I lean back, quirking an eyebrow up, not satisfied with her lackluster answer. The glare she shoots me would shrivel a weaker man's dick, but I love her feistiness. I trail one hand up her leg, slowly, meticulously teasing her by letting my fingers dance along the soft skin of her inner thigh, barely grazing the hem of her tiny shorts before pulling back. Her legs fall open wider, and I can see she isn't wearing anything under the skimpy pajama bottoms as I glimpse a patch of dark hair covering her gorgeous pussy. *Fuuuuck.* My resolve is being tested.

Time feels like it stretches for an eternity between us. We are frozen in this moment, and I want it to last forever. The moment we become us.

"I'm fucking perfect."

"Good girl." I let the smirk that was fighting to break free unfurl and ravel in the way her face flushes more at the praise. In one swift motion, I tug her shorts off and bare her glistening cunt to me. My mouth is on her in an instant. I am ravenous for her taste. The need to make her come apart is my only driving force right now. Her fingers dig into my hair, pulling until my scalp stings, so I burrow in further, desperate to make her come on my tongue. I lick, suck, savor, and fuck every inch of her pussy with my mouth until she lets out the most beautiful sound I've ever heard. Her body seizes up, those thick, luscious thigh muscles locking me in place as her release coats my tongue. *Euphoria.* That is the only word that can describe what I'm feeling right now.

When her orgasm finally relents, she falls back on the bed, panting. The dazed, blissed out expression on her face is now my greatest accomplishment in life. I take the opportunity to strip my clothes off, which results in a delighted gasp that is so goddamn girlish and sexy, it makes my cock twitch. I revel in the way her eyes seem to soak up every part of me, like she's committing my body to memory the same way I am hers. I can't stay away any longer.

I prowl onto the bed once more, settling back into my new favorite place to be, in between her thighs. I take my time dusting her skin with kisses and gentle nips with my teeth as I slowly make my way up her body. She's so responsive—her body responds to every touch, chasing the pleasure my mouth is bringing her. When I reach Everly's breasts, I lavish them with the same careful attention I gave her pussy. I suck on each nipple until they're as red and swollen as her lips. My cock notches against her pussy, just barely gliding along her seam, slick with her own arousal. Her hips jump at the teasing bit of contact, and I feel her body chase after mine, searching for more. Begging for more.

I release her nipple with a loud pop, then I surge forward and capture her mouth with mine. Her arms wrap around my neck, fingers digging into my hair again as she pulls me to her, a feral sort of need driving her movements now. I thrust my dick into her slick heat, just the barest inch, enjoying the way her body reacts to everything I do to her. Everly tightens her grip on my hair to the point of pain, letting me know exactly how much I'm frustrating her. Just as I think about sinking in one more slow, teasing inch, I feel her lips next to my ear.

"Dane! Fuck me. Please." Her husky request is kryptonite to my will power and my hips surge forward, sheathing my cock in her to the root.

"Fuuuck…" I groan.

She whimpers as she adjusts to the sudden intrusion, but before I can wonder if I hurt her, she begins grinding against me, seeking more. Aching to be fucked. And fuck her I do. I thrust in and out of her tight heat, snapping my pelvis against her ass in a steady rhythm. Her eyes close in bliss, and she drops her hands to her breasts to play with her nipples. Every moment of this is my new favorite memory. When I slide her legs over my shoulders and bend down to capture her mouth with mine, she lets out a groan of pleasure so erotic I'm afraid I'm going to come right then and there. Instead, I silence her with my tongue and thrust into the one spot I know will be her undoing. I swallow every cry, whimper, moan, and plea. Her sounds becoming so frantic and desperate I know she's almost there.

With a few more pounding thrusts, she comes with a shout. Her walls clench around my cock, triggering my own release. Her pulsing walls controlling the pulse of my dick. Coming into her is rapturous. Our bodies stay locked together as our kiss transforms from something animalistic to something sweet, languorous and comfortable. Our chests, hot and sticky with sweat, press together, and I collapse on top of her. I can feel her heartbeat, rapid as a hummingbird's, as clearly as my own.

When the sweat on our bodies cools and heart rates return to normal, I roll off her and pull her into my side to cuddle. She fits so perfectly in the curve of my shoulder, her head nestled under my chin. This is where we belong. This is home now.

CHAPTER 53
EVERLY

Dane and I are lying in bed facing one another as we eat the cold grilled cheese sandwiches that somehow miraculously didn't get eaten by the four-legged date saboteur that's currently snoring at the foot of my bed. The pasta salad must have actually satiated the beast.

I watch Dane lick butter off his fingers, and the wink he shoots me when he catches me staring causes my cheeks to heat. It's so easy with him. Lying in bed, eating cold sandwiches, just enjoying the moment as it is. There is a feeling of tranquility between us right now that is so comfortable and settled, I'm afraid I'm going to ruin everything with my next question, but it's the last hurdle we have to clear before we can move forward for real with a relationship. I know where I stand, but I also know Dane is much younger than me and may still have certain expectations for his life, and the last thing I want to do is rob him of any of his dreams.

I close my eyes and inhale a deep breath to fortify

myself in case I ruin everything with this next question. I commit this moment to memory. How perfect it is. No matter what else happens, we will always have this one perfect moment. When I open my eyes again, I find Dane staring at me—brows furrowed, eyes questioning, full lips turned down in a worried frown. He's sensed the shift in my energy. He knows I've got something on my mind. The way this man can read me never fails to stun me. Especially after how clueless Bryce seemed to be of my every emotion.

The way Dane can look at me and see *inside* me makes me feel vulnerable but seen in a way I've never felt before. This is why I have to say this now, before we get too far along and fall too deep and realize that this won't work. I need to know while I still have one foot still firmly planted in *I'm a strong independent woman and I can do it on my own* land. Once he's embedded into my soul for good, losing him will cleave me in two, and I don't know if I'll be able to recover from that. A girl can only be patched together so many times before she becomes just the shattered remains of what could have been.

"Do you want kids?" The question hangs in the air between us, heavy, almost corporeal. Thick like fog on the mountains before the sunrise. Dane studies my face, like he's trying to figure out if there is a right answer to the question. I bite back the urge to tell him I can't have children. My heart thunders in my chest from anxiety. I don't want to influence his answer. I have to know if it's something his heart truly wants. I don't want him to say what he thinks I want to hear.

Dane reaches up with his free hand and gently cups my cheeks, swiping away an errant tear with his thumb. I didn't even realize I was crying.

"I want *you*, Everly. Just you. If you want kids, I'll gladly give them to you. If you don't, then that's fine too. All I need is you."

His words cause my lungs to stop functioning. I was so scared he would say he wanted kids. That they would complete him. That I wouldn't be able to give him something he desperately wanted. It takes a long, long, moment for my brain to process his answer, for relief to replace the fear.

"Do you want kids, Ever? I'll put a baby in you right now. If you don't, I'll call and make an appointment to get snipped. Just say the word." I choke out a laugh at his offer. This man. He is so fucking perfect.

"I can't have kids. At least, I don't think I can. Bryce and I tried for years but nothing ever came of it. 'Unexplained infertility', the doctors called it. Neither of us seemed to want them badly enough to pursue the more invasive options, and Bryce wasn't open to adoption." Dane's eyes soften at my confession. He doesn't speak; he just lets me get this one last secret off of my chest.

"I'm almost forty now, Dane. My eggs, if they're viable, are considered geriatric in maternal fetal medicine. And honestly…I don't know if I do want to be pregnant at this stage of my life. I'm finally figuring out who I am, and…I'm enjoying that. I'm enjoying the life I want to live."

Dane shrugs and shoots me a lopsided grin. "Okay, so no babies then." I can't believe this conversation is going so smoothly. Surely he has to have some feelings on having kids.

"That's it? You're fine with not having your own biological child? You're young. You still have plenty of time to live your life and decide to be a dad when you're ready. I don't want to take that from you."

"I told you, Ever. You are all I need. If you can't get pregnant or don't want to get pregnant, that's not a deal breaker for me. If we decide down the road we would like kids, there's always adoption or fostering. Or we can raise a litter of food-stealing muppet dogs if we decide we don't have enough chaos in our lives. Please don't feel like you are holding me back. I haven't ever seriously considered children as a possibility in my future. It is something I'm willing to explore if and when you want to, but if it's just me and you, I'm sure Uly will keep us on our toes."

I laugh at his joke, more tears dampening my cheeks as the weight of his conversation lifts from my shoulders. I lean over the plate of the twice forgotten grilled cheese sandwiches and kiss Dane. It's a soft, languorous, unhurried kiss. I kiss him like we have forever to look forward to. Because we do.

When I pull away, I finally say the words I've been holding back until I knew it would be safe to confess them. "I love you."

"Fucking finally. God, Everly, do you know how long I've been dying to hear you say that? Fuck, I love you too."

I laugh at his excitement as Dane tosses the plate of food onto the floor so he can pull me into his body.

He covers me with his naked hardness, settling between

my legs. I feel his erection, heavy and thick against my pussy, but he doesn't move to enter me. He just revels in kissing, caressing and whispering *I love you* into my skin as he worships every inch of me. When we finally come together, it feels like the beginning of our forever.

EPILOGUE

2 YEARS LATER

DANE

"Yo, Roberts, you ready to go? I don't want to be late!" I stand from my desk the second I finish submitting the last of my arrest reports for the day, eager to get going. I'm in a hurry. Tonight is the ribbon cutting for Ever After, Everly's new passion project, and she will kill me if I'm late. I promised I would pick up the gluten-free, nut-free, allergy-friendly cupcakes for the reception. It's the least I can do, since Ever has been working long hours going straight from her day job at Whispering Grove, to cleaning, organizing and painting the small building located in the heart of downtown Birch Falls, while I've been splitting my time between working and getting my

Bachelor's in social work, with a focus in community outreach.

I look around for my partner and see her in Sargent Randall's office. Judging by her tense body language and the jut of her chin as she stares down Randall, Serena isn't happy. Immediately, I know this is Randall pawning a case off on her that he doesn't want to handle. He's been doing this for months now, sending Serena on calls that he deems unimportant and lower priority, doing his best to discourage Serena from continuing on with her career with the Birch Falls PD. Randall is old school, and he is everything wrong with our justice system. I decide to rescue Serena from Randall's patronizing, and head across the bullpen to retrieve her.

I knock once on the door before opening it, interrupting the standoff happening between Serena and Randall. "Roberts, it's quitting time. Ready to go?"

Randall cuts his glare toward me, clearly not thrilled with my interruption. Serena nods and moves like she's going to follow me, but Randall speaks up, halting her in her tracks.

"Actually, I was just telling Office Roberts there is a call she needs to respond to. A man called in claiming his wife is 'missing'. It's probably just some dumb bastard who won't admit his wife is cheating on him." Randall's tone strives for indolent and long-suffering, but I can tell there is an edge of challenge to it too. If Serena had hackles, they would be raised right now. A lesser man would be cowed by the glare she is directing his way. Clearly Randall see this assignment as beneath him and a punishment for

Serena for whatever insubordination he thinks she's guilty of.

"Shift's over, Boss. Can't one of swing shift guys handle it?" I interject, trying to keep the peace and get Serena out of there so she won't miss Everly's big night. She's been there helping when I haven't been able to, and I know this is as important to her as it is to me. She's been integral in helping Everly and Bethany with the community outreach aspect of Ever After, and she deserves to be there to help celebrate.

Ever After is going to be a small studio that specializes in providing therapy through art for teens, young adults and women who have experienced intimate partner violence.

The idea came about after Bethany, the Director at Whispering Grove, and seed investor for Ever After, realized how well Everly's approach of combining art with therapy worked for the residents on site, and thought it would fill a need in the community for at risk youth. Years prior, Bethany experienced the loss of a nephew to suicide after years of struggling with addiction and depression, unable to find the resources needed to help improve his mental health. Since then she had been searching for a way to help kids in similar situations. Everly also wanted to be a resource for women who had been through similar experiences to hers, so together they came up with *Ever After*.

Mental health specialists are hard to come by on a good day, even more so when children are involved. When Everly told me about what she and Bethany wanted to do, it ignited a desire in me to do more. To really help the people that need it the most, and not just keep upholding a broken system built on the backs of the disenfranchised and oppressed. I went into police work because I needed a job and wanted to help, but quickly became jaded at the power imbalance and use of police resources to uphold white supremacy that has been baked into our justice system for the last century. Sure, I helped put Dominick Reeves away, but how many more of him are out there? How many more Bryce Carmichaels are out there helping men like Dominick get away with their crimes?

After a strained moment where Randall and Serena ignore my clumsy attempt to break up the tension, Serena huffs out a frustrated sigh, "Go on, Dane. I'll catch up after handling this."

"But—"

"I said, go on. I'll handle this call that Sargent Randall has deemed himself too important to go on, then I'll see you at the reception." Serena's tone is icy, and I know her wrath is directed at the superior officer in front of her. Serena has tried her best to talk me into staying on the force, to help her with her mission of creating change from within, to fight against men like Randall, but she has her calling and I have mine. And mine is building a brand new future with Everly while helping as many people as we can. I can see that Serena's mind is made up, so I jerk a nod and back toward the exit, unwilling to risk being late myself. Tonight is too important, and I have more than one stop to make on the way to the ribbon cutting.

"Alright, I'll tell Everly you're still coming." As I turn to leave, Serena calls out a warning.

"Don't you dare do it before I get there."

"I wouldn't dream of it, Roberts." I bite back a grin as I think about the surprise I have planned for later.

"THANK you everyone for coming out tonight to help celebrate the opening of Ever After. This is the culmination of countless hours of working during every second of free time, to breathe new life into this decrepit old building, creating a safe haven for the most vulnerable of us in our time of need." I'm standing next to Everly as she addresses the crowd gathered in front of us. A few dozen of Birch Fall's most prominent citizens—local leaders, business owners, and teachers—along with our friends and family, are here to celebrate. I scan the crowd to see if Serena has arrived, and I spot her near the door, still in uniform, standing between Kai and my mom, her expression soft and beaming with pride. The stony, resolved officer I left at the station has been replaced with Everly's best friend, who happens to be soft as a marshmallow and proud as fuck of her. My heartbeat begins to drum faster as I realize I don't have to wait any longer to spring my surprise.

Everly gives my hand a squeeze as she turns to look at me, continuing on with her speech. "I couldn't have done this without the support of the community; my boss and business partner, Bethany; my friends; and my partner, Dane. Ever After is proof that good that can come from the darkest moments we are forced to endure. That our worst moments don't define us." Everly chokes up. Her hazel-green eyes shimmer, bright with tears that do nothing to hide the conflicting emotional cocktail of apology, remorse, and gratitude swirling within them.

She drops the mic so that her next words are just for me. "I love you, Dane. Thank you for being my light." She leans up and kisses me, sweet, chaste, and crowd-appropriate. It takes all my self-control not to deepen the kiss and to pull away instead, so that I have room to drop to one knee.

Everly's face is adorable as it morphs from confusion to shock as she realizes what I'm doing. Her right hand flies up to cover her gasp, but I don't let go of the left one. Instead, I pull out the ring I had tucked into my pocket.

The ring I had to stop and pick up after the metalsmith I worked with to make it, added the finishing touches. I spent an entire weekend with Kai, three hours away at a DIY make your own engagement ring workshop. Kai was making a new set of wedding bands for their anniversary, which has already passed, so Serena knows what I was up to. It's why she insisted on being present when I proposed. She said she had to see the ring before she'd let Everly say yes.

"Everly, I may be your light, but you've always been mine. Even when I never saw a way to capture it and make it my own, I cherished the light you brought into the world. Being with you makes me strive to be a better man every day. Your strength, courage, empathy, creativity, and kindness inspire me to be the kind of man that deserves to bask in your light. Will you grant me the privilege of always being in your light? Will you marry me?"

I slip the rose gold band, shaped to look vaguely like a tea rose on a vine, with three Moissanite stones, onto her ring finger. With the help of Christian, the metalsmith who ran the workshop, I designed and hand-forged the ring myself from start to finish—minus setting the stones and the polishing. It's not perfect by any stretch of the imagination, but with the way Everly's eyes light up when she sees the ring you'd think I just gave her the Hope Diamond. Everly's head begins to bob frantically as she drops to her knees in front of me, her face devastatingly beautiful, awash in happy tears and the biggest smile she's ever given me.

Everly leans in and whispers against my lips, the most beautiful words I've ever heard, "I'm yours forever, Dane Wilcox."

EVERLY

"Are you ready?" Serena comes up behind me, a concerned expression on her face when our eyes meet in the reflection of the mirror I've been planted in front of for the last five minutes. I was supposed to be following her outside to the garden to say my marriage vows to the most incredible man I've ever known. But one last "quick check" of my lipstick has turned into a minor existential crisis as my mind tries to sabotage what is supposed to be the happiest day of my life.

It makes absolutely no sense to be this nervous. I love Dane. I want to marry him. I have no doubts about him or how much he loves me. How *good* he is for me. How *perfect* we are together. Caroline has wholeheartedly embraced our relationship without a single hesitation. The last two years with him have been the happiest of my life. We are in sync in all things, and a romance novelist couldn't conjure a more perfect relationship than ours.

So why am I standing here, rooted to this spot, letting irrational terror hold me hostage with invisible tethers?

"Hey, Ever, you okay?" Serena immediately picks up on my internal conflict and plants herself in front of me, forcing my gaze to hers. The confident, reassuring warmth of her honey-gold eyes is an immediate balm to my nerves. "Talk to me, Everly."

"Why do I feel so scared? I want this. I want to marry Dane. I love him. Why do I feel like I'm getting ready to jump off a cliff?"

To Serena's credit, she doesn't just immediately start spouting platitudes about how everyone gets the pre-wedding jitters and true love, *blah, blah, blah*. Her eyes take on a thoughtful look as she considers my confession.

"Because you are." Her husky voice is very matter of fact, not pandering at all. "You have done this before, and it ended in just about the worst possible way imaginable. You know how awful it can get if it turns out to be the wrong choice. You've lived through it. You survived it, and you love Dane so much you are willing to do it again. You are willing to face the scariest thing you've ever lived through, head on again, for love. It's not easy to turn off that instinctual self-preservation after having to adapt to it. Give yourself some grace. You're allowed to be a little scared. It'd be silly not to be. But all the best moments in life are the result of doing something that scares us."

I think back to how scared I was when I first proposed the idea of Ever After to Dane, and how unsure I was if we would be able make it work. And now, I am doing the most rewarding work of my life. I think back to how scared I was when I decided to tell Dane the truth about his father's death, and how it was the first time in over a decade my soul finally felt unburdened. I think about how scared I was when I took the time for myself after Bryce's death and made myself find my own happiness, and how it made me the woman that was worthy and ready to accept Dane's love.

Nodding, I close my eyes against the sting of tears threatening to fall, in a desperate bid to salvage my eye makeup. "You're right." I pull Serena in for a hug as the fear that has been paralyzing me is overtaken by an overwhelming sense of assuredness, with a healthy side of excitement, to be marrying Dane. We hold each other for a solid minute as I will my racing nerves to calm. Once I feel calm enough, I give Serena one last squeeze before pulling away.

"Thank you."

Serena's lips quirk into a grin, "No problem. Now let's go get you married before he gets impatient and breaks down the door to come looking for you. You made him wait long enough as it is."

I laugh as I let Serena tug me out of bedroom I used to get ready in and through the back door to Caroline's back-yard garden. My breath catches in my lungs when my eyes find Dane standing under a trellis covered in lavender wisteria blooms. He's wearing a white button-down with his sleeves rolled up, topped with a waist coat, a blue so dark it resembles the color of the ocean under a full moon, and I am stunned by his beauty. And by the absolute unadulterated loving devotion shining from his eyes as he watches me march down the makeshift aisle, made by the friends and family gathered for our small, intimate wedding ceremony. With a guest list of only a handful of friends, Bethany, and our parents, and Kai officiating as a very freshly and very officially ordained-by-a-not-at-all-sketchy-website minister, this wedding is ten times smaller and infinitely more intimate than my wedding to Bryce, and I wouldn't have it any other way.

Kai doesn't even get to finish saying the sentence "You may now kiss..." before Dane's lips are on mine, and he is promising his soul to mine through this kiss. I return his kiss with fervor and make the same promise in return.

The End

BEFORE YOU GO...

Did you enjoy Duress? Please consider leaving a review on Amazon or your favorite book reviewing website. Even short reviews help with getting my books seen.

Recommending books you've enjoyed is one of the easiest ways to support your favorite indie authors. We are all just a bunch of pervs with praise kinks and reviews give us the motivation to keep writing.

ACKNOWLEDGMENTS

I've said it before, and I'll probably say it every time I write and publish a book; It takes a village for me to put my stories on page. From my alpha/beta readers, editor, cover designer, and author friends who keep me (semi)sane while writing, every single one of you helped me get this book into the world.

Thank you CWC for bring a source of unwavering support, friendship, accountability, and inspiration. I am so fortunate to have found such an amazing and talented group of people to call friends on this journey, and I hope we continue to push each other towards greater success.

Thank you, Allie and Jessica, for all your feedback and encouragement, and for pointing out when the garden gummies started working a little too well.

Amy, you've been with me since I started on this crazy journey to become an author, and I'm grateful you're not sick of me yet. Your tears are the best writing fuel ever.

Candice and Kristen, my honorary PAs, thank you for being such an amazing source of support on my first public signing as an author. You ladies make me feel like a real author!

Kelly, thank for you for being such a chill editor. I love

knowing I can trust your feedback, and that you won't strip away my voice (just all those extraneous commas).

I've experienced a lot of ups and downs on this writing journey, and without my friends, I don't know if I would have stuck with it. So even if I didn't name you specifically (because I suck at this), please know that if I talk to you even semi regularly you play a pivotal role in keeping me sane and motivated to keep telling stories. I'm so thankful for everyone I've met along the way, and I hope you will continue to go with me on future journeys into my imagination.

Thank you to every reader who has commented, shared, or DM'd me their thoughts on my books. Your reactions give me life and are the entire reason why I write.

Last but not least, thank you Kevin, for believing in me and never doubting my ability to write. You are the blueprint for all of my book boyfriends.

Until next time,

Poppy

ABOUT THE AUTHOR

Poppy Fitzgerald is an emerging author of romance novels. Poppy calls the beautiful Blue Ridge Mountains home, with her husband, two sons, mostly absentee cat, and overly affectionate Golden Doodle.

Poppy enjoys any and all romance genres and tropes, but loves to play around with popular tropes and turn them on their heads to come up with something not commonly seen.

When she's not writing she usually has her head buried in her kindle, reading smut. She also communicates fluently in GIFs and sarcasm and loves making her readers cry.

Want to know what's coming up next for Poppy? Join her newsletter at:

https://poppy-fitzgerald-author.kit.com/7b14b4ba11

THE BIRCH FALLS SERIES

Astray

What was supposed to be the typical "girls night out" with a couple of drinks, and a fun catch-up with her best friend, turns into something completely different for married, but lonely, Eloise Fitzpatrick. She wasn't expecting to get stood up by her bestie, or to have a tall, dark and dangerous stranger hit on her and steal a kiss under the street lamp.

Her unexpected night causes an eruption of conflicting emotions inside of her, including the crushing sense of betrayal to her husband. For the first time in years, Eloise finds herself feeling sexy, desired, wanted…But the guilt of these feelings threatens to consume her. Her husband, Caleb, may currently be married to his job, but she can remind him of why he married her first.

Eloise is determined to pour more energy into her marriage to make it work, and forget the handsome stranger with the heart stopping kisses.

Unfortunately for Eloise, the stranger has other plans, and they do not include a happily ever after with Caleb. His obsession isn't just leading Eloise astray… it is taking her down a dark path that may be the destruction of more than just her marriage.

Exile

Serena Malcolm is barely keeping her head above water.

When an accident kills her father and disables her mother, Serena's idyllic life in Birch Falls ceases to exist. Gone are the days of parties, study dates and a carefree life. At the tender age of 18, she finds herself stepping into a parental role with only her best friend, Kai, and an elderly neighbor as her support system.

After spending two years lost in a balancing act of caring for her mother, working two jobs, and graduating college, Serena forgets what it's like to be cared for. That is, until Dominick Reeves, a devastatingly handsome cop with a sexual intensity that cannot be ignored, swoops into Serena's life.

What starts as a whirlwind romance begins to turn sinister as Dominick increasingly asserts control over her world. Serena may have wished for escape, but she finds herself in exile.